THE NEW YORK TIMES

THE WASHINGTON POST

SOUTH FLORIDA SUN-SENTINEL

MILWAUKEE JOURNAL-SENTINEL

AMAZON • *BOOKPAGE*

CRIMEREADS • BARNES & NOBLE

THE NEW YORK PUBLIC LIBRARY

ONE OF *PARADE MAGAZINE*'S 101 BEST MYSTERY BOOKS OF ALL TIME

AN ABA INDIENEXT PICK

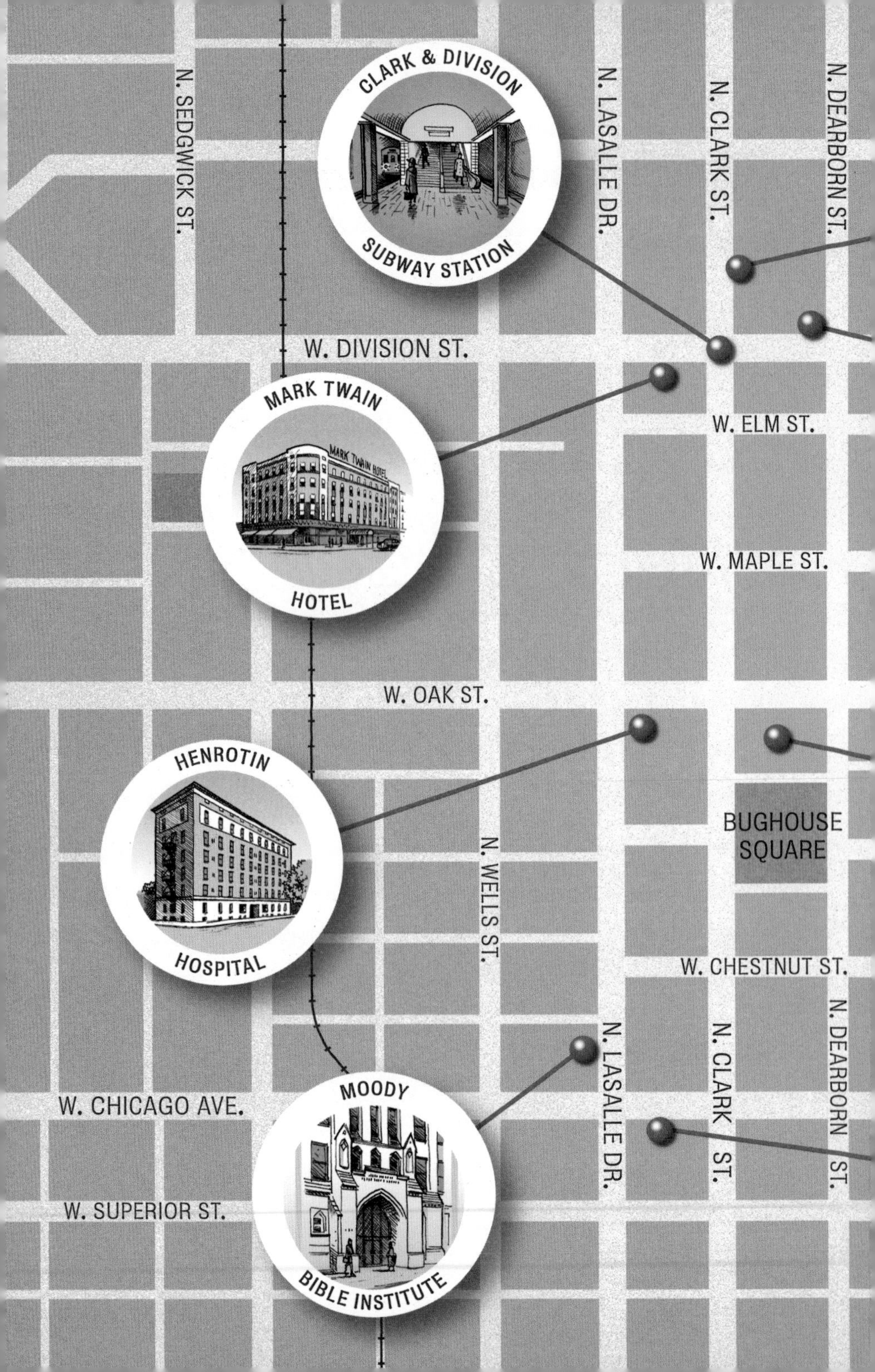

CLARK & DIVISION
SUBWAY STATION
MARK TWAIN
HOTEL
HENROTIN
HOSPITAL
MOODY
BIBLE INSTITUTE
N. SEDGWICK ST.
N. LASALLE DR.
N. CLARK ST.
N. DEARBORN ST.
W. DIVISION ST.
W. ELM ST.
W. MAPLE ST.
W. OAK ST.
N. WELLS ST.
BUGHOUSE SQUARE
W. CHESTNUT ST.
W. CHICAGO AVE.
N. LASALLE DR.
N. CLARK ST.
N. DEARBORN ST.
W. SUPERIOR ST.

1/4 MILE
KLANER
FUNERAL HOME
LAKE MICHIGAN
E. DIVISION ST.
N. LAKE SHORE DR.
TING-A-LING
Ting & Ling
ICE CREAM · GRILL · CANDIES
CANDY SHOP
E. ELM ST.
E. OAK ST.
E. LAKE SHORE DR.
NEWBERRY
LIBRARY
N. RUSH ST.
E. DELAWARE PL.
E. CHESTNUT ST.
LAKE SHORE PARK
N. STATE ST.
EAST CHICAGO AVENUE
POLICE STATION
E. CHICAGO AVE.
N. MICHIGAN AVE.
E. SUPERIOR ST.

Praise for *Clark and Division*

"Just as only James Ellroy could have written the Los Angeles Quartet and only Walter Mosley could have crafted Black Angelenos' experiences into the Easy Rawlins mysteries, crime novelist and research maven Naomi Hirahara was destined to write *Clark and Division* . . . The vibrant characters, the history and the aura of determined optimism that permeate the novel make it feel like the beginning of a saga not unlike Jacqueline Winspear's Maisie Dobbs mysteries."

—Paula Woods, *Los Angeles Times*

"Searing . . . This is as much a crime novel as it is a family and societal tragedy, filtering one of the cruelest examples of American prejudice through the prism of one young woman determined to assert her independence, whatever the cost."

—Sarah Weinman, *The New York Times Book Review*

"Hirahara has drawn a devastating picture of a family in crisis and a nation's monumental blunder."

—The Washington Post

"Engrossing . . . The best historical fiction shows how events affected the people who lived that era. Hirahara's *Clark and Division* ranks high."

—Oline Cogdill, *The South Florida Sun-Sentinel*

"Hirahara gives us a rich and vibrant portrayal of Nisei life in multicultural Chicago: the nightclubs, the hoodlums, the young people looking for connection, looking for their place in a world that up until previously had not merely excluded them but incarcerated them."

—Désirée Zamorano, *Los Angeles Review of Books*

"Beautifully written and deeply moving . . . Hirahara's novel is an accomplished and important story about a time in American history that I felt privileged bearing witness to."
—Carole E. Barrowman, *The Minneapolis Star-Tribune*

"Hirahara's most deeply felt and satisfying book to date."
—Parade Magazine

"This absorbing historical fiction, by the Edgar-winning author of the excellent Mas Arai series, vividly brings to life the experience of being Japanese American during World War II—a shameful chapter of casual racism, fear and distrust that continues to echo today." ***—The Seattle Times***

"The crime-solving is absorbing, but the novel works more compellingly as an informed portrayal of life in crisis among a group of American citizens who learned the hard way that, in certain circumstances, democracy doesn't apply to them."
—The Toronto Star

"Gripping . . . This immersive true-crime historical mystery novel takes place in Chicago in 1944, at the height of the mass incarceration of Japanese Americans."***—Ms. Magazine***

"Meticulous . . . A wonderful portrait of Japanese American resilience and struggle." ***—International Examiner***

"*Clark and Division* is a moving, eye-opening depiction of life after Manzanar. Naomi Hirahara has infused her mystery with a deep humanity, unearthing a piece of buried American history." **—George Takei**

"Crime fiction is at its best when telling a compelling story while also analyzing the shadowy foundations of human nature. Very few writers do that better than Hirahara."

—S.A. Cosby, *The Washington Post*

"A beautifully written novel. A telling and touching story that echoes across the decades. Naomi Hirahara uses the past to inspire us to be relentless in doing the right thing, right now."

—Michael Connelly, bestselling author of the Harry Bosch series

"Naomi Hirahara's *Clark and Division* opened my heart and mind to specifics of the experience of Japanese Americans during the Second World War. Rich in period detail, it is page-turning historical fiction, a tender family story, and a mystery that plays on two levels: *What happened to Rose Ito?* and *At what cost are Japanese Americans finally seen as full Americans?* It's a story that moved me deeply."

—Attica Locke, *New York Times* bestselling author of *Heaven, My Home*

"Hirahara's gifted writing is a master class in how to bring a historical epoch to life."

—Sara Paretsky, bestselling author of the Chicago detective VI Warshawski series

"*Clark and Division* does what crime novels do best: It uses a wonderfully wrought, ticking time-bomb of a story to illuminate a larger social issue, in this case the incarceration and resettlement of tens of thousands of Japanese Americans during World War II. A jewel of a novel. Buy it, read it, enjoy it." **—Michael Harvey, author of *The Chicago Way***

"The story of Aki Ito and her family, newly released from Manzanar, transports us to an often ignored moment in our own history, while holding a mirror to the present day . . . Aki Ito is the kind of heroine that belongs not just to the past, but to every generation. We see ourselves in her tenacity, her sense of justice, and her love for her family."

—Amy Stewart, *New York Times* bestselling author of the Kopp sisters novels

"One part mystery. One part historical fiction. In Naomi Hirahara's expert hands that 1+1 equation somehow equals 10, leaving you with a story that is enthralling, enlightening, and edifying."

—Jamie Ford, *New York Times* bestselling author of *Hotel on the Corner of Bitter and Sweet*

"Like no other work before, *Clark and Division* captures the day-to-day uncertainty of the post concentration camp Nisei world, where poverty, racism, and squalid living conditions co-exist with freedom, excitement, and dreams for a better future in wartime Chicago. Only Naomi Hirahara can mix a portrayal of a people in transition that feels authentic down to the smallest detail with an engrossing mystery filled with unexpected twists. Whether you are already a fan or are about to become one, this is not to be missed!"

—Brian Niiya, editor of the *Densho Encyclopedia* and *Encyclopedia of Japanese American History*

CLARK AND DIVISION

ALSO BY THE AUTHOR

• • •

The Mas Arai Mysteries

Summer of the Big Bachi

Gasa-Gasa Girl

Snakeskin Shamisen

Blood Hina

Strawberry Yellow

Sayonara Slam

Hiroshima Boy

CLARK AND DIVISION

NAOMI HIRAHARA

Published by
Soho Press, Inc.
227 W 17th Street
New York, NY 10011

Library of Congress Cataloging-in-Publication Data

Hirahara, Naomi
Clark and Division / Naomi Hirahara.

ISBN 978-1-64129-369-3
eISBN 978-1-64129-250-4

1. LCSH: Japanese Americans—Fiction. 2. Chicago (Ill.)—Fiction. 3. Murder—Investigation—Fiction. I. Title
PS3608.I76 C53 2021 | DDC 813'.6—dc23
LC record available at https://lccn.loc.gov/2021000576

Interior design by Janine Agro
Interior map by Mike Hall

Printed in the United States of America

10 9 8 7 6 5 4 3 2 1

To
Heather
Jane
and
Sue Kunitomi Embrey
(1923–2006)

CLARK AND DIVISION

CHAPTER 1

Rose was always there, even while I was being born. It was a breech birth; the midwife, soaked in her own sweat as well as some of my mother's, had been struggling for hours and didn't notice my three-year-old sister inching her way to the stained bed. According to the midwife, Mom was screaming unrepeatable things in Japanese when Rose, the first one to see an actual body part of mine, yanked my slimy foot good and hard.

"Ito-*san*!" The midwife's voice cut through the chaos, and my father came in to get Rose out of the room.

Rose ran; Pop couldn't catch her at first and when he finally did, he couldn't control her. In a matter of minutes, Rose, undeterred by the blood on my squirming body, returned to embrace me into her fan club. Until the end of her days and even beyond, my gaze would remain on her.

Our first encounter became Ito family lore, how I came into the world in our town of Tropico, a name that hardly anyone in Los Angeles knows today. For a while, I couldn't remember a time when I was apart from Rose. We slept curled up like pill bugs on the same thin mattress; it was *pechanko*, flat as a pancake, but we didn't mind. Our spines were limber back then. We could have slept on a blanket over our dirt yard, which we did sometimes during those hot Southern California Indian summers, our puppy, Rusty, at our bare feet.

Tropico was where my father and other Japanese men first came to till the rich alluvial soil for strawberry plants. They were the Issei, the first generation, the pioneers who were the progenitors of us, the Nisei. Pop had been fairly successful, until the housing subdivisions came. The other Issei farmers fled south to Gardena or north to San Fernando Valley, but Pop stayed and got a job at one of the produce markets clustered in downtown Los Angeles, only a few miles away. Tonai's sold every kind of vegetable and fruit imaginable—Pascal celery from Venice; iceberg lettuce from Santa Maria and Guadalupe; Larson strawberries from Gardena; and Hale's Best cantaloupes from Imperial Valley.

My mother had emigrated from Kagoshima in 1919, when she was in her late teens, to marry my father. The two families had known each other way back when, and while my mother wasn't officially a picture bride, she was mighty close. My father, who had received Mom's photograph from his own mother, liked her face—her strong and broad jaw, which suggested she might be able to survive the frontier of California. His hunch was right; in so many ways, she was even tougher than my father.

When I was five, Pop was promoted to market manager and we moved to a larger house, still in Tropico. The house was close to the Red Car electric streetcar station so Pop didn't need to drive into work, but he usually traveled in his Model A anyway; he wasn't the type to wait around for a train. Rose and I still shared a room but we had our own beds, although during certain nights when the Santa Ana winds blew through our loose window frames I would end up crawling in beside her. "Aki!" she'd cry out as my cold toes brushed against her calves. She'd turn and fall back asleep while I trembled in her bed, fearful of the moving shadows of the sycamore trees, demented witches in the moonlight.

Maybe because my life started with her touch, I needed to be close to her to feel that I was alive. I was her constant student, even though I could never be like her. My face was often red and swollen, as I was plagued by hay fever from the long stalks of ragweed that crept into every crack of concrete near the Los Angeles River. Rose's complexion, on the other hand, was flawless, with only a dot of a mole on the high point of her right cheekbone. Whenever I was near enough to look at her face, I'd feel grounded, centered and unmovable, less affected by any change in our circumstances.

While Rose was surrounded by admirers, she kept her distance just enough to be viewed as mysterious and desirable. This was something we learned from our parents. Although we were thought well of by other Japanese Americans, we were not indiscriminate joiner types, at least before the war. In school, our classmates were mostly white and upper-middle-class kids who attended cotillions or Daughters of the American Revolution events, activities that were off-limits to us. There were about a dozen Nisei offspring of florists and nursery operators—smart, obedient boys and immaculately dressed girls, who Rose remarked "tried too hard." Rose's style was effortless, and when she wasn't home, I'd shed my plaid dress and secretly try on her signature outfit—a white blouse, long knit khaki skirt and a thin lemon-yellow sweater, a color that most Nisei girls would avoid wearing. I'd study myself in the full-length mirror on the door of the wardrobe, frown at how the skirt bulged at my belly; it was also much too long, falling down to my ankles but covering my thick calves. And that shade of yellow made my own skin look sallow and sickly, further confirming that Rose's clothes were not for me.

When I wasn't in school, I spent time in Tropico going on long walks with Rusty. In those early years, we wandered past the tangles of deerweed, which resembled prostrate women, underneath willow trees where blinding-white egrets rested their elegant limbs, and heard the high-pitched song of the Western toads, which reminded me of the buzz of hot electrical wires. This was before the Los Angeles River flooded, causing the city to fill the riverbed with concrete. Afterward, we still heard the toads, but they weren't as loud.

I wished that my teen years could have been spent outdoors alone with my dog, but my growing up involved being around other people my age. As I didn't have that many opportunities to socialize with the *hakujin* girls outside of school, when I was invited to do so, it was a momentous occasion. One day in eighth grade, Vivi Pelletier, who sat next to me, handed me an invitation to her pool party. It was handwritten on off-white stationery with scalloped edges. The Pelletiers, who had moved to Los Angeles from Europe, were rumored to be connected to the movie studios. They lived in the Los Feliz Hills and were one of the first families in the area to get their own pool.

I held on to that invitation so tightly that it was moist when I showed it to Mom, who wondered if I should go. It would be a high-tone *hakujin* affair, and who knows how I could end up shaming the family. I was known to make faux pas, like running around with a stain on my shorts because my menstruation pad had shifted during an *undokai*, a sports event in Elysian Park for our Japanese-language school.

And then there was the matter of my swimsuit. I had an old striped cotton swimsuit whose fabric sagged around my *oshiri*, making me look like I was wearing diapers. That suit was good enough for Japanese potlucks at White Point, not far from the fish canneries on Terminal Island, where close to two thousand Issei and Nisei lived. It would not do, though, for Vivi Pelletier's pool party.

"Just let her go," Rose told my mother. "I'll take her to get a new suit."

We went to the dry goods store in Little Tokyo on First Street. Their selection was limited, but I found a navy blue one-piece that covered my ample buttocks.

I brought the folded suit in a bag with my present, a bath powder puff set, which I thought was appropriate for a girl originally from France. I had never attended a party for a *hakujin* girl and carefully watched all the guests so that I didn't make any serious mistakes. Quite a few mothers were also in attendance but I was relieved I had come alone. Being the only Japanese, Mom would have felt awfully out of place, and Rose would have been bored out of her mind.

We had finished eating egg salad sandwiches with the bread crusts cut off when Vivi's mother pulled me aside into a room she referred to as the salon. I feared that I had done something wrong again.

"I am so sorry, but can you come some other day to go swimming with Vivi?"

Did Vivi's mother think that I had come unprepared? "I have my swimsuit in my bag."

"No, no dear. That is not the problem." Mrs. Pelletier had wide-set eyes and a high forehead, which made her look like one of the forest animals in Disney's *Snow White*.

I finally figured it out. It was like Brookside Park in Pasadena; the mothers didn't want me to go into the pool with their daughters.

I fled out the front door without saying goodbye to Vivi. It was a long downhill walk, and my body shook as I stomped on the asphalt.

When I let myself into our back door, Rose turned from

the dress pattern she and Mom were cutting at the kitchen table. "Why are you home so early?"

I couldn't help but to burst into tears, and relayed what had happened.

"I told you not to go," Mom murmured in Japanese. When she felt slighted by her Issei friends, fellow immigrants from Japan, her anger would manifest itself like a hot streak, but when it came to *hakujin* men and women, my mother became deflated, half believing what they thought about us.

Rose was not having it at all. "I didn't waste an afternoon shopping for nothing," she muttered. She demanded that I go with her to confront Mrs. Pelletier. I tried to resist, but as usual I was overpowered by my sister, who dragged me to the car. When she insisted on something, my whole family eventually went along with it.

Rose pushed on the Pelletiers' doorbell multiple times in rapid succession. On the doorstep, she cut a striking figure—dress cinched at her tiny waist and her skin almost glowing. She didn't even give Mrs. Pelletier a chance to say hello. "Did you invite my sister to your pool party and then tell her not to go into the pool?"

Mrs. Pelletier's face turned beet red. She tried to excuse herself by saying that it was fine with her, but her guests were uncomfortable. "Aki is welcome to come and swim at any other time," she said.

But Rose, as usual, didn't back down. "This is unacceptable. You owe my sister an apology."

"Oh, dear, I am so sorry. Truly I am. I am new to America."

But we're not, I thought.

Rose didn't make any speeches about racial equality or anything like that. We remained silent on the drive home. I went to sleep early that night and after sundown she climbed into my bed and wrapped her arms around me. Her breath smelled sour from the *takuan*, Mom's prized pickled radishes, from our dinner. "Don't you let them ever think that they are better than you," she whispered in my ear.

The next Monday, Vivi, looking embarrassed, returned my bag with my folded bathing suit and a card in the same off-white stationery, probably a thank-you for my birthday gift. I barely acknowledged her and threw the bag in the hallway trash can without opening the card.

At school, I was able to make a couple of friends, but only with girls who seemed as isolated as me. The only thing that we had in common was our fear of being alone at lunch and recess. I couldn't wait until I was in high school, on the same campus as Rose. Our high school had been built five years earlier, a gothic structure that looked like Wuthering Heights, except it stood on a sunny hill instead of a foggy moor. When I finally entered tenth grade, I followed Rose and her groupies around like Rusty followed me from one room in our house to another. She'd barely acknowledge me in public—only occasionally remarking with an eye roll, "What can I do; she's my little sister."

Rose was the only Nisei girl in the drama club. One late afternoon she came into our bedroom carrying a bound script, her cheeks flushed. "I'm the lead, Aki, can you believe that?"

I waited for her to make an announcement at dinner, but she didn't, just gulped down Mom's *okazu*, a stir-fry of pork and tofu, faster than usual. "Why didn't you say anything to Mom and Pop?" I asked her when we both were in bed.

"I didn't want to jinx it. Or get Mom too excited."

That was indeed something to consider, as Mom was known to get on the phone or go into Little Tokyo or the produce market to "accidentally" run into people to *ebaru* about our latest accomplishment—well, specifically Rose's. I didn't mind that I wasn't the subject of her boasting. By being under the radar, I was free to be completely average.

I practiced the lines with Rose every night. Babette Hughes's *One Egg* was a one-act comedy, which surprised me because my sister wasn't the type to crack jokes. The play featured three actors in a café—a male customer, a female customer named Mary, and then the waitress.

As I read the lines for the man and the waitress, it became clearer and clearer to me that the two customers were fighting over something more than eggs. There was some charge of romance and it disturbed me.

"Are you sure that it's okay that you are playing Mary?" I finally asked.

"Why wouldn't it be?"

"I don't know." I couldn't put my apprehension into words. We were all used to invisible rules and taboos, breathing them in as they hung in the air of our houses, schools and churches. In California, Japanese could not marry whites, and I sensed that Rose's casting was a subversive act by the drama teacher. I was both excited and scared for Rose; her insistence not to be treated any different from anyone else could get her in trouble.

About a week before the production, Rose came into our room, her usually bright eyes red and puffy.

"What's wrong?" I asked, my stomach turning in anticipation of trouble.

"Nothing. Who said anything was wrong?" she snapped back at me. She stopped asking me to rehearse lines with her, and the script disappeared from our room.

The evening of the play, Rose made some excuse that she had to go to Doris Motoshima's house to plan a fundraiser for the school service club. I couldn't stay back and took Rusty for a long walk all the way to the high school. There were no windows in our auditorium, so I snuck into the lobby, only to have one of the ushers, a senior like Rose, stop me to say that dogs were not allowed. I grabbed the program, though. Outside I saw that Rose was listed as the waitress and Sally Faircloth was Mary. After tying Rusty to a tree beside the auditorium, I returned to the lobby.

"I think that there's a mistake here," I said to the usher, who I remembered was in the glee club. "My sister is playing Mary, not the waitress."

The usher shrugged. It was a minor detail that he obviously cared little about. Finding him utterly useless, I took a seat in the back. The seats were only half-full, mostly with middle-aged parents. I watched another one-act play in progress; the acting was earnest and saccharine. And then came the start of *One Egg*. Rose entered the stage as the waitress, wearing a simple light-blue dress that you'd see worn by employees in any greasy diner. That was the only thing about Rose's character that seemed subservient. She wore a pair of shiny black patent leather pumps—her best shoes, in fact—and her hair was immaculately curled with a big royal blue bow tied at the top. Her lips were painted bright red, no doubt her favorite Red Majesty shade. As I had read the play in my rehearsals with Rose, the waitress was a maddening, irritating service worker. In Rose's version on stage, she was a siren, teasing the male customer—"no sir, yes sir," and diminishing the female customer played by Sally Faircloth.

When she climbed in bed that night, she was still wearing her lipstick from the play.

"How did it go?" I asked, my head still on my pillow but my eyes alert and searching.

"I saw you sitting back there," she said. "You shouldn't have come."

"The waitress was the better role, anyway," I said, almost convincing myself of it. Rose didn't have to tell me that the switch was the result of some complaint. By this time, we understood how the world worked for us. To articulate the attitudes against us would give them power and credence. We preferred to release the pain silently, let it rise in invisible balloons that we couldn't see but we could feel, bumping against our foreheads and shoulders, warning us not to stray too far from what was expected.

After Rose graduated from high school, she went to work as a clerk at Pop's produce market, typing out orders from grocery stores. Pop left for work at dawn, receiving the crates of vegetables that arrived in flatbed trucks, vans and huge transport vehicles. Rose took the Red Car into work at a more sensible time, around eight. After graduating from high school, I would sometimes accompany her downtown when I started taking classes at Los Angeles City College. I was proud to sit next to her and tried to keep my ankles crossed like she did. When we arrived at the subway terminal building on Hill Street, though, I would realize my legs were wide open, my skirt taking up most of the seat.

The boss's son, Roy Tonai, was officially listed as the owner of the produce market because he was American born. He had a mean crush on Rose, and everyone said that they probably would get married, especially because Roy was already twenty-four and ready to settle down.

"I hear there's going to be a dance at Nishi this weekend," Mom said after dinner one evening. "Roy's mother told me that he will be driving in their new car. He wants to take you."

"I'm sick of this talk of Roy and me." Rose threw her napkin on the table. "I'm not marrying him, Mom. I know that will ruin your plans to lord it over everyone at the market." Her response to my mother initially surprised me as I observed that other Nisei girls would have been delighted to be in Rose's position. Roy was handsome, with a square jaw and a thick mane of hair that he combed back with oil. In spite of being the boss's son, he hauled crates of vegetables like any other employee.

But Rose was like our father; she didn't like to be boxed in. Whenever you tried to trap her in a corner, she'd get out. I think about that often now. How she must have fought that day in Chicago. Even all these years later I sometimes shut my eyes tight and try to transport myself back, to pretend that by willing myself there in my mind she might somehow have felt less alone.

CHAPTER 2

December 7, 1941, wasn't a typical Sunday for us Itos, starting at dawn, long before we knew what was going to happen. I was feeling poorly and so was Rusty. He was twelve, ancient for a golden retriever. He was practically deaf and had a bum rear leg; when he walked, he jerked like a car with a flat tire. Yet he soldiered on, his big mouth open in a smile and his wet pink tongue sticking out whenever I took his leash off a nail in the wall.

Mom, Pop and Rose left the house at five in the morning to help prepare for a wedding reception at the local Buddhist temple. The bride was a distant relative on Mom's side; most of Mom's relatives were in Spokane, a thousand miles away from us, so even a second cousin once removed was valued as a close blood relative if they lived in Los Angeles.

I, with my high fever, could not attend, so Mom had prepared me a pot of *okayu*, rice porridge, before they left. In fact, I was eating a bowl of the *okayu* with a red pickled plum floating on its glossy white surface when someone pounded on our door. I ignored it and so did Rusty, who couldn't hear a thing.

More pounding. Annoyed, I put down my chopsticks and tightened the belt on my bathrobe. Pop had drilled a peephole about three inches below the factory-made one to accommodate our height, and I pressed my eye against it. Floppy black hair and dark eyebrows. Roy Tonai.

I didn't want anyone, much less a man, to see me in my threadbare bathrobe, but Roy was practically family. I blew my nose in a handkerchief, stuffed it into my pocket and opened the door. "For God's sake, Roy, what's going on?"

My aching head couldn't grab hold of the words coming out of Roy's mouth. Japan had bombed Pearl Harbor in Hawaii. Killed American servicemen. This would definitely mean war. We knew plenty of produce workers who had come from Hawaii, dark men with melodious accents who had formerly worked on sugar plantations. I pictured Hawaii as a paradise of coconut trees and white sand beaches. It felt unbelievable that Japan would want to bomb such a place.

Within an hour, my parents and Rose had returned. The wedding had been called off because of the "incident." I felt faint. My mother put her hand on my forehead and ordered me to go straight to bed. I was happy to comply but I couldn't rest. Produce workers under Pop's leadership trampled in and out of our house expressing worry and dismay.

A day later, President Franklin D. Roosevelt officially declared that the US was at war with Japan. Our world shook and our friends began to disappear. Roy's father got picked up and was placed in a jail in Tuna Canyon with Issei Buddhist priests, Japanese-language instructors and judo teachers. Several days later the government sent him and the others on a train to who knows where. Since Pop didn't serve on any boards of language schools or other Japanese-type groups, he wasn't picked up, which he later took as an insult, as if he wasn't influential enough to be seen as a threat to national security like the others.

Even before this, after one too many cups of sake, our

father had spewed vitriol about the ways the world pressed against us Japanese. The Issei were already barred from buying land in California, and by 1920 the state was making it hard for them to even lease. Now with the war there was the curfew, which restricted the movement of all Japanese Americans. It wasn't fair that he couldn't leave the house before six o'clock in the morning; all his *hakujin* co-workers, even the ones from Germany and Italy, were free to go anywhere at any time. By six o'clock he would have missed out on multiple orders from the Midwest and East Coast.

Rose, meanwhile, hated having to be at home by eight o'clock every evening. "They've even canceled the flower market socials," she'd complain to me. The Nisei gatherings at the cavernous building on Wall Street, a few blocks away from the produce market in downtown Los Angeles, hardly seemed like a threat to the government to me.

Rose's connections with Nisei groups helped us know how to toe the line in Tropico at the beginning of World War II. Richard Tokashiki, whose father owned a flower shop on Los Feliz, told her where we should turn in our radios and our father's hunting gun, which he used to scare off rabbits. Richard was also the one who got Rose on the bandwagon to support a patriotic Nisei group, the Japanese American Citizens League. They would set up tables at different daytime events to recruit members. She kept trying to get me to come with her but I couldn't bear to be away from Rusty, who had stopped walking entirely and refused to eat. It was like he knew what was going to happen to us—or maybe he was absorbing the unspoken tension in the house.

One day I finally relented and manned a table with Rose to sign up new members after a talk by a JACL leader from Utah. I felt like such a fraud because I myself didn't bother to become a member. There was something about the oath of allegiance that we were supposed to sign, alongside our black-and-white headshot and a fingerprint of our right index finger. The statement announced that we supported and defended the Constitution, "so help me God." After getting their signature verified by a notary public, members were encouraged to carry the piece of paper in their pockets and purses, as if that documentation would be evidence that they were real Americans.

The campaign didn't sit right with me. Only the American-born could join the group. But what about our parents? They were the ones who'd had to struggle to build a life in America. They chose it, strove for it. Meanwhile Rose and I miraculously appeared here, magically American, without even having to journey across the Pacific Ocean.

I was among two hundred Nisei at Los Angeles City College. The other students were from Japanese communities in Uptown, South Central, Boyle Heights or Little Tokyo and often congregated in regional cliques. I didn't take school that seriously. Like Rose, I was spending most of my time working at the produce market in the winter of 1942. The market seemed different, as if a major earthquake had thrown it off its foundation. The men seemed rougher and more impatient. Some customers dropped their accounts for no reason. In one case, the operator of a chain of grocery stores specifically said it was because we were Japs.

Pop didn't seem overly worried. "Everyone needs food. They need to eat. And everyone knows our vegetables are number one," he told Roy and all the other workers. But his grin disappeared as soon as the men left his office.

I was afraid to bring up Rusty's decline in health because everyone in the family was so preoccupied with this war business. One Friday afternoon I was watching him breathing so hard in the backyard that I couldn't stand it. It took me three awkward and painful attempts to hoist Rusty into a wheelbarrow from our shed. Bumping him down Glendale Boulevard past the rail yard, I transported him to a plain storefront where there was an animal doctor who usually treated horses.

The veterinarian delivered the bad news that I feared. My dog's heart was failing. Rusty looked up at me knowingly. He was ready to let go.

It was getting cool by the time we were home. Rusty lay under a cedar tree, his breathing becoming even more labored. "Rusty, I love you. I love you," I repeated as I buttoned my heavy coat and lay down next to him. I smelled his stinky breath together with the earthiness of dirt, a combination that still haunts me today.

Through the windows, I could see the silhouettes of my parents and Rose clearing off the dining-room table as it was getting dark. I couldn't discern Mom's staccato of Japanese words, but I did hear my name. I knew that I should get up and tell them where I was but I didn't want to leave Rusty's side. I was so tired and let myself doze.

When I awoke, Rusty's body was stiff and cold and I knew that he was no more. I couldn't bear the thought of raccoons or coyotes clawing or tearing at his flesh. Using an old shovel from the shed, I found a spot of loose dirt where Mom planted her *shiso* plants every spring. I began digging a hole, hitting hardpan about midway but using the nose of the shovel to break though. In the darkness, I buried him.

When I walked into the house, I was completely covered in dirt.

"What happened to you?" Rose asked, almost dropping the plate that she was drying.

"Rusty's dead."

No one said anything, not even scolding me for being out of the house during curfew.

I first saw the exclusion order nailed to a telephone pole near a popular Scottish-themed restaurant on Los Feliz Boulevard in March. I was terrified by the black type calling out, INSTRUCTIONS TO ALL PERSONS OF JAPANESE ANCESTRY. The order stated that we "aliens and non-aliens" had to report to a Civil Control Station at an address in Pasadena in the beginning of May. We were instructed to bring linens, toiletries and clothing, only in bundles that we could carry. Where was the government taking us?

Since many of the male Issei leaders were already gone, their wives came by our house, bereft, afraid, confused. Mom extinguished any flames of panic. There was no time for emotion. We had to cross an unknown body of water in a rickety rowboat. If we paused to cry or ask questions, we were bound to sink.

We packed up our belongings in cardboard boxes, the straw trunks that our parents had brought when they first came to America and, of course, wooden produce crates. One German farmer let us use his barn in San Fernando to store most of our boxes. A Mexican produce worker held on to our silverware and Pop's tools. A church in Glendale agreed to keep our photo albums. As parts of me were being cut off and scattered in different places, I was quickly learning not to be too sentimental about anything.

Roy, as the owner of a produce market, was privy to inside information from local politicians and businessmen. One day he came by to tell us that he, his mother and sister were going to report early to an assembly center in the Owens Valley in hopes that we would not be displaced to an unknown location in another state. Called Manzanar, it was about a four-hour drive toward Death Valley, and surrounded by the Sierra Nevada mountain range. "At least we'll be in California," he said to my parents and Rose while they stood in the middle of our empty living room.

Rose, who normally wouldn't give Roy the time of day, listened intently and nodded. "Better to know where we'll be," she agreed.

Pop handwrote a list in pencil of where all our belongings were stored and slipped the paper in the ribbon band of his felt hat. "We will all come back before you know it," he said. Pop's emotions ran hot and cold, depending on how much he drank, but when it came to the family and business, optimism had been his key to success so far.

I had no such hope. I walked along the concrete riverbank in search of a last song from the toads. I laid some wildflowers at Rusty's grave, my mother's former *shiso* patch. Like Mom, I was pretty sure that we wouldn't be back again and in the remote chance we were, we wouldn't be the same.

The frames of the more than five hundred barracks were already standing when we arrived at Manzanar in late March 1942. We drove up in a caravan with military police tailing us. When I emerged from Pop's Model A, I felt my heart clamp down into my chest. The wind howled and blew through my hair, forcing my skirt to hide in between my legs. The military police immediately confiscated the Model A and Pop's face fell, as if he finally understood what would be taken away from us.

The camp was divided into thirty-six residential blocks, which comprised fourteen barracks, twenty by a hundred feet in size, arranged in two rows of seven. Each barrack was divided into four rooms. We lived in a room with Roy's mother, widowed aunt and older sister, while Roy stayed in a bachelor barrack, also in Block Twenty-Nine. Through my window I could see the Children's Village, a special unit that housed orphans from three prewar children's homes, including one called Shonien, which wasn't far from Tropico. The orphans, who ranged in age from toddlers to nearly adults, were a mystery to us as they had their own kitchen and kept to themselves, for the most part. Issei nurserymen eventually planted a garden and cherry blossom trees around the Children's Village as if plants could heal the wounds of displacement.

Each block had a set of lavatories, separate for men and women. I was completely horrified when I first stepped into ours because there were no separations between toilets. Mom, Rose and I took our bathroom breaks together because we could take turns holding up our coats or towels to shield the person on the toilet. Our periods, which used to occur at about the same time while we lived in Tropico, disappeared altogether while we were in camp, a sign of the terrible stress that we were under. Even though we didn't voice our complaints out loud, our bodies knew our truth.

In the beginning our family stayed together, enduring the completely foreign environment as a tightly knit unit. But as the weeks passed, our ties loosened. Rose's cool magnetism attracted both sexes. It was only a matter of time before a Nisei group, Just Us Girls, known as JUGS, recruited her to be one of their members. Now most of her meals and evenings were spent with them. I was so hurt to be excluded that instead of forcing myself on Rose and her new friends, I avoided her circle entirely.

Camp took its toll on my parents. Without his title of produce market manager, Pop began to wither and turn inward. Woodworking or gardening, which many of the Issei men embraced, were futile activities, he believed. Instead he started drinking more heavily, hanging out with other old miscreants who were intent on making the best bootleg alcohol out of corncobs or anything else they could find in camp.

Mom continued to keep up appearances. Little baby gray hairs began to sprout along her hairline, and she spent most mornings either plucking them out or having me or Rose do the tedious chore. She made sure to have a list of things to do every day. As she completed each task, she wrote a check mark beside it. I heard her explain to the other Issei women that's what they needed to do, too, to not lose their minds.

I got a job with the Supply Department, which issued jackets and blankets when the weather got cool. That's where I met Hisako Hamamoto, who was from Terminal Island. Hisako was a bit plump, but she didn't care. She even made fun of the extra roll of fat around her waist, poking it after we shared a meal. In the early mornings, we'd walk to the Victory Garden to help Roy and some sons of flower growers prepare the soil for seeds of lettuce or spinach. One day as we were sitting in the dirt, Hisako yelped in pain. The culprit? An evil scorpion, which I flattened with the heel of my shoe. Hisako's upper thigh, where the scorpion had injected its venom, was bright pink and swollen, and I helped her to the closest mess hall, where I cleaned the wound and made a cold compress of ice.

"No sign of its stinger, so you'll be all right," I reassured her, explaining that Rusty had not been so lucky on one of our walks by the Los Angeles River. Pop showed me how to remove the scorpion horns from Rusty's paw with a pair of tweezers and treat the wound.

"You'd be a good nurse," Hisako complimented me as she pulled her skirt down. "You're good in an emergency. I myself can't think straight." Actually, I was a crybaby, but when immediate danger loomed, I was able to access another part of my brain and complete tasks that I never thought I could do.

Hisako's observation stayed in my mind and when I heard about the nurse's aide program at the Manzanar hospital, I enrolled. I never saw Rose much, anyway, as she would stay out late to make paper flowers for special events at the mess hall at night: weddings or send-off parties for Nisei soldiers in the US Army. Some of my father's roguish new friends eviscerated the JACL leaders who had lobbied for our boys to be drafted in the first place. Why did we have to spill our blood on the battlefield to prove that we were loyal Americans? Let us out of our cages first and then maybe we'd consider military service.

I was sympathetic to their viewpoint, but could not say anything to Rose, who was spending most of her time with the pro-JACL Nisei. I even heard rumblings that she was an *inu*, an informant who was ratting out the Issei or Nisei who had been educated in Japan, sending them to Department of Justice detention centers like the one Roy's father was in. That accusation was preposterous, but camp was becoming polarized between the accommodationists and the dissenters.

By the spring of 1943, the government was starting to push the "loyal" Nisei out of camp into the general population of free Americans, as long as they stayed away from the western military zone. Instead of returning home to California, we had to move into unfamiliar towns and cities in the Midwest or the East, anyplace that needed cheap labor to replace the men who had been sent to fight overseas.

Of all the regions, Chicago was the promised land. It was the second-largest city in the US, full of factories and manufacturers that needed laborers. In camp we were shown a series of promotional black-and-white films about the merits of the city, "Hello, Chicago." Rose's eyes widened when she saw the skyscrapers and the river cutting through downtown, the *hakujin* and black women wearing hats and high heels as they crossed the busy streets. That scene frightened me, as I'd almost forgotten what it was like to be surrounded by *hakujin* people and boulevards. Somehow I had gotten used to the searing wind cutting through the haunting Owens Valley and the landscape of jagged mountains surrounding our barracks, the home for 10,000 Japanese Americans.

In June 1943 the War Relocation Authority recruited Rose to be among the early Nisei to go to Chicago. Responding to an official invitation, she attended an informational meeting and returned to our barrack with a resettlement pamphlet, which she tossed on top of her bedspread. I grabbed it and studied every instruction on how to best assimilate into mainstream life.

"Don't bunch up in numbers more than three," the resettlement literature stated.

There are four of us, I thought. *Would that make us one too many?* "I guess they don't want the Japanese to be too conspicuous."

"They want us to be invisible," Rose said and laughed. "That's plain impossible."

If we could not help but be seen, we had to be the best Nisei specimens, the ones with broad white smiles and spotless suits and dresses. I understood the resettlement agency's strategy. If I were working for the government, I would send hundreds of Rose Itos out into the wide plains of the Midwest or the villages of New England. If anyone could convince a suspicious public that we Japanese were patriotic Americans, it would be my older sister. Judging from the shine on her face, I knew that she had accepted the call.

I have replayed the day that she left Manzanar in September 1943 over and over in my mind, as if I'd remember some new details if I thought about it enough. I'd cried because I didn't want to be separated from Rose. Everyone made fun of me for being overly weepy at twenty years of age. I wasn't known to say much of anything, but sometimes emotions welled up inside of me and escaped before I could shut that door.

"Take care of Mom and Papa," she said, gripping her tan suitcase. The dust swirled around her—on anyone else it would have looked gross and dirty, but Rose looked like an angel covered in gold dust. She was wearing her favorite dress, white polka dots on dark blue, and a hat on her perfectly styled hair.

I nodded and swore that I would, not realizing how tough that would really be. I handed a farewell gift to her that I had been working on ever since she had announced that she had been approved to leave. It was a diary covered in some wood that I had salvaged from a box that once held toilets. From the old Issei who did woodworking in camp, I had received a bit of sandpaper and stain. He also used a drill to make three holes on the two wooden panels, which I threaded with an old shoelace to keep the notepaper together. On the cover I had burned in the name ROSE as well as the image of the flower.

"Oh, Aki, it's beautiful," she said. "Not sure if I'll write anything in it—you know me." Noting my crestfallen response, she tried to assuage my feelings. "Ah, but I adore it, I really do. I'm going to stick it in my pocketbook so it'll be with me the entire train ride."

She got on a bus with some Nisei men assigned to a sugar-beet farm a few states away. She waved furiously at us and at first I wouldn't lift my head to really say goodbye. I was afraid if I did, I'd wail and never stop. But finally when the bus began to move, I looked up. Rose's face was already fixed toward where she was going next.

"I'm going to be in Chicago soon, too," Roy announced as he delivered mail to our barrack around Christmas 1943. He had been voted our block manager and distributing the mail was probably the best part of his job. We never got much mail, but since Rose left, we received postcards from her. This one was of Chicago's Moving Stairs, an escalator to the newly built subway. Another one was of the Mark Twain Hotel, located at 111 West Division, the corner of Clark Street. The hotel was apparently walking distance from the apartment that she shared with two other Nisei girls. She had gotten a job with a famous candy company that made these chocolate logs covered with peanuts and caramel. I pictured her enveloped in sweetness as she filed papers or whatever she did as an office clerk. On this postcard she wrote that she'd been searching for a unit for our whole family for when we were to be reunited in Chicago.

"You're not supposed to read our mail," I scolded Roy in jest.

"It's a postcard. I can't help but read it," he said.

"Has Rose been writing to you, too?"

Roy's face reddened, and I couldn't figure out if it was because Rose hadn't corresponded with him or perhaps because she had.

He didn't answer my question. "I gotta get out of here," he said, adjusting his mailbag. "A guy can die too early in this place."

Within a month, in January 1944, he had gone to Chicago. Eager to follow both him and Rose, I prepared our leave clearance papers, revisiting questions that didn't make much sense. Like would we foreswear any allegiance to the Japanese emperor— Who said that we bowed down to him in the first place? If you didn't answer the questions in a particular way, you would be labeled "disloyal" and forced into another exodus, this time to a harsher camp close to the Oregon state border. More than ever, we wanted to get out of Manzanar into the free zone.

As Rose had been the one who always handled our official family's English-language government paperwork, that responsibility now fell on me. I felt myself withering under the pressure. I kept crossing out certain answers and reread the simplest questions multiple times. Whenever I gave my parents instructions on what we needed to do next, they would gaze at me dumbfounded as if they couldn't quite recognize me. "And, Pop, no staying out late at night," I warned my father. We couldn't afford any kind of setback.

A week before we were due to leave, I noticed my father up in the middle of the night, slipping on his worn-out shoes.

"Where are you going?" I sat up in my bed but he was out the door before I could stop him. I lay down, unable to fall back to sleep, listening to the short and sharp breaths my mother inhaled in her slumber, as if there wasn't enough oxygen in the room.

Around dawn, our barrack shook with the arrival of two men—a drunken Pop with his arm around the shoulder of our local camp policeman, Hickey Hayashi. Mom immediately got to her feet and together they hauled him to his bed, where he collapsed in a drunken stupor.

"You know that he's not supposed to have this, Ito-*san*." Hickey produced a pint-size glass container that I knew Pop stored his bootleg sake in.

My stomach fell. Could this criminal incident mean the end of early release for us? I was ready to get on my knees and beg for mercy when Mom stepped in. Using an elevated Japanese reserved for addressing kings, Mom apologized profusely while standing in front of Hickey in her nightgown. From underneath their bed, she retrieved a pair of new shoes for Pop that we had ordered from the Sears Roebuck catalog for our move to Chicago. Those shoes were supposed to replace his holey ones that he was wearing right now, on top of his bedsheets. Mom offered them in exchange for the camp policeman's silence.

Hickey shook his head. "No, Ito-*san*, no need for that."

"This is a token of our appreciation. We've benefited from your service to us over these months."

After three rounds of this back and forth, Hickey relented and departed with Pop's new shoes. A week later, we were on our way to Chicago.

We traveled by train. It was so strange to be on a train after being restricted to a square mile in the middle of Owens Valley for so long. After months of living in a concentration camp, I felt that our lives had been compressed in one of those snow globes and the world as we had once known it may have been a figment of our imagination. But no, here we were, with the glorious mountain ranges of Colorado and then the flatness of Nebraska passing by our windows.

We were close to the Iowa border when I got sick. A twisting pain grabbed my insides and it took all my strength to pretend that it wasn't there.

"Aki-*chan*, I told you not to eat that sweet that your mess-hall friend made," my mother said, noticing my discomfort.

Hisako had pressed the *koge*, burnt rice, with a sprinkle

of sugar—a most precious commodity—as a special treat for our long trip. Mom thought it was disgusting, but I was touched by the gift.

Finally I was able to make my way to the restroom. It was quite embarrassing as, by that time, sweat was dripping from the sides of my face and my legs were shaking. While I was in the ladies' room, I almost blacked out. I thought I heard my sister's voice in my ear, *Take care of Mom and Papa*, not as a memory, but as a new directive. *I am*, I thought, annoyed that my family's low expectations of me would seep into my subconscious.

When I returned to our seats, most of my makeup was on my handkerchief, as I'd cleansed my face with some cold water. Pop had already fallen asleep, the brim of his hat lowered over his eyes. Sticking out from the band was the edge of the paper, now completely yellowed, that listed the location of our earthly belongings in Los Angeles.

"I wonder if Rose will meet us at the station," Mom said. We hadn't heard from Rose for a couple of weeks. I had sent her a telegram with our Chicago arrival date, but didn't receive a response back. We weren't worried at the time. It wasn't like she could call us in camp. Mom suspected Rose was lovesick about some young man in the city. On the train, we saw Nisei GIs, handsome in their pressed uniforms, and I imagined that someone like that had captured Rose's heart.

As we got closer to our destination, I could tell Pop was getting excited. He was sitting straight up as the train lurched back and forth; he kept looking out the window and back toward the passengers leaving and entering. Oh, to see the flash of Rose's smile, that in itself would be enough for me.

When we finally arrived at Union Station, Pop was the first out the door with his one suitcase. The train station was so huge and grand, with majestic white-colored marble walls. A huge war bonds poster was on display below the clock while the flags of military allies—the United States, Great Britain, France, and Australia—hung down by the vertical beams. In the center of the station was a USO desk to serve all the soldiers who were on leave and needed instructions on the best accommodations and recreation.

As we stumbled into this mass of humanity, we saw a group of Japanese Americans walking toward us. I recognized one of our former Nisei camp leaders, Ed Tamura. Ed had hightailed out of Manzanar as soon as he could. His face was round and smooth; if he had to shave every day, I would be surprised. Then I spotted Roy and his slicked-back hair, drooping a bit in the May heat.

I first felt embarrassed that there was this welcome party for us. We were simply the Itos, a former Los Angeles produce manager, his wife and younger daughter. I searched the group for my sister. But there was no bright smile, lipstick applied perfectly in spite of the humidity.

"Something's happened." I could barely hear Mr. Tamura's voice over the hubbub in the building.

Roy couldn't look at us. "There was an accident at the subway station last night," he said.

Before he could declare, "She's dead," I knew. I had felt it in my bones when I was getting sick on the train. Rose had departed this earth, as dramatically as only she could have done.

CHAPTER 3

None of us got any sleep that night, even though we were already exhausted from our long bus and train journey from Manzanar. We didn't touch our suitcases, which Mrs. Tamura and Roy had placed in front of the fireplace of our one-bedroom apartment. We should have opened up the windows to let the night air cool the bedroom, but we didn't have energy for that. Still in our street clothes, we lay on beds side by side, my parents in one and me in the other, exactly like in camp. Even though I was by myself, I stayed on the right side, careful not to cross over to where Rose was supposed to be. Was she really gone forever?

The next day I prepared to go to the coroner's office to see Rose's body. We didn't have to; Roy had already identified her for the authorities. But I wanted to see her. Not that I needed to be convinced that Rose was dead, but as long as her body remained aboveground, I didn't want her to be alone. And since I was going, my father decided that he should, too.

No one had witnessed exactly what had happened, only that someone had been run over at the Clark and Division subway station. The police had reached the scene fifteen minutes after the subway was stopped. The police had found

Rose's pocketbook down on the tracks. The contents were intact but the handle had been torn off by the incoming train.

My father and I were practically sleepwalking as we got into a taxi. I wasn't aware of my environs until we walked into the morgue. The smell was wretched, both sour and chemical at the same time. A sheet covered Rose's body, which was probably naked and broken. The sheet was pulled up to her chin, but the top of her shoulder was exposed, revealing that her arm had been severed. Pop also noticed how brutally mangled Rose's body was and crumpled to the floor. I didn't pull him up. We both were in shock.

I felt my whole body stiffening. Was that my sister's face? All her beauty—the pink blush in her cheeks, the fullness of her lips, the playfulness in her eyes—was gone. Now this face I knew so well resembled animal hide stretched over a human skull. Even her black hair, always immaculately styled, seemed to have lost its sheen. Her beauty mark was still visible on her right cheek, confirming that this body had once been inhabited by the soul of Rose Mutsuko Ito.

I couldn't move, even as Pop lurched to his feet and stumbled out of the room.

I don't know how long I stood there, but the coroner's voice finally broke through the noise of the revolving fan. He asked me if I had had enough, and I nodded. He covered Rose's face with the sheet.

"May I talk to you, Miss Ito?" He led me to his office. Piles of manila folders loomed on the floor and on a desk in the middle of the room.

He directed me to a squeaky wooden chair with wheels, which rolled a few inches away from his desk when I sat. Nothing was stable or level in my life, even the floor of this government office.

He picked up a manila folder and licked his index finger

to turn the pages of a form, but then got right to the point. "Your sister had an abortion. It was recent. Perhaps a couple of weeks ago." His blue eyes were the color of marbles that a neighbor in Tropico had played with.

"You have made a mistake," I said. My declaration surprised even me. I usually would not tell any authority figure, especially a *hakujin* man, that he was wrong. Why was he mentioning an unspeakable criminal procedure like an abortion when my sister was dead? "A train ran over her."

"The evidence of an abortion is undisputable. I have to put it in my report. But it was not the cause of death, which was definitely suicide."

That he could pronounce that Rose had taken her own life so definitively without even knowing her was unbelievable. I wanted to shout in his face, *My sister didn't kill herself. Not on the day before we were coming to Chicago.*

The coroner looked at me silently, and I knew what he was communicating. She had taken her own life *because* we were coming—probably out of shame for her situation.

"Rose wouldn't do that." In my mind I had made the declaration at the top of my lungs, but the words from my mouth were barely audible.

"I'm so sorry to be the one to tell you this," he said. I could tell that there was no convincing him otherwise.

"I'd like her things." I didn't want the coroner's office to hang on to anything that was Rose's.

"The police have the contents of her purse."

"Her dress—"

"We had to cut it off of her. There was a lot of blood."

"I want her dress."

"They have that, too."

I stared at him. Was he telling the truth? I couldn't tell. "I need the address of the police station."

The station was located at 113 West Chicago Avenue—I made him write it for me on a slip of paper. After he did so, he stood up. "Well," he said, "we'll send the body to the mortuary as soon as we hear from them."

Pop was waiting for me in front of the building, his hat flopped over his swollen eyes. It was obvious that we would never be the same again.

We took a taxi back from Ogden Avenue. I had to give the driver a big chunk of the money in my purse. The apartment Rose had secured for us on LaSalle was in a building with more than a hundred units, and the one vacancy was on the top floor. Mr. Tamura had apologized over and over for that when he'd let us in the day before. "Housing has been such a challenge with so many being released from camp." But there were two rooms: a bedroom and dining room—a luxury when most people were living in studios, sometimes six to a room.

I had to jiggle the key in the lock to get the door open. The air was warm and stuffy. My and Pop's suitcases were still in front of the fireplace. Roy, who had said that he'd be over after his work, sat alone at the table, which was made of wood, maybe walnut. Our beds and two chairs were the only other pieces of furniture. On the table were a couple of cans of beer, an open newspaper, three ration books and some brochures that Mr. Tamura had left for us. We didn't have a full kitchen, merely a kitchenette with a sink, hot plate and a refrigerator that was in need of a block of ice. It wasn't much, but it was more than we had in camp.

I didn't bother to say hello to Roy. What was the point? "Where's my mother?"

"She went to bed. The doctor gave her something to make her sleep."

I wished that one of our Issei doctors from Southern

California was in Chicago to look after us. But most of them were still in one of the ten concentration camps across America. There were more than a hundred thousand Japanese Americans who needed their help there.

"I bought some sandwiches," Roy said.

"Pop. Food," I said to my father, who was still standing by the door as if he had entered a stranger's home. "Roy bought us some sandwiches. You need to eat."

Pop slowly made his way to the middle of the dining room. He bowed from his hip until the top of his head almost grazed the edge of the table. In Japanese he said, "Thank you for all you have done for us."

"It's nothing, *Ojisan*. I'm so sorry." I thought I heard Roy's voice crack.

I went to retrieve the box of sandwiches from the counter. When I turned back around, Pop was gone, as was one of the beer cans. I scowled and was going to go into the bedroom and scold him for drinking on an empty stomach, but Roy stopped me.

"Let him be, Aki. He needs some time alone." He drained his last bit of beer. "It was bad, huh? To see her like that."

I felt strangely protective of Rose in her deceased state. Why did Roy have to make a comment about how she looked? "What happened? Were you with her?"

Roy shook his head. "The police went by her apartment and one of her roommates called me at work. They told me that it was probably suicide."

"You know that Rose would never have killed herself."

"It must have been an accident then."

I didn't dare bring up the abortion with my parents in the next room. "Did Rose have a boyfriend?"

Roy frowned. "Not that I know of. What, did she mention something to you?"

I heard the bedroom door swing open and then my father's footsteps in the tiled bathroom.

"I better get going."

"I need to talk to you. Soon," I said in a hushed tone.

Roy got the message that I didn't want my parents to be part of the conversation. "Well, maybe we can have a drink sometime."

"I'm not going to a bar with you, Roy." In camp I had sometimes heard that Roy was a bit fast, getting too close to girls at dances.

"I'm working at the candy company tomorrow. There's a diner nearby. Maybe there." He recited the name and closest intersection, which I recorded in the notebook I kept in my purse.

We made arrangements to meet the next day.

Leaving the empty can on the table, he gestured toward the newspaper. "There's an article in there about Rose. You might not want your parents to see it." Those were his last words before he was out the door.

The article in the *Chicago Daily Tribune* was brief, the size of a matchbook: a woman had been fatally run over by a train car at the Clark and Division station. There was no name or physical description. The police were investigating the incident, which had occurred at six o'clock in the evening two days before.

For my family's sake, I hoped that there wouldn't be a follow-up article. But on the other hand, I couldn't let Rose disappear in a two-inch box.

I felt like collapsing, but I knew that I wouldn't get a wink of sleep in a bed next to my parents. It had been bad enough in camp, but now with all this grief surrounding us, I wouldn't be able to breathe. I had to do something.

It was only seven o'clock and still light outside. I took a

pen from my purse and, using the edge of the newspaper, I wrote:

> *I went out. I'll be back soon.*
> *Aki*

I folded the page with the story about Rose and put it in my purse, then took out Rose's latest postcard, the one of the Mark Twain Hotel. On the postcard was her return address, an apartment on Clark Street. I went through the resettlement's "Welcome to Chicago" brochures until I found a Triple A map of downtown.

I made sure that the door was locked behind me.

CHAPTER 4

I knew that Rose had had a couple of roommates, a Pasadena woman named Louise from the Gila River camp and another from San Francisco whose name I couldn't remember. If I couldn't get any clarity from Roy now, I would go to the women who had lived with her.

As this part of Chicago was arranged in a grid, I could easily figure out where I needed to go on the map. Our apartment building was on LaSalle, which ran north and south. Clark was the next parallel street over and after that was Dearborn. Division cut through going east to west. Since I was used to wandering around Los Angeles and Manzanar on my own, I had erroneously thought navigating to Clark and Division would be a breeze.

Once I faced LaSalle, the smell of car exhaust overwhelmed me, and the passing traffic blew debris into my eyes. I tried unsuccessfully to blink away the dirt; a stubborn speck remained, causing my eyes to water further. I was a complete mess and had lost all sense of direction.

I walked the wrong way for two blocks. The grand Chicago of those promotional films we saw in camp was absent during my trek. Here, twilight lacked the comforting glow that seemed to embrace Tropico and the outlying brown hills back home. The gray boulevard seemed unfriendly, full of haggard people scurrying to their next destination.

For a second I thought about returning to the apartment. Then I found myself standing at the intersection of Clark and Division across from a grand-looking building, newly constructed: the Mark Twain Hotel, the building on Rose's postcard. To be in the presence of my sister's touchpoint—a landmark that she identified with, enough to mail me an image of it—was a sign that bolstered my spirit. The street on the other side of the hotel, Clark, was more lively—*nigiyakana*, as Mom would have said. There were various businesses tightly bound together—restaurants, bars, barbershops and plenty of rooming houses. In the middle of the block, sandwiched in between a cleaner and bar, was my sister's three-story walk-up.

At the foot of the stoop were Nisei boys in zoot suits, loose pleated pants and boxy jackets with wide lapels and chains hanging from their belts. I'd seen the pachukes back in Los Angeles, around downtown or Boyle Heights, where a lot of Japanese Americans lived alongside Mexicans, Russians and Jews. I heard stories in camp that the boys would steal the chains connected to the sink stoppers in the block lavatory to adorn their outfits.

I hugged my purse to my chest and for a second I regretted making this trip on my own.

"Hey, Manzanar girl. Twenty-nine," a boy on the stoop called out, causing me some confusion until I recognized our block number.

I had no idea who this boy was, but I wasn't in the mood to talk to him. In camp, there were certain boys you knew you needed to steer clear of. With the Issei elders all around, there were lines that they couldn't cross. But that wasn't the case in Chicago. I got the feeling that young people ruled here.

I put my head down and continued up the stairs. I had

trouble opening the glass door, and the same boy came around and jimmied the latch. He smelled strongly of musky cologne that almost made me sneeze. "That's how it's done," he said. I tucked my chin away from him and pushed the door open with my left shoulder.

I went up the carpeted stairs to the second floor. A cockroach skittered by and I remembered Rose writing that the city was infested with bedbugs. I suppressed the urge to scratch my ankles. Insects were the least of my worries.

On the left side of the stairs was number four, my sister's residence. I almost dissolved into tears but I took two big breaths. *Ochitsukinasai*, I ordered myself. I needed to hold it together for Rose's sake.

Two firm raps with my knuckles, the rattling turn of a lock, and the door opened to reveal a thin Nisei woman with brownish hair curled up around the nape of her neck. Although it was dark in the hallway, there was soft light from some lamps inside. The woman, who looked a little older than me, wore a fitted tan dress and raspberry-red lipstick. She seemed to know what looked attractive on her skinny frame.

"I'm Rose's sister," I said.

The woman's face fell. Her eyes and red lips sloped down and she seemed frozen for a moment.

"I'm so sorry," she finally said. "Come in, come in."

The room held three twin beds, two of them on opposite sides and another that almost blocked the door. Dresses on hangers were suspended from nails high on the wall. The wallpaper beside one of the beds had peeled off, revealing a long crack, stained brown by a possible water leak. There was a small refrigerator and hot plate in a corner but no sink.

"Aki, right? I've seen a photo of you. Rose spoke about you all the time. I'm Louise."

The door opened again and another woman entered, a

towel around her neck. She had big eyes and heavy eyebrows that seemed drawn on, but were probably all natural. She looked like one of those healthy farm-girl types that could outwork most men.

"Hello," she said enthusiastically upon laying eyes on me.

"This is Rose's sister," Louise said in a hushed tone. "Aki."

"Oh. I'm Chiyo." She extended her hand. It felt pillowy and soft until she squeezed.

I frowned for a moment. Chiyo didn't seem like she was from San Francisco, and I didn't recognize her name. "I think there was another roommate."

"Oh, you must be talking about Tomi," Louise said. "She moved out a few months ago. She's a house girl in Evanston now. Couldn't deal with the big city."

"I took Tomi's spot. I was living in a hallway before, so this sure is a thousand times better." Chiyo folded her towel on a hanger and placed it on one of the nails on the wall. When she turned back around, her cheeks were a little flushed. "I didn't know your sister that long. We didn't talk much. But I sure am sorry."

Was this the way it was going to be from now on? People looking pitifully at me and my parents? I dipped my head in response.

Louise was bringing me Rose's tan suitcase. "She had packed all of her things in here—"

"Her toothbrush and cup are still in the hall bathroom," Chiyo added. "I'll go get them."

My head was spinning and Louise must have noticed that I was feeling unwell.

"Here, sit down." She gestured to the bed that stood awkwardly in the middle of the room, and I sunk into the mattress. The box springs wheezed from my weight. *Is this where my sister slept?*

I felt Louise's eyes all over me as I tried to catch my breath. Her attention made me feel more agitated than grateful.

Chiyo returned with a red toothbrush and a jar that looked like it had once held strawberry jam. Why I would want that, I didn't know. But I accepted the items, gratefully.

"What a terrible accident," Louise said.

"Is that what people are saying?"

Louise and Chiyo exchanged glances. "Well, of course, what else could it be?"

"The coroner thinks that Rose committed suicide."

"What?" Louise seemed genuinely disturbed. Chiyo, on the other hand, didn't.

"Rose wouldn't have done that." She wouldn't have abandoned me. "Can you tell me how she was that day?"

"She hadn't been feeling well lately," Chiyo said.

"Yes, she had been spending a lot of time in bed," Louise added. "I figured that she caught the flu."

My sister, who was strong as a horse. She hadn't even gotten sick from the inoculations in camp, which had sent others to the latrine every hour.

"Did she go to the doctor?"

"No, she refused." There was regret in Louise's voice, as if she should have forced the issue. "Some of the hospitals won't accept us Japanese."

"But there's plenty who will treat us, too," said Chiyo.

I needed to understand what had been happening with Rose. "Can you tell me who she was spending time with?"

"Well, Roy, of course. That's why I called him when the police came by," Louise explained.

"Anyone else? Was she seeing someone?"

"Not that I know of," Louise said. "There was really no one else. I mean, all of us would go out to dances and things in a group. And you know Rose, always surrounded by the fellows."

Chiyo didn't confirm Louise's observation. "I don't go to dances that much."

"She and Tomi spent a lot of time together, before Tomi moved out to Evanston."

"Can I get Tomi's phone number?"

"Of course. I have to tell you, though, the lady who she is working for doesn't like her to get many phone calls."

"Then her address?"

Louise sucked her cheeks together as if I was now really inconveniencing her. She knelt by the bed where I sat and pulled out a box from underneath. She leafed through a green address book, then recited an address which I wrote down on the folded newspaper I'd tucked in my purse. As she returned the box to its place under the bed, I saw a stack of books and gasped.

"Oh, those are Tomi's old books. We've been telling her to pick them up," Louise said.

But I had recognized the spine of the diary I had given to Rose as a farewell present. "That's Rose's."

Louise looked incredulous as I pulled the diary from the middle of the stack, causing the top ones to fall onto the hardwood floor.

"I made this for her." I clutched the rough exterior of the diary, my hand covering the letters, ROSE, that I had burned on the cover.

"Oh, it's wonderful that you spotted it," Chiyo said as I opened Rose's suitcase and pressed the diary into her folded clothes. I took out a scarf, one that she had ordered from the Sears Roebeck catalogue for the cold Owens Valley winters, and wrapped it around the jam glass. That and the toothbrush also went into Rose's suitcase.

"Yes, we wouldn't have known that she even had a diary." Louise stood up and wiped the dust from her fingers and dress. "I never saw Rose write much, except postcards."

As I re-latched the suitcase, there was a faint knock on the door.

"Another *okyaku-san*!" Chiyo seemed elated. They must not get many visitors.

It turned out to be another woman around our age carrying a powder-blue suitcase. I almost fainted when I got a look at her. She was a doppelgänger for Rose. She was tall with a long face and a quick smile that would soften any Issei curmudgeon or Nisei bureaucrat. Her voice, however, was much sweeter, completely extinguishing the initial resemblance.

"Hello. I'm Kathryn. Came from Rohwer, Arkansas. The American Friends sent me. I'm sorry that it's so late, but they thought there might be an opening here."

First an awkward silence, but then Chiyo rebounded, introducing herself and Louise. She hesitated when it was my turn, and I came to her rescue. "I'm Aki."

Kathryn took note of Rose's tan suitcase. "Oh, are you the one moving out?"

"Ah, no." I rose from the bed. "I need to go."

Chiyo nodded, as if my time was indeed up.

"I'll walk you out," Louise said.

"You don't have to." I felt hurt that Rose was being replaced so quickly. Would her roommates even feel her absence tomorrow?

"Well, at least out to the staircase."

Kathryn said a bright goodbye, and I wondered if anyone would tell her what happened to the girl whose bed was now hers.

I followed Louise out, noticing the door's heavy-duty deadbolt, which still looked shiny and new compared to the other hardware in the decrepit apartment.

At the foot of the stairs, I had to say something. "Rose didn't kill herself. You knew her the longest, Louise. You know what I'm saying is true."

"I didn't really know her." Louise tugged on the top button of her dress. "She was off in her world and I was off in mine. I'm so sorry."

I said nothing more. I held my purse and Rose's suitcase with one hand as I went down the stairs, lightly touching the banister with the tips of my right fingers. *This is the banister Rose touched*, I thought.

Despite her polite and polished veneer, I didn't completely trust Louise. Why did I have to push to get Tomi's contact information? And hale and hearty Chiyo too easily accepted the coroner's theory that Rose had committed suicide. How could they have recovered from Rose's death so quickly to welcome a new roommate? Did my sister's life mean anything to them?

Tomi. Tomi might be the key to Rose's secrets.

The entrance of the Clark and Division station appeared in front of me so suddenly I didn't realize at first what I was looking at. Stairs descended from the street into the bowels of the subway terminal, like the skinny mouth of a monster. I wanted to go down and see the platform where Rose had been standing when she took her last breath. But I had the suitcase and didn't want to lug it up and down. *I'll come tomorrow*, I told myself. Maybe around six o'clock, the time the newspaper article said she had been killed.

I transferred the suitcase to my right hand. It was getting heavier over each block. Men loitering outside bars, smoking cigarettes and cigars, called out to me.

"Baby."

"Tokyo Rose."

"Sweet thing."

"Come over here."

"Let's talk."

It was dark now and I didn't feel safe.

A person wearing an evening gown and heavy makeup—and more than six feet tall—barreled down the street and through the doors of the Mark Twain Hotel. I was starting to figure out that I couldn't take anything in Chicago at face value.

After I let myself into the apartment, I still felt unsettled. I took off my heels and crept through the apartment in my white bobby socks. Through the bedroom door, I could hear the familiar snoring of my father. At least my parents were having a respite from the nightmare of our reality.

In the dining room, I slowly unpacked everything from Rose's suitcase. There was a small linen closet in the hallway, but otherwise no storage space to speak of. I'd probably have to refold everything and put it back, but that didn't matter.

I carefully laid everything out. A few pairs of silk stockings, a precious commodity. She hadn't had those in camp, for sure. Three other dresses, including a fancier one that I had never seen before. Her polka-dot dress was missing. An album for war bond stamps—I remembered that she had purchased that in Los Angeles before we left for Manzanar. The album had spaces for 187 ten-cent stamps, red ones featuring a minuteman from the American Revolutionary War. Rose had neatly mounted dozens of them until there was one open page left. I carefully unwrapped the strawberry jam jar from Rose's scarf and placed it on our table, a sign that Rose was still with us, somehow.

What I was most eager to look at was the diary. Had Rose actually used it? She wasn't the type to write things down and reflect about what she had done. I opened it and a piece of torn paper fell to the ground. The ripped fragment had a red number, *20*, printed on it. The number was meaningless to me and I figured that Rose had used the paper to mark a page. After placing the scrap in the back of the diary, I started flipping through random pages.

The sight of her familiar long and loopy handwriting made me dissolve into tears. With all the emotion pressing down on me, I didn't think that I would be able to read anything tonight. As I closed the diary, I noticed that there was a gap in the binding. Pages had been ripped out and I couldn't help but wonder if they had held some secrets to why my sister was now dead.

CHAPTER 5

Today is the first day of my new great adventure. Chicago.

Back at the produce market, I would sometimes make calls for Papa to Chicago. I'd make my voice high-pitched and refined so that I sounded Caucasian instead of Japanese. My high school English teacher said I had a nice voice, that I could have been a radio announcer, even. Can you imagine such a thing?

My sister, Aki, made this diary for me, so I suppose I should try and use it. She knows that I'm not one to write things down, but maybe I'll prove her wrong. There's no one to talk to in this train, anyway. Oh, but it's lunchtime, so maybe I'll check out the dining car. I've never dined on the train before.

I couldn't get out of bed the next day. Mom and Pop had risen early and were dressed in their second-best clothes—their first-best clothes had been the ones they'd worn on the train to Chicago.

"Where are you going?" I wiped the sleep out of my eyes and watched as Pop fastened his watch and Mom retrieved her purse. I had taken the time to roll my hair in pin curls the night before, and as the bobby pins had come out, the curls hung loose like giant spiders around my head.

"The resettlement office. *Tou-san* and I need to find jobs."

I pulled myself up from the bed and followed them into the dining room in my cotton pajamas. This would be the first time my mother had ever looked for paid work. But we certainly needed the money. There was literally nothing to eat or drink in the apartment. The tap water from both the bath faucet and the sink were brownish. And the refrigerator was still in need of a block of ice.

All night I had debated whether I should tell my parents about what the coroner had told me. What if there was a follow-up story in the newspaper that mentioned the abortion? What a shock that would be. Abortion was against the law. I had heard of girls in my high school getting pregnant, but they were usually sent away to some relative's house in the middle of nowhere. One of Rose's classmates apparently got an abortion from her doctor, but it was so hush-hush that most of us could not even speak of it.

In camp, I had read out loud a brief story in the JACL's house newspaper, the *Pacific Citizen*, about an Issei doctor in the free part of Arizona who had been sentenced to prison for performing an abortion on a *hakujin* woman. "*A-la-la*," my mother pronounced in judgment. More than by the word "abortion," she was scandalized by the words "prison term." It was clear that if you had an abortion, you didn't speak of it and certainly shouldn't get caught.

How could I say anything to my parents?

I'd stored Rose's suitcase in the linen closet so that my parents wouldn't encounter it right away. Their hearts and minds were so tender that they didn't need further reminders that she wasn't with us anymore.

"The funeral arrangements still need to be made," my mother said before leaving.

"I'll take care of it," I said. My mother's crease-ridden face immediately softened. "What day should I request? The weekend?"

"The sooner, the better."

"You mean even as early as tomorrow?"

Mom glanced at Pop, not for guidance, but to monitor his state of mind. "Tomorrow will be fine—"

"Unless we find *shigoto*," Pop chimed in.

Mom and I knew that it would not be easy for two old Japanese immigrants to find a decent job, specifically one that didn't involve cooking or cleaning.

"Well, *ittekimasu*," my mother said—just as she did every time she left the house; so normal, so everyday. The Japanese phrase felt like a warm salve on my neck. Pop, on the other hand, bobbed his head as if I were a random acquaintance he happened to pass on the street.

I took a quick shower in the brown water and had changed into one of my cotton dresses when I heard a knock at the door.

"Who is it?" I asked, fastening the last button, closest to the hollow of my neck.

"Harriet Saito. I live on the second floor." The voice sounded bright yet firm, reminding me of a grammar school teacher's.

I unlocked the door. Harriet was an average-sized Nisei woman like me with an updo of dark-brown curls. I was embarrassed of my disastrous pin curls. I needed to know who did her hair.

"I work with Mr. Tamura in the resettlement office."

She offered up a thermos and something in a brown bag. "I thought that you might need some food."

Gratefully receiving the items, I invited her in. In the thermos was hot coffee and in the bag were a copy of the *Pacific Citizen*, a loaf of bread, some strawberry preserves. I recognized the jar: it was the same as the one Rose had been using as a cup.

"Oh, thank you so much." These mundane gifts felt more valuable than gold.

"And don't worry about Rose's death being mentioned in the *Pacific Citizen*. I overheard Mr. Tamura saying that he was planning to talk to them. He'll work to keep it out of the *Free Press*, too."

I didn't know how to respond. While I wanted to protect my sister's memory and my family's privacy, especially from the gossipmongers in camp, were we doing Rose a disservice by erasing her death?

Harriet must have sensed my discomfort because she directed her attention to our kitchenette, checking our hot plate and opening the rickety refrigerator. "You'll need some ice," she declared, and recommended an iceman in one of Mr. Tamura's directories.

We sat down at the table and I absorbed all the daily living resources that she had to share. For hairstyling, she recommended a couple of beauty shops, including the one in the Mark Twain Hotel. "The family was in Amache, the camp in Colorado. They'll give you a discount as you settle in."

I slowly sipped the coffee in the thermos cup, letting each bit of it energize my body. Harriet looked down at the floor. "I lost my brother in the war. I know what you are going through."

My eyes grew wide. "In Europe?"

She nodded. "Italy. A month ago."

"That's so awful."

"My parents had a memorial service in camp. I was here, so I couldn't go. Isn't it strange that once you leave camp, they make it so much harder to get back in?"

The irony of that burned in me. I also couldn't stand the thought that Harriet's parents had to say goodbye to their fallen son behind barbed wire.

"He knows that I love him." She used the present tense, as if he was still alive.

She was trying to console me, but instead I felt a stab of anger. Why did our siblings have to die while we were torn away from our homes?

I screwed the cup back on the thermos. "I plan on going to the police station today," I announced.

"Why?"

"I need to collect my sister's belongings."

"Mr. Tamura can get all of those things for you. So you don't have to deal with all that ugliness."

"No, I need to." Harriet might have been able to make her peace with her brother's death from a distance, but I wasn't like her.

"Mr. Tamura also says that he can loan your family the money for the mortuary and funeral."

Pop would resist the offer, but it wasn't like we had any alternatives. We'd each been given twenty-five dollars from the WRA when we left, and I had about ten dollars from my job in the Supply Department at Manzanar. Most of that had gone toward the apartment.

"Go to Klaner's. It's a couple of blocks away," Harriet said. "Mr. Tamura has already spoken to them. You'll be our first—" She couldn't finish her sentence and I wasn't going to help her. She pushed herself from her seat and awkwardly excused herself, saying that she was going to be late to work.

I told her that she probably would be seeing my parents, who had set off for the resettlement office an hour ago.

"Good thing that they went in early," she said. "Sometimes the wait can take all day."

"If you happen to run into them, don't mention anything about me going over to the police station."

"Of course, of course. I understand." Harriet gave me a faint smile tinged with worry.

According to the map, the police station was only about six blocks away. LaSalle was full of rooming houses and historic churches with high-pitched steeples and rounded wooden doors.

The police station was in a three-level rectangular structure made of giant brick blocks. A row of seven long windows lined each floor, and steps led up to the covered front entrance. As I had rarely set foot in a police station in Los Angeles, entering one in a massive foreign city like Chicago shook me to my bones. I took a couple of deep breaths before going up the stairs.

The doors burst open, revealing three *hakujin* women wearing tight clothing, their hair in disarray and their mouths smeared with lipstick. A couple of black men, one in a priest's collar and holding a Bible, followed, but they didn't seem at all connected with the women. Even before noon, the East Chicago Avenue police station was bustling.

No one behind the counter batted an eyelash when I stated I was the sister of the woman killed at the Clark and Division train station. I was in a place whose business was tragic endings.

I had to wait for at least half an hour. I watched as men, both *hakujin* and black, shadows of stubble on their faces, were escorted in by police officers in dark uniforms and caps. Finally, an officer with jet-black hair came my way. "Eat-o." He pronounced my last name with a strong accent that I hadn't heard before. As he drew closer, I saw his face was deeply lined, making him much older than I'd first thought.

I stood up from the bench. "I'm Aki Ito."

He introduced himself as Officer Trionfo. His eyes were like a serpent's as he scanned my body from my tan pumps to my blue day dress. The humidity was doing crazy things to my hair, and from the corner of my eye, I spied a stray curl springing out from my head.

I explained that I was Rose's sister and had come to collect her belongings.

"You don't want them," he said. "All bloody and crusty. Pretty disgusting. Have your father or the War Relocation Authority man pick them up."

"No." Pop was hanging by a string. I wasn't going to subject him to this. And Ed Tamura was a bureaucrat. He was nice enough, but he wasn't family. "No, I'd like to collect them myself." I was embarrassed to hear my voice was thin and shaking, and the police officer responded with a knowing smile, as if he knew that I'd back down.

This would not do at all. I was here as Rose's advocate. And I wasn't going to abandon her.

Before I knew it, I was practically shouting. "Give me my sister's things!"

The policeman, perhaps shocked by my burst of emotion, grasped hold of his night stick. I imagined a rain of blows coming my way. I welcomed them—perhaps physical pain could mitigate the pain that I held inside. I squeezed my eyes shut but nothing happened. I opened them to see a middle-aged *hakujin* police officer standing between us. He wasn't wearing a hat and his short-cropped hair was the color of honey.

"What's going on?" he asked Trionfo.

"Ito's kid sister. She wants her purse and dress. They're all in tatters."

"Why don't you get them out of the safe."

The officer locked eyes with this man I assumed must be his superior.

"Officer Trionfo." The blond man's voice was stern.

The policeman shook his head and took off down a staircase to the basement.

"Thank you." I pressed down on the pleats of my dress.

"I'm Sergeant Graves." Whereas Trionfo's jacket had bunched up around his burly arms and middle, this man's uniform rested flat on his lean body. All his visible skin was marked with faint freckles.

"Aki Ito."

He seemed amused by my name, as if it were some kind of joke. He gestured toward the counter. "We'll need some information from you to claim the items."

I filled out a form with my name, how I was related to Rose, and my address. I hadn't had time to properly remember the street number and had to go into my purse to retrieve the information. "We arrived in Chicago two days ago," I explained.

The sergeant responded as if this was not news to him. "Well, welcome. I'm sorry that you had to arrive in our fine city like this."

"My sister didn't kill herself," I told him. "She wasn't the type."

"You people have gone through a lot these last couple of years."

To hear it declared so plainly by a *hakujin* astonished me.

"Yes," I replied. "Yes, we have." I waited to see if he would assure me that the investigation would be ongoing, but he was silent, a patient smile on his lips. Since he wasn't making any promises, I felt like I needed to push more. "You will find out what happened to my sister."

Graves nodded. "Of course. This case isn't closed. I have your information, so I'll make sure to send a man to your apartment if there's anything new."

I wasn't optimistic that he would follow through, but at least he seemed more accessible than the other officer.

"Where are you heading now?" he asked.

"The mortuary. Klaner's, I think they call it."

"Well, you'll be in good hands there." He excused himself, saying Officer Trionfo would return shortly with Rose's belongings.

"Thank you, Sergeant."

He gripped my hand goodbye. His fingers felt cool and comfortable, like he was used to gripping the hands of grieving women.

Trionfo reappeared a few minutes later.

"Here." He threw a brown package in my face, grazing my forehead. More than anything I felt embarrassed to be treated so disrespectfully. I looked around to see if anyone had witnessed it, but everybody was fixated on other problems that seemed more immediate than mine.

Klaner's turned out to be an impressive facility at 1253 North Clark Street. It was a block north of Division Street and expansive, with its own elegant funeral parlor.

Mom and Pop weren't regular churchgoers and probably skewed more Buddhist than anything else, but Rose and I had attended the local Japanese Christian church in Glendale from time to time. All of us had written that we were Christian on our leave papers. It was easier for us that way.

The funeral director, who had terrible pockmarks on the sides of his face, was attentive and called the coroner's office to find out when Rose's body could be released. My exposure to church in Glendale helped me answer his questions about the service. "Psalms for the scripture reading," I told him. "Something about God leading us to green pastures."

I couldn't think of any hymns besides "Amazing Grace." "Can we dispense with singing?" I finally said. "Maybe the organist can just play something." The funeral director seemed a bit surprised by my request, yet wrote my directions down in his files nonetheless.

"And she'll need a resting place."

"Ah, we can cremate her and put her remains in an urn. You probably would like her close to you."

"We might want to bury her."

The *hakujin* man lowered his eyes as if he couldn't bear to look at my face. He got up from his desk, spoke to another employee, and then got on the phone.

Finally he returned. "You can have the funeral service here, but interment may be an issue." I tried to keep up with what he was saying. "We'll have to insist on cremation. Then you can determine where to place the ashes."

"Is it because we're not from Chicago?" I asked.

The funeral director's hunched shoulders slumped further. His body language reminded me of Vivi Pelletier's mother and all the others who messaged that the Japanese were not welcome. And sure enough, forced into a corner, he articulated what I feared. "At this particular time, cemeteries are not accepting Japanese bodies."

I didn't have the energy to protest; if they were going to refuse Rose, I didn't want her to be buried anywhere near here.

"I recommend that you speak to these people." He

handed me a paper on which he had written *Chicago Japanese Mutual Aid Society* and a phone number. We made arrangements for the funeral to be held the day after next to allow time for them to get Rose's body from the coroner's office.

After that appointment was over I headed for the diner, where I was supposed to meet Roy. I felt like a soggy tissue. From the desolation of Manzanar, Chicago had seemed like a light in the distance. But now that we were here, I could see it was a mirage of what we had desperately hoped for.

What my mother always said about completing tasks, though, was true. I did feel a sense of accomplishment after making the arrangements for Rose's funeral, despite the harrowing and disappointing encounters in the police department and the mortuary. Maybe these Chicago institutions had momentarily knocked me off my feet, but in a few minutes, I would be sitting in a restaurant, which I hadn't done in more than two years.

As I entered the diner, a server near the door handed me a small box of Milk Duds. I wasn't quite sure what I was supposed to do with it and stood there like a silly goose until Roy called me over to one of the front booths.

"They handed me this." I held the yellow box in front of Roy.

"It's a Greek tradition to receive something sweet before a meal."

I slipped into the booth across from Roy. He was wearing a tie and some of his hair had gotten loose from the front of his oiled pompadour. I didn't waste any time and popped the Milk Duds, one after another, in my mouth. They were the medicine I needed, transforming me into the Aki that Roy had known before all this had happened.

We both ordered coffee and after much prompting from Roy, who said this was his treat, I added pancakes, my favorite. The pancakes in camp were so doughy that I almost choked on them; as a result, I'd sworn them off for the past two years.

"What's in the package?" he asked, as I carefully placed it next to me on the vinyl seat.

"Rose's clothing and belongings from the police."

"What the hell, Aki? What are you doing, carting around her things all over Chicago?"

"I came straight from the station. And the mortuary." I didn't want to relive my encounter with Officer Trionfo and chose not to get into the details. "The service is the day after tomorrow at eleven. So can you spread the word?" I figured that the crowd would be small because most people would be working, but Roy assured me that he would be there.

"She'll be cremated," I announced, my voice getting shaky again.

"That's no surprise. No *hakujin* cemetery wants a Jap body. Same as Los Angeles."

"I thought Chicago would be different."

Roy snorted in response.

"I'm supposed to contact the Japanese Mutual Aid Society to store her remains at their mausoleum."

"It's at Montrose Cemetery. You'll be able to keep her there for a while."

"Is it far away?" I couldn't imagine leaving Rose too far from us.

"It's pretty far north. A German fellow bought some prairie land for it. But it's still in Chicago."

"Is that close to Evanston?"

"Why, you planning to go to Northwestern or something?"

"That's where Tomi lives."

Roy frowned.

"You know Tomi, Rose's old roommate."

"Why do you want to see her?" Roy's voice sounded unnecessarily harsh.

"To ask her about Rose."

"I don't think she'll know much. She and Rose didn't talk much recently."

I didn't know why Roy was pouring cold water on my plans. My face must have revealed my irritation because he pushed a large box across the table. "Here. This is for you and your family."

It was a box of chocolate-and-caramel logs, twenty-four of them, according to the printing on the box.

"Did you steal this?"

Roy started laughing and I started to do the same. I hadn't heard Roy laugh since before the war. "You know that I work at a candy factory, don't you?"

My pancakes arrived and I felt like crying. They were perfect brown discs, steaming hot with a big pat of butter melting on top. I kept pouring the maple syrup atop the stack until Roy told me to stop. "You're acting like you're a hobo off the street."

"I don't care what anyone thinks," I said. My mother had always chided me for unladylike behavior, and I was tired of people telling me to rein in my natural inclinations.

In between bites, I told Roy about my visit to Rose's old apartment and the discovery of her diary.

"I didn't know Rose kept one of those. She didn't seem the type." He brought his coffee mug to his mouth and before taking a sip, asked, "Did she write anything about me?"

"No," I lied. I needed more time to pore over her diary, but I knew Roy was mentioned several times. "At least nothing much."

Roy drummed the surface of the Formica table with his fingers. Was he nervous about what Rose could have written about him? If the coroner's assessment was true, someone had gotten Rose pregnant. And Roy was the one male that Rose was the closest to in Chicago.

"I'd like to see that diary someday," he said.

I kept dabbing at my sticky lips with my napkin. I had no intention of showing Rose's diary to him. "Most of it was everyday things. Traveling within Chicago. Getting her hair done at the Beauty Box in the Mark Twain Hotel. Regular Rose stuff."

"So mostly about her."

I ignored Roy's insult. "From her diary, it didn't seem like she was depressed. I don't believe that Rose would commit suicide; do you?"

Roy ran his fingers through his hair. "Being out of camp does things to you. You're finally free but you're not. It's like there are invisible bars caging you in. You do something you're not supposed to do and you hit a wall."

"Like what?"

"Like asking for a promotion because you've been working harder than any other man on the line." Roy's jaw tightened. "If it weren't for my mother, I would have enlisted by now."

I remembered the fate of Harriet's brother. "But you might be killed."

"I'm no namby-pamby jellyfish. I know what people are saying." Roy's family was depending on him, especially in communicating with the men—Roy referred to them as vultures—who had taken over the Tonai produce market. Roy's father was still being held in an alien detention center in Santa Fe, New Mexico. There was little chance that the government would approve an early release for him, so the female Tonais decided to stay in camp, at least for now.

The waitress came to take away my empty plate. I had completely devoured every crumb and drop of syrup.

Two Nisei women who had entered the diner stopped at our booth. The taller one was pulling at the arm of the shorter one to prevent her from addressing us, but it didn't work. "It sure didn't take you long, did it?" The woman's voice was scratchy like a smoker's. She wore a wide-brimmed hat, accentuating the round shape of her face.

Roy shaded his eyes, as if he didn't want to look directly at the women. "This is Rose Ito's sister. Aki." The two women fell silent.

I exchanged greetings with them but only retained the shorter woman's name, Marge. "I didn't know Rose had a sister," she rasped. The taller one, who wore a pair of cat-eye glasses, gave me a once-over.

After awkwardly excusing themselves, they took refuge in a booth on the other side of the restaurant.

"What was that all about?" I asked.

Roy pulled at the front piece of his hair. "I dated one of their roommates. Things didn't work out so well."

"How about you and Rose?"

"What about us?"

"You know."

"We were friends, Aki. Friends from back home. Only that. She was actually a lot nicer to me here in Chicago. Probably because you and your folks weren't around. There was no one else she knew from Los Angeles."

"Did she have any boyfriends? Did she go on any dates?"

"You know Rose." He stared into his empty coffee mug. "She was always surrounded by people, but no one really knew her. No one could get close. Maybe you were the only one who knew the real Rose."

This whole conversation was a dead end. For all the years that I had known Roy and the Tonais, could I trust him? Rose had obviously had a relationship with someone, and if it hadn't been with Roy, then who? I was annoyed that he hadn't shed any light on what had been going on in Rose's life. I let Roy pay because I didn't have enough cash to cover my pancakes. He promised to take me to a Chinese restaurant next to eat chop suey.

Before we went our separate ways, I told him, "Remember the day after tomorrow. Rose's funeral."

My legs were tired from all the walking, so I hopped on the subway, even though I would ride it for only one stop. It was getting to be rush hour and I was almost crushed in the movement of men in scratchy suits and women in high heels. Hot air pressed through the train car and at certain moments I felt nauseated as I inhaled the stench of the brown evidence package. My stomach had always been weak, too responsive to my emotions. Before I knew it, the stationmaster was calling out, "Clark and Division," and my heart leapt. My eyes filled with tears as I clutched Rose's things. I had intended to scrutinize the activities on the train platform where Rose could have been standing the evening of May 13, but instead I was pushed forward by a stream of people, as if I was completely uprooted and unmoored.

CHAPTER 6

Some girls found a job at a bra factory. I thought that might be fun if we get free samples. But it turns out that you have to work in a room without any windows and the bras are pretty cheaply made, with hooks that dig into your back.

My roommate Tomi works at the big candy company in town and said that there may be an opening for me. I interviewed with a round man with a waxed mustache, the kind that you see in Westerns. I was trying to keep from laughing, so I think I might have been smiling the whole time. I got the job.

To prepare for the funeral, my mother and I went out to get our hair done. It had only been a week since we had gone to the camp beauty parlor in Manzanar to make sure that we looked presentable for Chicago. Now we needed to be *chanto*, in perfect order, to say goodbye publicly to Rose.

I took us to the beautician inside the Mark Twain Hotel. It was close and Harriet had recommended it, but the real reason was that I knew Rose had gone there.

We left Pop alone in the apartment, reminding him that the iceman was on his way. As soon as we walked outside, we felt heat rising from the concrete and soaking us in a messy, sweaty stew—and it was only mid-May. I never thought that I would look back longingly at our summers in the Owens Valley, where the blinding and unrelenting sun darkened our faces, arms and legs if we didn't cover them. But at least it was dry there, not humid like this.

Compared to our apartment, the Mark Twain was grand, stretching out on the corner like a bird in flight. It was at least five stories high. It even had a lobby with a couple of workers behind the desk. One looked like a Nisei; he had a wide chest with a head of curly hair. As we passed, he didn't smile or ask us any questions, simply stared, as if he knew that we were fresh out of camp.

The Beauty Box was toward the back of the first floor. There were a couple of tall chairs facing round mirrors and drawers. "We don't have appointments," I apologized to the Nisei proprietor, who was getting paid by a client, a *hakujin* woman who looked like she was walking around in a pink nightgown and robe.

"No worries, no worries. The rest of my afternoon is open."

The beautician, who introduced herself as Peggy, surveyed my mother's hair. "Your hair is so healthy and black. You must eat a lot of nori."

Mom smiled, the first time in a long time. She did pride herself on her hair. "I am Yuri," she said, careful not to mention our last name. "And this is my daughter, Aki."

"Yuri and Aki. Those names are easy to remember. And are you new in town?"

We both nodded. I wanted so much to ask her about Rose, but I knew that Mom wouldn't want me to bring her up with a stranger.

Peggy didn't ask us a lot of questions about our background. We did tell her that we had come from Manzanar, and that was all she needed to know. She took Mom first, expertly taming the cowlick that sometimes made her look like a cockatiel. She put Mom under the salon hair dryer and then studied me.

"You might look good with a shorter hairstyle. It'll be easier to take care of in this Chicago humidity."

I don't know how Peggy figured out that grooming was one of my weaknesses. Or perhaps it was painfully self-evident. I had kept my hair shoulder-length, because that's the way Rose kept hers.

"Ah—"

Mom lowered her head from the vroom of the dryer. "Yes, Aki-*chan*, cut. It will be *sukkuri* for the summer."

I didn't care how refreshed I looked. "Don't make me look like a boy," I said in a soft voice to Peggy.

The beautician laughed, a peal that was as delightful as wind chimes. "Even if I shaved your head, you would still look like a girl. But trust me, you're in good hands. I'll make you pretty as a picture."

As Peggy clipped away, I felt pampered in a way I hadn't felt in . . . maybe ever. She put my hair in curlers and then sat me under the dome of the hair dryer, too. When she removed the curlers, she rearranged my hair with a fine-tooth comb with a sharp tail that could have poked my eye out. In the mirror my face transformed from a less attractive version of my sister's into someone I had never seen before.

"Oh, why are you crying? Do you hate it?" Peggy pulled out a couple of facial tissues from her drawer and held them out to me.

During this time, Mom had been watching me like a bird of prey. I knew what she was thinking. *Don't you dare say anything. Keep your mouth shut.*

I dabbed at the wetness. "I'm a crybaby. It usually takes more time for people to find out."

"Oh, you've been through so much. Coming from camp to this big city. It's a shock to your system. It was to mine, too." She went through the drawers in her station and dug out three hair rollers that she said I could have for free. "Just put these on when you go to bed."

"Aki-*chan,* we are going to be late," Mom said, even though we had no pressing appointments. She settled the bill and practically dragged me from the chair.

In the hallway she murmured to me in Japanese, "Our family business is our business. No one else needs to know." Tomorrow, though, we were having a funeral, and everyone would know that Rose Ito had died.

My parents didn't expect many people at the service. The weather reports predicted a thunderstorm later in the day; in Chicago showers seemed to come out of nowhere and threatened to drench our beautiful hairdos because we still hadn't purchased umbrellas.

The mortuary attendant, who had given us the coroner's death certificate in an envelope, told us to sit in the first row of the funeral parlor, in front of the urn that held my sister's ashes. Since Rose's world in Chicago had been such a mystery to me, I opted to stand at the door and greet every person who entered, to gather information about who she could have had a relationship with. My parents, on the other hand, followed protocol, my father slumped over in his suit, while my mother kept looking behind her to see what she was missing.

I was genuinely shocked to see how many people came in for the late-morning funeral. First of all, it had been pulled together in only forty-eight hours. And also, it was right in the middle of the day, when the Nisei should have been working in factories or at desks pushing papers. Back in Tropico, we made sure to have the funerals in the evening, after the produce workers had completed their shifts and had time to take a bath.

Funerals, even more than births or even weddings, were absolutely mandatory to recognize. Back in California, we made sure to place cash called *koden* in envelopes to leave with the receptionists before we entered. Although its roots are in Buddhism, almost every old-timer, regardless of religion, gives *koden* in the Japanese community in the United States. If someone dies, the community rallies around and gives money to the deceased's family members to pay for the funeral costs. And in return, when the time comes, the survivors will pay the same exact amount to those who gave them *koden* during their time of need.

So far, Klaner's had had very few funerals for the Japanese. It made sense as most of us were young and relatively healthy. Pop, in fact, seemed like one of the oldest. The head mortician had told me that the German and Polish immigrants also have a tradition of mutual aid for funerals, but nothing as prescribed as *koden* for the Japanese. I asked the attendant for a lined accounting sheet and told him to make sure each envelope had the name of the giver and a return address.

Roy was one of the first to arrive. He came with his roommate, Ike, a tall Nisei with thin, hooded eyes. Although Roy's hair was neatly combed back and he was wearing a tie, there was something about his face that didn't look right. His eyes, usually clear, were terribly bloodshot, and his lips seemed thick, as if they had been stung by a mosquito. He offered to be an *uketsuke*, a receptionist for the *koden* money, even though before the war that job was usually assumed by young women or old men. I told him that a mortuary worker was handling that responsibility. I'm not sure why I was suddenly concerned with appearances, but I didn't want Roy to look weak in any way. I hoped that he would sit up front near my parents, but he chose to sit in back to keep his eye on me, as if he was expecting trouble to walk into the funeral.

A steady stream of people began arriving shortly thereafter. Even Louise and Chiyo, wearing brown and navy dresses, respectively, were a welcome sight. I accepted Chiyo's bear hug and Louise's tight elbow squeeze. A *hakujin* woman about our age with flaming red hair and a couple of men in perfectly tailored suits and hats sat with Roy. I assumed that they all worked together at the candy company. A few *hakujin* people even showed up.

Ed Tamura arrived with his wife and an older man wearing a minister's collar. Harriet was right behind them.

"I didn't expect you all to come," I said.

"Mr. Jackson said it would be okay and that he and the Quaker women would cover for us," Harriet explained. I had heard that this Mr. Jackson was the man who ran the War Relocation Authority office.

Mr. Tamura introduced me to the minister, who was in charge of a small Japanese congregation at the Moody Bible Institute on LaSalle and Chicago. With thinning hair that looked like it was raked into place, the Reverend Suzuki had a long face and square jaw; I wondered if he could have been half *hakujin*. "I meant to meet with you and your parents this week," he said. "We were surprised that you had planned the funeral so soon."

I refrained from saying that we wanted to get the funeral over with, because that would sound callous. But more time would have forced us to consider protocol for informing our relatives in other camps, and so on. I had no idea if I would even let Hisako know; our camp exit was supposed to give the imprisoned hope. By having the funeral so quickly, we could dispense with such decisions and considerations, at least for right now—as long as Mr. Tamura succeeded in keeping our tragedy out of the *Manzanar Free Press*.

"I didn't know your sister," the Reverend Suzuki said apologetically. "May I get some quick biographical information for my eulogy?"

We took a few steps back in the hallway and I told him the first things that came to my mind. That Rose was always the first to try something new, whether it be the Lindy Hop, a new type of chewing gum or spaghetti in a can. That she never seemed scared even when she might have been deep inside. That her favorite color was orange, even though she was careful to never wear it because she claimed that it looked awful against her skin. And that she was my older and only sister.

"Where was she born?"

"Tropico. California." I told him her birthdate and repeated my parents' names, Gitaro and Yuri Ito.

The organist started playing, a cue for us to get situated for the service. As we passed through the velvet curtains, two zoot suiters entered behind us. "This funeral is for Rose Ito," I told them. Roy immediately came to my side, as if he were expecting the two Nisei men.

"We know," one of them said, and I remembered him—the one who'd approached me outside Rose's old apartment. This time, instead of averting my gaze, I took him all in. His skin was dark, as if he had spent a lot of time in the sun. There was a crescent scar by his eye. Could it have been from chicken pox, or something more nefarious?

"We want to pay respects," he said. "More than you ever did, Tonai." The scarred man's companion was much larger, with a doughy face. He said nothing but nodded in agreement. They brushed against Roy as they found seats in the back row.

When they were out of earshot, I whispered to Roy. "What did he mean by that?" *More than you ever did.*

"Those guys are trouble."

"How did they know Rose?"

"Maybe she took pity on them."

I made a slight face. We both knew that Rose didn't pity anyone.

Placing the small bundle of *koden* envelopes collected by the mortuary worker in my handbag, I took my seat beside my parents, while Roy planted himself a couple of rows back with his roommate.

The organ music stopped and then the minister began talking. I couldn't pay enough attention to absorb what he was saying. I heard words—Tropical, not Tropico—and something about how Rose liked to dance and eat spaghetti. It all didn't make any sense and I felt my mother's body stiffen next to me.

Finally the attendees made their way to pay respects to Rose's ashes and offer their condolences to my parents and me. Besides Roy and the Tamuras, there was really nobody who knew us. Their words of sympathy seemed especially hollow. Did they realize what we had really lost?

A heavy mustached man who resembled Teddy Roosevelt bent down to address Mom and Pop. He said that he had been Rose's supervisor at the candy company. "She was such a good worker. A fine human being." He spoke slowly and enunciated each word as if my parents wouldn't be able to understand him.

Louise and Chiyo were next in line. I introduced them to my parents, who bowed their heads to their chests. "We are indebted for all you have done for our daughter," my mother said in Japanese.

"So Tomi didn't come," I said. I was deeply disappointed as I wanted to meet the girl that Rose had been the closest to in Chicago. In a note I had slid underneath the door of their apartment the day before, I had asked them to somehow let Tomi know about the funeral as well.

"It's the end of the school year, so I think she has a lot of responsibilities around the house for the professor and his wife," Louise said.

We'll see about that, I thought to myself, already planning a trip to Evanston.

The line moved quickly. Soon most of the attendees, including Roy and his roommate, left to return to work.

A bespectacled *hakujin* man stood in the back with a small notebook the size policemen use. He jotted notes with the stub of a pencil. He was thin and wore wire-rim glasses that made him almost look owl-like. He was the type of man who could look handsome in one instance and decrepit in another.

He didn't bother to offer any condolences and I was suspicious of why he was here. If Roy had been there still, I would have asked if he knew the man. I took a deep breath and headed across the room toward him. Just as I reached him, he turned and exited the building.

"The minister screwed up the funeral."

Realizing the comment was directed to me, I turned, seeking the speaker. Almost hidden by the red velvet curtain was the zoot suiter with the scar.

A part of me thought he was right, but it hadn't been Reverend Suzuki's fault. I straightened up and looked the boy in the eye. "What is your name?"

"Hammer."

Given the tragic circumstances, I tried not to smile. The Nisei had all sorts of funny nicknames like Bacon and Nails, so why not Hammer?

"My real name is Hajimu," Hammer said sheepishly. He seemed more embarrassed by his given Japanese name than his informal moniker.

"I'm Aki. Thank you for coming and thank you for helping me with the door the other day."

My calm demeanor seemed to throw him off for a moment because he couldn't offer a response. He was wearing a mustard-color zoot suit with a cigarette behind his ear. His friend, who I learned was called Manju, shifted his massive weight from one leg to another in a plaid suit that seemed a bit too small for him.

"How did you know Rose?" I finally asked.

"From the neighborhood."

"Rose was very friendly," Manju said.

I frowned. I didn't like what he seemed to be insinuating.

Hammer could tell that I had taken offense. He excused himself and practically pushed Manju out the door.

My mother had finished settling the mortuary bill and drew near me.

"Why were you talking to those boys?"

"They knew Rose. They were paying their respects."

Mom didn't seem to believe me. "Never shame us. All we have is our reputations."

Outside the sidewalks were wet, but the sun was out as if the sudden late morning downpour had been the universe's joke on us humans. Nothing could be trusted in Chicago, especially the weather.

Back in our apartment, I opened the death certificate, which included the basic details of Rose's life.

Name: Rose Mutsuko Ito. Birthdate: July 3, 1920.

Under cause of death it stated, *Cardiac arrest from torn*

brachial artery in subway collision. From my nurse's aide training, I knew that the brachial artery was the major blood vessel in the upper arm.

Below that, *Suicide.*

There was nothing about the abortion, but I felt like I had to say something. Reveal what I had heard about Rose.

I gave the *koden* envelopes to my father. Now it was our job to compile a list of people who had attended and given us money. We couldn't wait until morning; this was a duty that needed our attention now. It was imperative that we do *okaeshi*, return the money that was bestowed to us when the giver's time of loss came.

Pop had filled our newly cold icebox with cans of beer and grabbed one to help tackle our task. I went and got one for myself. I'd had a beer only once in my life before. After being released with a church key, the fizz of beer punctuated the quiet of our apartment. My parents were too distracted to comment.

We'd often taken care of the funerals for Pop's bachelor employees, so we already had a system in place to count *koden*. Pop counted the bills and wrote down the sum on the outside of the envelope. Mom wrote down the sum and the person's names, both Japanese and English, on a piece of notebook paper. It used to be Rose's job to check the names against the list from the funeral, to make sure that no envelopes were missing. I sat in Rose's place, drinking the beer right from the can, feeling its bitterness catch in my throat.

No revelation came out of my mouth that night, but in the morning at breakfast, over bread and strawberry jam, I blurted it out. "The coroner says Rose recently had an abortion."

Pop froze, some jam hanging down his chin, while Mom blinked as her mind adjusted to the information I had shared. "*Shikataganai, desho*," she said. "Rose is gone and there's nothing we can do about it. She'll want us to carry on. And we will. We won't talk about this ever again."

CHAPTER 7

The WRA office is in a very grand building, with many floors and fancy doodads around its windows. I would have loved to report to such an office every day. The War Production Board is also in there, so the elevators are full of men, high-tone types in suits, but also soldiers and workmen in overalls and boots. They have all kinds here.

Since I was planning to go to the WRA resettlement office later that day, my mother made me bring hastily written thank-you notes for Mr. and Mrs. Tamura as well as Harriet Saito. Neither of my parents had secured work yet, but they wanted to spend the rest of the day completing their letters on lined paper. With the *koden* monies we received, we could pay Mr. Tamura back for the mortuary fee as well as sundries like envelopes for our notes. Postage would be an additional cost; we decided to hand-deliver as many of the thank-you notes as possible.

The office was about a mile and a half away at 226 West Jackson. My parents had walked there—my mother said that spending money on a subway ride was *mottainai*, wasteful, but I suspected that it was more because they didn't want to imagine Rose dead on the tracks. My shoes were scuffed and dirty with hardly any tread, but I decided to walk, too, to get fresh air and escape the stifling mood of our apartment.

It felt so good to be ignored. Nothing you did went unnoticed in Manzanar. But now nobody from Block Twenty-Nine was going to call out and wonder if I was going to the mess hall or, God forbid, the lavatory. There were no guard towers or barbed wire. I could step lively on the concrete sidewalk, my purse underneath my arm, a young career woman reporting for a very important assignment.

My destination, the Chicago and North Western Office Building, loomed at least thirteen stories high. Everything that I had known in Los Angeles up to that time, in contrast, was spread out like a reclining fat man who didn't care how much space he was taking up.

I'd brought one of Pop's handkerchiefs and blotted the perspiration on my forehead and underneath my nose. I always sweated buckets, at least on my face, and often when I pulled out a compact to check myself, I'd see an unattractive red bloom on my cheeks. "Aki, why are you always a mess?" Rose would tease me, nary a blemish on her countenance except for that single beauty mark, no matter how stressed or tired she was. These were moments when I'd wondered if we truly were related.

Out in the hallway were folding chairs which were all occupied by Issei and Nisei newcomers seeking work or lodging. A *hakujin* woman came through with a tray of water and paper cups, offering everyone refreshments for the long wait. The woman wore a full-sized apron with a tiny flower pattern over her plain kelly-green dress. Other *hakujin* women milling around the office wore the same apron, a sign that they came to serve. They were most likely Quakers, I figured—Friends, as they called themselves.

I had first heard of the Friends back in Los Angeles. I'd thought they were simply friendly *hakujin* people, but my sister quickly corrected me. "It's a religion where they sit in a circle and don't even have a minister or anything," Rose said. She had gone to a Friends meeting in Pasadena with a classmate and found the experience quite uncomfortable. People silently waited for the Spirit to visit the room and Rose had no idea of who or what to expect.

The Friends seemed to help anyone in trouble. Some of the Friends drove on dusty roads for four hours to visit the detainees in Manzanar, bringing fresh pies or personal items found in storage. Their sense of charity and compassion overwhelmed me. I know that I should have felt appreciative, but instead I felt shame that we were in that kind of position in the first place.

But here in Chicago, I accepted the cup of water from the Quaker woman. In hindsight, it was probably the start of my soul's demise: the fact that I'd accept anything to help me and my family's survival here in Chicago.

I sat in the last folding chair, holding that paper cup, which was becoming soggier and more formless by the minute. I finally gulped down its contents like a cowboy taking a final swig of whiskey. That was when I noticed a familiar person standing in front of me.

"Aki, I didn't know that you'd be here today." Harriet, who was wearing an A-line dress that camouflaged her thick waist, grabbed ahold of my elbow and practically lifted me onto my feet. For a woman my size, she was surprisingly strong. She led me to the front of the line.

This favored treatment did not go unnoticed.

"Hey, what gives?"

"What's so special about her?"

"Yeah, she the queen of Spain or something?"

Worse were the silent, disapproving frowns of men and women of my parents' generation, some of them toothless, their cheeks pulled in like decaying jack-o'-lanterns.

As we finally entered the office, I practically had to climb over people seated in wooden chairs. I almost ended up in the lap of an Issei couple when I tried to allow room for two Nisei women to pass by on their way out.

My face reddened. I appreciated Harriet's kindness, but I really didn't want to stick out in any way.

A whisper rolled down the line, gathering volume. "She's the one whose sister died? Really?" I heard one Issei woman say to her friend as we moved to the head of the line. The same people who had glanced at me with such disdain bowed their heads.

"You didn't have to, Harriet," I told her as she plopped me in a chair at a desk in front of Mr. Jackson, the head honcho of the WRA office.

Grabbing the wet ball of the water cup from my hands, Harriet shook her head, signaling me to accept her favor, and left me with Mr. Jackson. In back of me was a young Nisei man with long hair that drooped over his eyes as he perused a magazine. He didn't even seem to notice that I was being helped before him.

Mr. Jackson wore glasses and had a mustache of brown and gray, which seemed to include remnants of his morning breakfast—toast and eggs. At another desk was Ed Tamura, talking in broken Japanese with an Issei couple.

Harriet had already given Mr. Jackson some forms she had filled out for me. I felt grateful for that. From the time we entered camp, we were always filling out forms with questions that sometimes didn't make any sense.

Mr. Jackson rolled my form into his typewriter. "What kind of work have you done?"

"Well, I worked in the produce market for about a year."

He began typing. "What were your responsibilities?"

"I answered the phone and took messages. And then in camp I worked in the Supply Department. I had to keep an inventory of items. I also went through training as a nurse's aide." We had left, however, before I was able to work at the Manzanar hospital.

"Excellent. And I suspect that you have good penmanship and can type."

Actually my handwriting was lousy and my father often had to lecture me because somebody misread my order. And my typing? It was henpecking at best. Mr. Jackson looked pretty deliberate with his keystrokes. I didn't say anything to contradict him, though.

Mr. Jackson glanced at a list of openings on a mimeographed piece of paper, then handed it to me.

I read the list. Almost all of the job descriptions called for an English-speaking Nisei, except the ones that involved janitorial work. "What is the Newberry Library?"

"It's right down the street from where you are living. They need another reference assistant."

The Nisei man in back of me broke his silence. "It's right next to Bughouse Square."

"Are there a lot of pests there?"

"No, they call it that because of the wackos who stand on soap boxes." The man pushed his hair back from his eyes. He looked familiar and I wondered if he had been in Manzanar.

Harriet had returned to my side. "Don't listen to him. It's a nice park with benches. You can bring your sack lunch and eat it there."

"So yes, you're interested in the job?" Mr. Jackson seemed eager to move me along.

I glanced at Harriet, who was vigorously nodding.

"I'll take it."

As Mr. Jackson got on the phone to communicate with my future employer, I felt a pang of guilt. Being the younger sister of a dead Nisei woman gave me an advantage over all these other people. I didn't want any special consideration, but I had my parents' well-being to protect. I had to accept.

I was to submit my paperwork to the head of the library's public service department. Harriet had drawn me a map, which was totally unnecessary. Walking north on Clark Street, I couldn't help but run into the Newberry. It dominated the block, a palatial four-story building that demanded respect. As I walked through the doors, I feared that either the structure or its keepers might spit me out.

The immaculate floors were so polished that my pitiful worn heels slid as I approached a guard standing by a bronze bust of a man. WALTER L. NEWBERRY, the statue read, and I figured that he must have been some incredible big shot even though I had never heard of him before. The guard directed me up an impressive staircase—I swear that I felt like Cinderella before she was transformed. My heart almost stopped beating. After sleeping in dilapidated wooden barracks and suffering through sandstorms, I couldn't quite reconcile that I was inside a place like this. And to think that I might even be working here. I came close to stumbling on those stairs a couple of times.

I finally reached a large open room with dozens of wooden desks, light streaming through long rounded windows. There was a reception desk where a man was checking in his briefcase with a blonde woman about my age. She wore a sky-blue dress, and her hair was the color of corn silk.

When it was my turn, I handed her the paperwork. She studied me curiously and asked me to wait as she consulted with her co-worker, a black woman carrying a stack of books, her glossy hair arranged into two rolls atop her head. She wasn't shy about giving me a once-over, either. At the produce market I had been around whites and even some blacks, but they had all been men who hadn't paid me much mind.

The *hakujin* woman made a short phone call, then returned to the receptionist table. "Wait a minute, okay?"

The supervisor in charge eventually appeared, a middle-aged man wearing a light-colored suit. Mr. Geiger had an easy smile. He asked me a few questions before he announced, "You'll be working here under Mrs. Cannon. Her other assistants will be training you. You'll start on Monday. Nine o'clock. Don't be late."

And with that I was hired.

I could have headed north back to the apartment, but returning to that dreary place didn't seem appealing after moving through the expanse of the Newberry Library. Across the street was the park—what the young Nisei man had referred to as Bughouse Square. I was curious about these "wackos," as I had seen my share of men mumbling to themselves on the streets of Skid Row next to the produce market in Los Angeles.

As I crossed the street, I felt normal for a moment, like I used to feel walking around my neighborhood in Tropico. A butterfly flew by. A squirrel scampered to an oak tree. I almost forgot that Rose was gone—that is, until I started thinking that I wanted to bring Rose to the park. I was overwhelmed again by sadness, an emptiness that would never quite be filled.

A long row of wooden benches wrapped around a fountain. I picked a spot and sat for I don't know how long. Political speakers took turns stepping up on the soap box or standing on the lawn, talking about the evils of fascism and how the Socialist Workers Party was being victimized by the government. Some merely recited recent headlines about the Allied forces winning back Cassino, Italy, from the Germans. My eyes started to flutter. I didn't want to be seen dozing on the bench like a common vagrant, so I stood up and straightened my dress.

I surveyed the park to make sure no one I knew had spotted me. Sitting on the other side of the fountain was the same strange *hakujin* man from the funeral, taking notes again. I felt the blood leave my face. What was he doing here? Maybe he was some kind of spy, keeping tabs on us Japanese Americans for the FBI. I felt a need to get out of Bughouse Square pronto.

I was walking at a fast pace down Clark when I heard someone behind me call, "Hey, hey, you—"

I turned to see the blonde reference assistant, breathing hard in her dress. I noticed that she was wearing flats, which was a relief. I couldn't imagine retrieving and carrying around stacks of books in high heels.

She obviously didn't know my name, so I introduced myself. Her name was Nancy Kowalski.

"So what are you? Chinese?"

I lowered my eyes. "No, Japanese. I'm a Nisei." I wasn't sure if Nancy would understand that term. "Born in America to Japanese parents."

"My friends are out in the Pacific, fighting the Japs. But I know that you aren't one of them. I've heard about you. The ones on the West Coast who were put in camps. The *Tribune* has been running all these stories on you. That we shouldn't be scared of you."

As she spoke a mile a minute, she gestured frenetically. I didn't know how to respond to all that she said.

"You'll like working here." She looked me up and down. "You seem like you'll fit in. Problem with me is I like talking so much. Sometimes I get in trouble for making too much conversation with the patrons. I put my foot in my mouth a lot. I'm constantly offending the other girl, Phillis. By the way, you spell her name *P-H-I-L-L-I-S*, without a *Y*. If I say something I shouldn't, tell me, okay? And I'll apologize in advance. I've probably said something offensive already."

I shook my head. "No," I lied. "You've been kind. And very helpful."

"And how do I say your name again? Achy?"

"It's Ah-key. It means autumn in Japanese."

"Autumn, I like that. I could call you Autumn—no, forget I said that. Achy. I got it."

I was walking on Clark when I saw Hammer kneeling by Rose's apartment stoop, throwing a coin against the wall. He had two cigarettes coming out of his mouth, as if one would not be enough.

I hugged my purse against my chest and tried to speed up, hoping that I would not be noticed. Of course, Hammer had a sixth sense about women walking by him.

"Hey, Manzanar."

Darn it. I could have been rude and ignored him, but I didn't want him to pursue me. I stopped and turned around. "Aki, remember? And I'm from Tropico." I didn't want to be identified by the concentration camp that had held me.

"Okay, Tropico then." The cigarettes he had held in his mouth were not lit because he stuffed one behind each ear. He was wearing the same mustard-colored suit and it was starting to smell in this humidity. Maybe that was why he used so much cologne.

"You look happy."

"I got a job."

"Where?"

"The Newberry Library."

"That fancy-pants place across from Bughouse Square." He rubbed his nose with the side of his hand. "Makes sense. You're so prim and proper. Ito-*san*'s daughter."

"Do you know my father?"

"Worked in the produce market for a little while. Before I was fired."

I raised my eyebrows.

"I'm not the type to wake up at the crack of dawn."

I was sure he wasn't. A couple of Nisei women walked past us, exchanging knowing looks. They probably suspected Hammer and I were an item, but that wasn't going to stop me from talking to him. "Where are you working now?" I asked.

"I'm in between jobs, you might say."

A wad of bills was stuffed in his top shirt pocket, causing the fabric to sag.

"Seems like you have plenty of money for someone between jobs."

"A man has to live." Hammer grinned, revealing a rotten eyetooth. "And no one is going to help us Japs. We gotta help ourselves."

"Where are you from?"

"Here, there, and everywhere."

"Stop being like that. Seems like you know plenty about my family and I know nothing about you."

Hammer rolled his tongue in his mouth as if he were sucking on hard candy. "How about I tell you one fact about me," he finally offered.

"Okay. But it can't be silly like what color socks you're wearing."

Hammer straightened, tossing the coin into his palm. He said nothing for a while and I turned to leave.

"I'm an orphan." He said it to my back, like he didn't want me to feel sorry for him. But I immediately did. I wondered if he might have been in that Manzanar orphanage, the one we called Children's Village. I didn't know what to say, so I stopped in my tracks and turned around to at least acknowledge that I had heard him. Apparently that was the right response because he grinned again.

Hammer was a bundle of contradictions and I didn't know quite what to make of him. Since he had made himself more vulnerable to me, I pushed forward with my inquiry. "What did you mean by what you said to Roy Tonai at the funeral? Something about you treating Rose better than Roy had."

"Ah, nothing."

"No, really, I want to know."

"Tonai has a short fuse. I don't know if you knew that about him."

I had seen Roy in all types of situations at the produce market. One time a grower from Long Beach tried to sell some soft cucumbers to my father and claimed that Roy had approved the transaction during a poker game. My father sent me to find Roy. When Roy heard what the farmer was claiming, I thought that he was going to blow his lid. He nearly pushed the farmer and his crates off the loading dock.

"So that's it? Are you saying that you saw him get mad at my sister?"

"I didn't say that."

Hammer was hiding something and I was getting nowhere with him. The sun was going down; my parents were probably wondering where I was. I couldn't wait to tell them that I had found a job. Maybe it didn't pay that much, but it was a lot more than the twelve dollars a month that I'd been making in camp. And it was someplace gorgeous, less than a mile away.

"Well, I have to go. My parents are waiting for me." I hoofed it down the sidewalk.

I was a few yards away when I heard him yell out, "Tropico, I like your new hairstyle."

CHAPTER 8

There are some wild nightclubs here in Chicago. There's one with a Hawaiian name that many Nisei men like to go to. Women—Caucasian, black and Japanese—loiter out front in their low-cut dresses, practically daring passersby to enter. It's common to see men lying down in their own vomit on the sidewalk from overdrinking. Mom would find it so disgraceful.

After my first week at the Newberry, Nancy was still calling me "Achy," but I didn't correct her. She was trying her best, and under the circumstances, her best was more than enough. Phillis Davis, the other assistant, kept her eyes on me constantly. It was as if she had never seen a Japanese person before. Then again, maybe she hadn't.

Both of them were good at explaining what our duties were. We checked briefcases in and out, answered the telephone and went into the stacks to retrieve books and ephemera that were ordered by the reference librarian on behalf of the patrons.

The patrons were mostly older *hakujin* men who might

have been professors at the local colleges. Not all of them, though. One woman regularly checked in a large lattice bag filled with parcels from local department stores. I knew in fact that she was the mother of a young child, because once she told me that time had gotten away from her and she was going to be late picking up her son from the school across the street. Another patron, a sharply-dressed black man, arrived with a different pocket square every visit.

There was a room where we could take our breaks, but I preferred to sit outside in Bughouse Square. Our lunchtimes were staggered so that at least one person would be working the desk.

Near the end of my first week of work, I was finishing a butter sandwich when Nancy joined me on my bench. I was a bit disappointed for my lunch sanctuary to be discovered but smiled at her nonetheless.

"So this is where you go off to. I sometimes take photos over here." She pulled out her own paper-bag lunch. "Kielbasa; have you had it?" Wrapped in wax paper was a long sausage in a roll. "Here." She broke off one end and handed it to me.

The boiled sausage looked so delicious; I couldn't turn it down. And sure enough, it was salty and meaty. I hadn't had anything so tasty in quite a while.

As we ate, we watched a few people rant and rave on the grass. One was a regular—a grizzled, shrunken man about my height who warned against the evils of American fascism. While I'd heard him repeat the same message twice already, today his scraggly red beard was shaved off, making him look twenty years younger.

After he jumped off his apple crate, I finally summoned the courage to bring up something that had been on my mind. "I don't think Phillis likes me much."

"Oh, she's like that. She doesn't wear her emotions on her sleeve. I thought that she completely loathed me and then I've come to find out that she doesn't mind me. I think that's the best you can do with Phillis."

"Does she live close by?"

"She's on the South Side. You know, the part where most of the Negroes live. I'm over in West Town near the Polonia Triangle." Nancy chewed quickly, a ball of sausage and roll expanding her right cheek. "Her brother is in the service. Army, I think. She won't talk much about it. But she's always sending letters to him. I see her putting the envelopes in the mailbox on the corner."

I wondered what Phillis thought of me. Maybe I was the enemy in her mind.

Nancy went on to talk about her family, which seemed to multiply many times over during our conversation. I actually enjoyed her prattling trivia about who was married to whom and how many children they had. "Do you have any brothers and sisters?" she finally asked.

I didn't know how to answer that question. Out of habit, my mouth said, "Yes, a sister. She's three years older than me." And then my head kicked in. "But she's not here in Chicago." I glanced at my watch and then got up abruptly, saying that my break was over.

I felt numb as I went to relieve Phillis. I think that she may have been annoyed that I was a few minutes late, but in that moment, I couldn't have cared less.

When I got home from work, Mom was cooking. She had found a part-time job, cleaning a Clark Street barbershop operated by the Bellos, two Filipino brothers. With all the stray hair and dirty tools, the shop needed to be cleaned every day. Pop didn't want her to go in late at night, so the Bello brothers and Mom struck a deal that she'd go in bright and early every morning around seven o'clock. With that arrangement, Mom was able to make dinner for us every night.

Using the electric burner in our kitchenette, she simmered scraps of beef and carrots in what smelled like a sukiyaki sauce. I wasn't sure where she got the soy sauce and rationed sugar, but the sukiyaki wasn't even the best surprise.

"We have *gohan*!" I exclaimed as Mom raised the cover of another pot, the steam lifting the stray strands of her hair.

Splendid rice—the sticky kind, not the type the *hakujin* ate with butter, all *pasa-pasa,* loose like sand. We had had rice in camp, too, but mess-hall rice was its own special creation. Sometimes it clumped together like some kind of swamp monster; other times, it looked okay but tasted like cardboard.

"Where's Pop?"

"He was going to the WRA office. To see about a job."

We waited for half an hour until six, but neither one of us could last longer than that. The meat was already getting overcooked, the sauce too reduced.

"I'm sure he's fine," I said, giving us permission to enjoy our first sukiyaki meal in our apartment in Chicago. I spooned the food onto two mismatched china plates, donations from the Friends. Before the sauce spilled over the lip of my plate, I was able to scoot some of the rice to absorb it.

Even though the sukiyaki didn't quite taste like the kind Mom used to make in Tropico, it was the best meal that I'd had in at least two years. *Enryo*, self-restraint, was a Japanese cultural value that Mom emphasized, and it took as much *enryo* as possible not to eat Pop's share.

Mom picked at her food, checking out the window for

Pop, even though it was too dark to identify the people walking below.

I dragged my spoon on the surface of the plate to make sure that there was no remaining sauce. Because of Pop's absence, Mom couldn't settle down and fully enjoy her dinner. "I'll check with Harriet. Maybe she knows something."

I went downstairs to the second floor and knocked on Harriet's door. I heard rustling, perhaps even low voices, before the door was opened an inch, revealing Harriet's right eye.

"Oh, Aki," she said.

I'd thought Harriet would let me in, but she positioned her body right in front of the crack in the door. I actually didn't know much about Harriet—if she lived with her parents, was married or had a boyfriend.

"Ah, I was wondering if you saw my father in the office today."

"I'm so sorry that it didn't work out."

I frowned and Harriet seemed regretful for revealing some information that she perhaps shouldn't have.

"It's hard to find a position for a man over fifty who isn't a native speaker," she explained. "The factories don't want him. And housewives don't want Issei men inside of their homes. You understand."

"So he didn't get a position?"

Harriet hesitated before admitting, "No."

"He hasn't come home tonight, so we were worried."

"Oh, I'm so sorry. He left the WRA about three o'clock, I think."

That was more than four hours ago.

Harriet apologized that she needed to take care of something quickly and closed the door. "The milk boiled over," I heard a male voice say. Who was she hiding?

When I returned to the apartment, I told Mom a white lie. I said that Pop had gone in for an interview.

"Maybe they hire him," Mom said, lifting an overflowing spoonful of rice toward her mouth.

Later, as I washed the dishes, I tried not to worry. No matter how much I studied the Triple A map, I still didn't understand Chicago. There were the special attractions by Chicago Harbor—the Field Museum, the lagoon, Grant Park, the Art Institute. And farther north, beaches and Lincoln Park, which had a zoo and golf courses. Everyone talked about the Loop, but I still didn't have a clear understanding of what was loopy about downtown.

Most impressive to me was Chicago's big powerful river, nothing like the Los Angeles River, a faint trickle in the middle of the concrete bank. The Chicago River, in contrast, asserted its dominance by cutting through the most elegant and expensive parts of the city. No one was going to control its waters, and I respected the river for that.

Chicago was divided into ethnic neighborhoods that weren't necessarily identified on my Triple A map. There was West Town—the Polish neighborhood where Nancy lived—and then the Greek, German and Italian districts. The blacks and the Irish both lived in the South Side but in different sections. Chicago even had a Chinatown; the restaurant Roy had promised to take me to was known for its *pakkai* and chow mein. My mouth was watering thinking about eating sweet-and-sour pork with noodles right now.

I told Mom to rest while I cleaned up. She had lost quite a bit of weight since we arrived in Chicago. Pop had, too. I hadn't, although I could probably stand to lose five pounds.

After washing our one pot and the dishes, I cleaned every spot of grime and dirt from our kitchenette. Mom had purchased a big carton of baking soda, which was more for cleansing than baking. Our icebox was a Coolerator, almost four feet tall, with a rectangular top compartment for a block of ice that needed to be replaced once a week. Our Coolerator was an old one that unfortunately leaked melting water into the main compartment, so we had to make sure to securely wrap our vegetables and meat in wax paper.

When the kitchen was clean, there was nothing left to do. No radio to listen to, nobody else to talk to. I wasn't much into knitting and sewing. Instead, I went to the closet and took out Rose's suitcase. Whenever I was alone in the apartment, I would do this, removing her clothing and refolding them. I was most curious about a dress with white cranes on a teal-green background. It was gorgeous but too gaudy for Rose's taste. I sniffed the collar; it smelled musky, like the scent of a man's cologne.

Also part of my routine was to take out her journal and reread the pages for one hint about how she had gotten pregnant and where she might have gone for an abortion. I sat on the floor, using the wall by the closet as a back support. The first part of Rose's journal was a confection, whipped cream with no dark pit. Rose didn't reveal that hard kernel inside of her. The entries about halfway through were more sporadic and brief, sometimes only one cryptic sentence. I had also removed the contents of Rose's purse. A round cracked mirror; her favorite lipstick, Red Majesty; her Citizen's Indefinite Leave card featuring her black-and-white headshot; and a coin purse with a few dollars.

I fell asleep on the floor, her dresses and slips strewn on my lap for comfort.

I was startled awake by the sound of a chair scraping our linoleum floors. Pop had come home and was attempting to sit down. He had left our apartment door open and I rose to lock it.

I glanced at my watch. It was close to midnight. "Where have you been?" I asked, but based on the smell of alcohol on his clothing and body, I could pretty much surmise what he had been doing.

"I got *shigoto*." His speech was rough, like the way the produce workers sometimes spoke to each other when they were in a hurry.

"You did?" I didn't mean to sound so incredulous, but I must have, because Pop practically sneered at me.

"Don't believe?"

"Where, then?"

Pop didn't answer right away. "At Aloha."

"Aloha. It sounds like a bar."

"Wassamatter with bar? Chicago's full of 'em. And look. I got *okane*." He took out a wad of dollar bills from his pocket.

"Pop, are you sure that you should be working at a place like that? I mean, at Manzanar, you did get into some trouble."

"*Damare*!" Pop shouted. Shut up! He had never said such a harsh word to me. By the look on his face, he was shocked by his own fury, which wasn't yet spent. He grabbed the closest thing to him—the strawberry jam jar that Rose had used to gargle with—and tossed it toward the other side of the room as if it were a grenade. It shattered, the broken pieces scattering on the linoleum floor. A shard glittered near my bare feet.

My mother emerged from the bedroom, her hair bundled close to her head. "What happened?"

I was too stunned to speak; I'm sure that Pop would have run out of the apartment if he wasn't so drunk. For a while, the three of us stood frozen in place, my sister's belongings lying in a pile by the closet. We were afraid to step on broken glass and didn't know where to go from here.

CHAPTER 9

I don't know why, but I've always had problems becoming close friends with girls. So many of them want me to play by their rules, but I never agreed to follow along in the first place. I hate when they demand something of me or say that I'm not being considerate. I mean, I can't read people's minds. The girls' club in Manzanar was all right because I needed something to while away the time. Doing the craft projects and planning dances was fun. It's not like we had to tell our deep dark secrets.

Ever since Pop's blowup, my parents seemed to be unified against me. My mother blamed Pop's anger on me—how could I question the legitimacy of his job when employment was so hard to find for Issei men? He cleaned a bar, while she cleaned a barbershop. *Souji*, or cleaning up, was perfectly respectable, and perhaps I needed to do some soul cleaning myself.

I wasn't sure what they wanted from me. When I was in the apartment, I felt that I was walking on eggshells when either one of them was there. One evening when I was alone, I went to retrieve Rose's suitcase from the closet, only to discover that it was missing. I knew that confronting my mother about it would only start an argument. At least I had hidden away Rose's journal between my mattress and the box spring. The bloody dress that I had received from the police turned out not to be her favorite polka-dotted one, but a tan one with miniature butterflies I had never seen before. It was starting to smell, so I threw it out. It was not missed.

I used the business card the funeral director had given me to contact Mr. Yoshizaki, a representative of the Japanese Mutual Aid Society. We made arrangements to meet at a coffeehouse by the Lawrence el station on a Saturday afternoon.

I was still a bit confused by native Chicagoans' use of the term *el*. It referred to Chicago's famous elevated train that rumbled over different parts of the city. But even the train that stopped at a new subway station like Clark and Division was called the el.

When it departed the underground station the ride was smooth, but as soon as the train car reached the elevated track, the journey became loud and bumpy. I could feel practically every rail tie as we moved forward. There were times when the train car sped a few feet away from tenement windows. I had a close-up view of clothing hanging from balconies and sometimes could spy on people sitting down for breakfast. We had complained about the cramped housing around Clark and Division, but seeing how other people were living, we didn't have that much to *monku* about.

As Mr. Yoshizaki had explained over the phone, the coffeehouse was right next to the stairs from the station. The neighborhood, which I later learned was called Uptown, held signs of a lively nightlife—theaters and bars adorned with neon. Right next to the platform was a beautiful Spanish-inspired ballroom.

I didn't have time to wander because I noticed an elderly Asian man waiting outside the coffeehouse. I assumed this was the Mutual Aid representative and quickened my gait.

"Are you Mr. Yoshizaki? I'm sorry to keep you waiting."

"Ah, Ito-*san*," he said and bowed. His voice had a familiar gentle lilt, reminding me of the Issei bookkeeper at the produce market. Mr. Yoshizaki had hardly any hair on his head. His heavy eyebrows and even eyelashes were all white.

We sat at the only open table, surrounded by *hakujin* customers. He told me that I could order anything I wanted, but only asked the waitress for a cup of coffee with cream for himself.

He spoke mostly in Japanese. "I'm beyond sorrowful that this awful incident has befallen your family."

His earnestness touched me deeply. To have an elder on my side meant the world to me. He didn't ask many prying questions but wanted to make sure that all our needs were met.

"I have a good job," I told him. "We're all working, in fact." I didn't reveal the embarrassing details of my parents' blue-collar situations.

"Ah, *yokatta*."

We slurped our respective coffees. The waitress returned to check on us and Mr. Yoshizaki waved that we were fine.

I cleared my throat to broach the reason I had asked for this meeting. "It's my sister, Rose. We have no place—"

Mr. Yoshizaki motioned for me to stop talking. "Your older sister's ashes can be stored in the mausoleum at Montrose Cemetery. And don't worry about the cost. The Mutual Aid Society will take care of everything. I will contact the mortuary today and have the urn transferred by tomorrow."

"Thank you so much." I grasped hold of his calloused

hand without thinking. We Nisei never did that to our elders, even the ones who we were related to.

"The Mutual Aid Society was started for those Japanese who were in America all by themselves. No relatives," he explained. "Our mission is to help. You can keep her ashes there as long as you want."

I was relieved that Rose's urn would have a sacred place to rest, even though it would be next to the remains of Japanese immigrants who had no one else in their lives.

As I climbed the stairs to the station on my way home, I was overcome with a great sadness. Mom, whenever she remembered her life in Kagoshima, spoke about *kurou*, which could be translated to "suffering." But the English word seemed to skim the surface, whereas *kurou* went deeper. It referred to a guttural moaning, a piercing pain throughout your bones. Even though Mr. Yoshizaki had said nothing about his life, either in Japan or America, I sensed that he knew *kurou*.

We had now been in Chicago for three weeks and the heat was becoming more oppressive. Although I was committed to finding out what had happened to my sister, the intense weather squelched my zeal. Sometimes I felt that I couldn't breathe, with the hotness pressing on all sides of me. My only refuge was work in the air-conditioned, protected tomb of the Newberry Library.

This particular Friday Roy came by our desk. He had the graveyard shift that evening but had the weekend off. I saw Nancy and Phillis exchange glances. *He's just a friend*, I wanted to immediately tell them, to dispel any notions they might have had.

"What are you doing here?" I asked. Even though he had a degree from USC, I knew that Roy wasn't much into books.

"The Californians are going to have a dance tomorrow night at the Aragon."

That was that fine building I had seen when I was on my way to visit Mr. Yoshizaki at the coffee shop near Lawrence station. "I thought we weren't supposed to gather in numbers more than three."

Roy rolled his eyes. The activity around Clark and Division was proof that the rules communicated in camp were out the window.

"It would be a good chance for you to check out the social scene in Chicago. I tried to call the pay phone in your hallway, but no one picked up."

I didn't know who the Californians were (later I learned that they spelled their name with a *K*). But if it meant time away from our apartment, I was all for it.

"This is not a date, Roy." That much I had to make clear.

"Are you kidding me? You're like my kid sister. I know Rose would want me to watch out for you."

We made arrangements to meet in front of the Mark Twain Hotel at seven on Saturday evening. Our meeting time was late enough that I could still carry out my plans for earlier that day: to go to the mausoleum where Rose's ashes were stored.

On Saturday morning I bought some flowers from a shop not far from the station. I knew that Rose would want something brilliant and red, roses, of course, but I found some yellow chrysanthemums that would weather the humidity better. Hearing what it was for, the florist wrapped the bouquet in white butcher paper. With my flowers, I went down the escalator of the Clark and Division station.

I had gotten used to going to the station where Rose

had been killed. One day I didn't even think about her. The realization surprised me, and then I felt guilty. My mother said Rose would want us to go forward with our lives, but I sincerely doubted that. It had been so important for Rose to be center stage, the hub that united us all. She would never want to be forgotten.

According to the Triple A map, Montrose Cemetery was actually not that close to Evanston, but at least it was in the general direction. North. I was determined to meet Tomi today.

I would have to take both the train and a couple of buses. And also do a lot of walking. A taxi was too expensive and I wasn't about to ask Roy to borrow a car to drive me, especially to talk to Tomi. He obviously wasn't that keen on her and would have probably tried to convince me not to see her.

I disembarked at the Lawrence station and circled until I found the bus that traveled about three and a half miles to a boulevard called Pulaski. Then it was a straight shot but a very long walk to my destination. In the humidity, my mums seemed to be shrinking and wilting. Sweat ran down my forehead and stung my eyes. I was starting to think that this was not a good idea.

Once I reached the sign for Montrose Cemetery, my outlook completely changed. The grounds were so green, helped by the summer storm a couple of days before. Flowers that people had left behind for loved ones seemed to be flourishing in the moisture and the sun.

My feet were killing me, and I checked the soles of my shoes. My right one was so thin that I was concerned a hole would appear, like on my father's shoes. I tore some of the butcher paper from the bouquet of chrysanthemums, folded it into a square and stuffed it under my foot. Voilà!

I then searched for someone to direct me to the Japanese Mausoleum. I saw workmen in the distance shoveling a new gravesite. I didn't relish walking through the wet grass to approach them, so I wandered around, glancing at the headstones and obelisks. A tall young Asian man washing the face of a concrete monument caught my eye. The monument had a pitched Japanese-style roof featuring a Rising Sun image. Underneath the roof it read, JAPANESE MAUSOLEUM.

I stood there, my bouquet of flowers in my hands, and watched him for a minute or two. He was wearing khaki work pants and a white sleeveless T-shirt. He must have felt my gaze because he stopped work and looked at me. "Oh, hello."

"Hello," I said.

"Are you here for the Japanese Mausoleum?"

I nodded.

"I'm pretty much done. I'll give you some time to yourself." He took his bucket and rag and walked toward a pickup truck parked nearby. He held his shoulders erect, as if he wasn't ashamed to be washing headstones in a graveyard. A part of me hoped that he didn't drive off without talking more to me.

There wasn't any kind of container to hold the chrysanthemums so I scattered the blooms across the front of the mausoleum. Rose's ashes were supposed to be inside, and I had to trust that Mr. Yoshizaki had placed her urn on a shelf like he said he would.

Visiting gravesites was a big deal for us Issei and Nisei. Our only blood relatives were in Spokane, Washington, but Pop still stopped at a bunch of cemeteries throughout California to pay respects to former employees and colleagues who had passed away.

I pressed my hands together and lowered my head. Sadly, I didn't feel that Rose was anywhere near this mausoleum, but I nonetheless prayed for her and all the others whose ashes were stored inside.

I opened my eyes and took in the structure again. I wanted to know how to describe it to my parents—that is, if we were still talking.

When I turned around, the clean-up man was still there, leaning against his truck, his gloves off. He had put on a plaid short-sleeve shirt over his undershirt.

"My father's with the society," he explained, and I imagined that he was referring to the Mutual Aid Society. "He usually organizes clean-up crews, but he can't walk that well anymore. Besides, the government officially banned us from gathering together."

No more than three Japanese in one place—Rose had been right, it was plain impossible. Obviously the government authorities had never been to Clark and Division, or at least had turned a blind eye to our growing Japanese community and our Nisei dances. Who knows which rules were enforced and which were not?

I asked him about the man whom I had met, Mr. Yoshizaki.

"Oh, Yoshizaki-*san*. He's like an uncle to me."

"Are you from Chicago?" I was curious. There was something different about him. With his high cheekbones and wide jaw, he looked like he was ready to face any obstacle in front of him.

"Born and raised. We're on the South Side."

"South Side? I thought that the Negroes and Irish live there."

"They do. The Japanese are sprinkled in. There used to be only a few hundred of us over here. At that time, I knew all the Japanese in Chicago." His eyes didn't leave my face and for some reason, I felt embarrassed. "I take it you're not from here."

"Los Angeles. Via Manzanar. My family lives around Clark and Division now."

"Oh, the Near North. The Mutual Aid Society has a hostel there, although it hasn't been open to the public for a while. Have you been here long?"

I shook my head. "Only about a month."

We were both silent for a while and I figured that he wanted to know why I was there at the Japanese Mausoleum. I gave him credit for not asking me.

"Well, I guess I should be going." I had written down the instructions for getting to Tomi's employers' house in Evanston and took them out of my pocketbook. It required more walking and transfers to different lines of transportation.

"Where are you heading?"

"Evanston."

"Evanston? That's in the opposite direction of Clark and Division."

"I know. I need to visit with someone there."

"I can give you a ride. I have no plans this afternoon."

"Oh, no, I can't ask that of you."

"I don't know if your shoes are going to last that trip."

I could feel the wad of butcher paper slipping inside of my shoes. I was on my way to getting some massive blisters. "Well, at least I need to know the name of the guy who will be driving me."

The man cracked a smile and held out his right hand. "Art Nakasone."

His hand was rough and callused. "Aki Ito."

We didn't say much during the drive to Evanston. Art wasn't one for small talk and neither was I. I didn't want to say anything about Rose because I didn't want to be that tragic girl, the surviving sister. I wanted to be a normal girl—well, as normal as a Nisei woman could be under the circumstances.

I did find out that Art was attending the University of Chicago and planning to major in journalism. I thought that was interesting because he didn't seem particularly chatty or nosy.

Being a native Chicagoan, he quickly figured out the route based on my maps and didn't even look at them as we drove. After about thirty, forty minutes, he slowed in front of a beautiful dark brick house with a rounded archway that led to a door with black hinges. Two large bushes with pink flowers framed the archway.

He parked and turned the engine off. "This is it," he said.

I checked the house number on my piece of paper. During the drive, I had mentioned a few things about Tomi, that she was a house girl for a professor here in Evanston.

"I wouldn't go through the front door," he said. "Try the back one."

I appreciated his advice. It was obvious that I was a bit in the dark about rules that applied to domestics and their guests.

"I can drive you back to Clark and Division. I'll wait for you here."

Normally, I would have protested, but I had no other options and gratefully accepted his offer.

I jumped out of the truck and smoothed my wrinkled, moist skirt as much as possible. This humidity was really the death of me. As I neared the house, I heard the deep bellow of a dog—probably a big one—and then the sharp yaps of a smaller one.

I rapped on the side door a couple of times—first, tentatively, and then more insistent, causing the barks from within to increase in volume. "Quiet!" a female voice commanded, and the pets obeyed. A woman appeared, slim like Louise but shorter, with porcelain skin. Her delicate facial features looked like they had been applied with a paintbrush. She reminded me of the classic Japanese beauties my family saw on the screen of the Fuji-kan Theatre in Little Tokyo before the war.

"Are you Tomi Kawamura?" I heard the panting of animals, perhaps from another room.

"Yes."

"I'm Aki Ito. Rose's sister."

As soon as I said Rose's name, Tomi began to shut the door.

"Please, no—" I called out, but before I knew it, she had disappeared. "Please, I need to talk to you. For Rose's sake." I banged on the door with my open palm. The dogs resumed their barking rampage, disturbing the serenity of the tree-lined street.

The door opened, revealing the beauty of Tomi's profile again. "Keep it down. Do you want me to get fired?"

"I'll be quiet. Let me talk," I begged.

"I can't have guests without prior notice."

"Five minutes. Give me five minutes."

"Three." Tomi folded her thin arms. She was obviously not going to let me inside.

I tried to make it fast. "You were my sister's friend. Maybe her only one in Chicago, according to her diary."

"Her diary?" Her cheeks flushed pink.

"She left it at the apartment. It was with your books."

Tomi couldn't speak for a moment. When she regained her voice, she said, "Why are you here?"

"To find out what happened to her before she died."

"I had already moved out here—"

"You must have known her secrets. You know, the big one." I swallowed. "That she was pregnant."

"You're insane." She pulled at the door again, but this time my body was in the way.

"Meet me somewhere, away from here." I was only a few inches from her face, so close that I could see her small nostrils flare out. "I work at the Newberry Library. It's safe there."

She yanked on the door again, crushing my left foot. I yelped in pain and fell forward into what looked like a mudroom. Two dog leashes and some raincoats hung on wall hooks, and rubber boots were lined up underneath a bench. Behind a set of French doors with paneled windows, a black Labrador and a white poodle leapt up, their nails making click-clack noises against the glass. Their tails were wagging.

"You can't be in here," Tomi said, attempting to both pull me up and toss me out.

Outside a car door slammed shut. Tomi turned to the street. "Who's that?"

Art had gotten out of the truck, probably in response to our scuffle.

"Oh, he's a fellow I ran into at the cemetery. He gave me a drive here."

"A fellow? You mean you don't know him?"

"He's Art. Art Nakasone. He's from Chicago. Lives on the South Side."

"You got into a car with a stranger? And brought him here? Have you lost your mind?"

"His father is with the Mutual Aid Society. He's a college boy."

"You're just like Rose. No common sense." Her scolding caught me off guard, and Tomi used my loss of equilibrium to push me back outside, slamming the door behind me. The dogs bid their farewell with a burst of barks, which subsided only as I got into Art's truck.

CHAPTER 10

The Nisei dances here in Chicago have been pitiful, maybe even worse than the ones in camp. At least in Manzanar we had the Jive Bombers and Mary Nomura. Nobody seems to be able to sing at these dances. The bands are so makeshift, as if the organizers found the musicians on the street. And at least two of the dances I've been to have ended in a brawl with men drunk out of their minds. Roy says that they are going to get more organized and better, but I'll be the judge of that.

The drive back to Clark and Division was even quieter than the ride to Evanston. I didn't mind because I wasn't in the mood to make small talk with Art Nakasone. My mind was full of why Tomi had soundly rejected me. I was the little sister of her dead roommate. I hadn't wronged her in any way; we were strangers. But something about Rose's life in Chicago had frightened her. Maybe Rose had fallen into the wrong crowd, although I thought that would be highly unlikely. Roy hadn't mentioned anything. But perhaps Tomi, a close female roommate, had been privy to information unavailable to anyone else.

By the time we reached Lake Shore Drive, I thought that I owed Art some kind of explanation. He had taken the time to drive me, after all. "You know back at the mausoleum," I said. "I was there for my big sister. She was the one who got killed by the subway car. The girl in Evanston was her roommate."

Art, his long fingers light on the steering wheel, nodded once. He turned to me when he stopped at a red light. "Sorry about your sister," he said. "That's really terrible."

"Did you hear about it?"

Art nodded again. "It isn't often that a Nisei girl is killed in Chicago."

I don't know if it was the gentle tone of his voice, but tears started to run down my face. I tried to contain my sadness, but the more I suppressed it, the more I cried. I was a mess.

"Do you need some water?" Before I could stop him, Art had pulled the truck over next to Oak Street Beach. He got out and hoisted himself onto the back of the truck. He returned to the cab with an old canteen that looked like the ones cowboys carried on their saddles.

I really didn't want to drink from that rusty canteen, but I didn't want to offend him. I took a swig and it tasted surprisingly clean and refreshing.

"Thank you." I took out a handkerchief and dabbed at my eyes. I would have taken out my compact and checked my face, but I figured that it was a lost cause. "I cry pretty easily. That's one of my biggest weaknesses," I told him.

"I don't think that's a weakness," he said. "I'm close to my younger sister. If something happened to her, I don't know what I would do."

I took some deep breaths. Leaning my forehead on the

passenger side window, I gazed at young people in their swimming gear, heading for Lake Michigan. Even though the war was going on, they seemed so carefree. I was envious of that ease, that lack of worry.

When he dropped me off in front of my apartment building, Art hesitated a moment, as if he was going to ask me something.

A group of Nisei women gathered at the stoop turned to shoot us looks and then whispered and laughed among themselves.

"Thanks for the ride," I told him.

"Yeah, see you around."

I pulled open the door and jumped out onto the curb. The toes on my left foot were still a bit tender, but luckily the pad of butcher paper had served as a layer of protection.

The girls parted like the Red Sea to let me through to the front door of the apartment. "Art Nakasone, huh?" one of them teased. I was surprised he was so well-known.

When I entered the apartment, I discovered that neither Mom nor Pop was there. I was thankful to be alone as I got ready for the dance. I found a few *onigiri* wrapped in wax paper in the icebox and ate the rice balls with a bit of cold chicken. Mom would have disapproved of me eating standing over the sink instead of sitting down with a plate and fork, but I was in a hurry.

After I took a quick shower, I examined my wardrobe. It was in such a sorry state. The dress I had worn that day was my favorite cotton one, but it was sticky with sweat. I had to go with a plain striped one. Something that I would have worn to a doctor's appointment and not a social occasion.

As I tried to give my hair some kind of shape with bobby pins, I dropped one onto the bedroom floor and crouched to retrieve it. The wayward pin had landed right beside Rose's tan suitcase, which my mother had placed under her bed next to a large dark-brown luggage case that had recently shipped from storage in California. There was a whole wardrobe in that tan suitcase—one that was much nicer than mine. I couldn't. Wasn't it disrespectful to my sister's memory? But I could hear Rose: "Don't be such a chicken. Those dresses aren't helping anyone stuck in a suitcase."

I pulled out the suitcase and undid the latch. Rose's dresses were rolled in tight, neat bundles, my own handiwork. My eyes were drawn to the fabric of the white cranes on the teal-green background.

Since I had never seen that dress on Rose, I felt that I had permission to try it on.

The dress was a wraparound that tightened at the waist and had a flounce on the side. Since we didn't have a full-length mirror, I used my compact to get a sense of how I looked. I barely recognized my body. I was no longer the girl who was overwhelmed and washed out by Rose's high school ensembles. In this dress, I had curves in all the right places. Did I dare? I recalled the looks those girls outside had given me, nosy and judgmental but tinged with a little respect. I had never received that from my peers before. I kept the dress on, closed the suitcase, and placed it underneath my parents' bed.

I checked myself again in the cracked mirror above the sink in the bathroom. It was almost time to meet Roy. Ready or not, here I come.

"Hey, Aki, over here!"

Roy was practically hanging out of the passenger side of a black Oldsmobile. The car was filled with people. Once I got closer, I recognized his roommate, Ike, in the driver's seat. His fine hair was cut in an unfortunate way so that it stuck out like the bristles of a broom. In the back were Louise, Chiyo and their new roommate, Kathryn.

Roy got out and gestured for me to sit between him and Ike in the front seat. I was hoping for a quiet ride in which I could pepper him with more questions about Tomi, but that obviously wasn't going to happen tonight.

I waved at the girls in back and squeezed myself into the front. It was a bit snug in between the two men, and I twisted my arms together so that I could make my body smaller.

"You remember Ike, right?" Roy said once we were back on the road.

"Yeah, is this your car?"

"My uncle's. He's in the import-export business."

"In other words, *okanemochi*. At least before the war." Roy made a circle with his index finger against his thumb, a Japanese hand gesture for money.

The three girls in back twittered.

"I told you to stop using those boochie words. We 'mericans have no idea what you are saying."

"Ah, stop your highfalutin' talk. You know the *hakujins* don't see you as one of them. If they did, University of Chicago wouldn't have a one-Nisei quota in your med school class."

"Are you from Chicago?" I asked.

"Wisconsin. My father is an onion farmer."

"My father worked for Roy's family at the produce market in LA."

"That's what Roy was saying."

Ike seemed sunny and agreeable. I could tell from the energy in the car that the women were more interested in Ike than Roy. A Nisei man who was on his way to becoming a doctor. Who wouldn't be impressed?

Within minutes, we entered a familiar neighborhood

bursting with lounges and clubs. This was Uptown, where I had been this morning to transfer from the train to the bus, only its character had completely transformed at night. Cars crowded the streets and men and women dressed in their Saturday finest sashayed on sidewalks. Everyone seemed to be making a statement.

Ike circled the block a couple of times before he found an empty parking spot next to a condemned building.

"I hope my uncle's car is still here after the night ends," Ike said as we piled out of the Oldsmobile. The last to emerge was Kathryn, who fluffed out her skirt and then took a long look at me underneath the lamppost.

"What a beautiful dress," she commented, and everyone stared at my outfit without saying a word. They must have recognized the dress as Rose's. I felt both embarrassed and curious. Maybe someone could tell me the story behind the dress because the fabric was certainly one of a kind.

ARAGON was spelled out vertically in lights outside of a familiar grand building; I had first noticed it when I met Mr. Yoshizaki. I felt excited to be there. After Roy handled the payment for our tickets, I was shocked to see how crowded the ballroom was. Were there this many Nisei in Chicago? Other than the people in our small group, I didn't recognize a soul at first. Then a few feet in, I spotted Harriet, whose face fell as soon as she saw my dress. "Oh, Aki," she only managed to say.

"C'mon, let's jive." I felt someone pulling at my hand. It was Roy guiding me to the dance floor. I was a passable dancer, only because Rose would use me as her partner when she practiced the Lindy Hop in our house.

I hadn't gone to many dances at Manzanar. Frankly, I hadn't wanted Mom to be by herself as Pop cavorted with his bootleg friends into the wee hours. To now be engulfed by the music, hearing the trumpet screech and feeling the wooden floors jump with our footsteps, transported me. I was like those couples along the shore of Lake Michigan, not giving a damn about anything.

The song ended and Roy whooped, sweat falling down from his oiled head. "You can jive!" he called out to me. He said it like he was seeing me for the first time.

He went to get us something to drink. I tried to find a place to rest, but the ballroom was filled with bodies and no chairs. Ike was surrounded by the trio of Louise, Kathryn and Chiyo, who all seemed to hang on every word he said.

When I'd first met her, Chiyo mentioned that she didn't frequent many dances, yet here she was, looking longingly at Ike. She seemed totally smitten and was asking him a question when I approached Louise, who was lagging toward the back of the group.

"I saw Tomi," I told her.

Louise, fanning her face, gave me a blank stare. "Really? How did that happen?"

"I went to the house where she works."

"How did she seem?"

"What do you mean?"

"Did she seem well?"

I frowned. "What happened to Tomi?" When Louise started to purse her lips, I rushed in to say, "Tell me this one time and I promise that I won't bother you again."

Louise glanced back at the group—both Kathryn and Chiyo were too mesmerized by Ike's account of his recent surgical rotation to pay us any mind. Maybe she was feeling too much like the fourth wheel, or thought this was the opportunity to get me off her back forever. For whatever reason, she pulled me a few yards away so that we could talk more freely. "She had a bit of a breakdown," she said in a hushed tone. Her eyes remained on the trio whose company she had temporarily left.

"A nervous breakdown, you mean?"

Now that she had come this far, Louise had to offer more information. "She was afraid of everything. Staying alone in the apartment. Going out late at night. Rose knew what was going on with her. But they didn't confide in me. I'm not sure what happened, but one night Rose and Tomi had a terrible argument—broken dishes and yelling. The next day Tomi had moved out. Rose didn't mention her again. It was better when Chiyo moved in. Things got a lot simpler."

A beanpole Nisei with a faint mustache tapped Louise's puffy sleeve and asked her to dance, and Louise seemed relieved to be able to end our conversation. I, on the other hand, felt totally left out in the cold. What had Tomi argued about with Rose? Could it have had anything to do with Rose being pregnant? How could I get Tomi to talk to me?

Although I was in the presence of other young people like me, I was starting to feel alone again. Where was Roy? He probably was chasing another girl, forgetting about me and our drinks.

I wandered around the edges of the dance floor, trying to spot that head of thick oiled hair. Instead I ran into Harriet, standing with the *hakujin* man with the wire-rimmed spectacles. He, like Harriet, seemed surprised to see what I was wearing. This was getting ridiculous.

I went straight to him, putting my hand out as if I were pursuing a business transaction. "I'm Aki Ito," I introduced myself. "You were at my sister's funeral. And I saw you at Bughouse Square the other day. You sure like to write things down in your notebook."

Harriet had no choice but to play the diplomat. "Ah, Aki,

this is Douglas Reilly. He's an anthropologist employed by the War Relocation Authority."

His handshake was a bit torturous, too sweaty and too long. "I'm sorry that I seem so obtrusive," he said. "My job is to observe and make reports. It may seem that I've been in a lot of places that you have, too, but rest assured, I'm not following you."

"We work together in the WRA office." Harriet attempted to explain their connection, but I was getting the feeling that their relationship went beyond the office.

"I would like to interview you sometime," he said to me.

"What about?"

"Moving to Chicago from Manzanar. How it's been for your family."

"I don't think that our story would be of any interest to the government." I was loath to explore Rose's death and its impact on the three of us. We were a house divided right now, hurting and confused. Why would I want to talk about that, especially to a bureaucrat?

"Douglas is doing it to help us. To guide resettlement policy in the future."

I didn't care about policy or the future. All I cared about was now and how we could keep our heads above water. I declined the interview as politely as possible, but before I left their presence, Harriet attempted a cheery smile. "I'll talk to you back at the apartments," she said.

I was so irritated by the encounter that I almost crashed into someone. "Hello." The voice I remembered, but he appeared very different. Instead of a sweat-soaked undershirt, Art was wearing a crisp white shirt, a gray suit and a maroon tie with two black stripes across its center. As soon as I recognized him, my whole body started pulsating.

"Hello."

"I didn't know that you were going to be here," he said.

"I didn't know that you were going to be here," I replied, and we both laughed. We sounded like idiots.

"I guess it never came up."

"Do you come here every weekend?" I pressed on the sides of my face, hoping that beads of sweat wouldn't appear on my hairline and ruin my makeup.

"Nah, I haven't been in a long time. I guess it's my lucky night."

I was struck by his last comment. Was he flirting with me? I wasn't used to hearing such talk and let it sink in before murmuring a response. "My first," I said.

"What?" It was hard to compete with the din of the lousy music and the sound of hard heels hitting the wooden floor.

"My first time," I repeated, louder.

A low yell shook the ballroom. As if pulled by a giant magnet, the crowd moved to the door. Everyone seemed to have lost interest in dancing in favor of gawking at an unexpected occurrence.

"What is going on?" Art asked a couple of guys who were rushing toward the action.

"It's the *yogores* again," someone answered.

"What?" I interjected.

"Hammer Ishimine. He's going at it with Roy Tonai."

There could be only one Hammer. Without explaining anything to Art, I ran into the eye of the crowd, pushing lookie-loos aside to find the source of the hubbub.

By the time I reached the center, the scuffle was in full force, a flash of mustard yellow, thuds of fists and hoots from the boys in the crowd. Older men ran in to break up the fight. Roy finally emerged, his nose and lip bloody and his right ear swollen. Hammer's face, on the other hand, was undamaged, but the collar of his zoot suit was completely mangled. In a protective stance was his ever-faithful companion, Manju.

An older mustached man in his thirties pointed a finger at the zoot suiter. “That’s it, Hammer. You’re not allowed at any of our events in the future.”

“Ah, who the hell cares? These dances are chicken shit, anyway.” He then noticed me standing there in the circle. “Hey, Tropico, let’s get out of here.”

How dare he address me like I was his girl? I didn’t move or say anything.

Hammer howled as if it was all a joke and strutted out of the Aragon with Manju at his side.

I went over to Roy, who was spitting out a tooth. Luckily it wasn’t a front one. I handed him a handkerchief that I had stuck in the pocket of the dress.

“Tonai, you’ll have to go, too,” the Kalifornian told him.

“I was defending myself.”

“Heard that you’re just as much to blame as Hammer.”

By this time, Ike had found us and examined Roy’s lip. “C’mon, let’s go. You’re going to need some stitches.”

Without thinking, I went with them, momentarily forgetting about Art. I wanted to run back and convey a proper goodbye, but it was all too late for that.

CHAPTER 11

There are nights when I miss my parents and Aki. And our dog, Rusty. Rusty was more Aki's dog than anyone else's. But when Aki wasn't around, he would stick close to me.

The mood in the crowded Oldsmobile was much more somber than on the way over. Kathryn, for some reason, seemed the most distressed. She kept sighing and making popping sounds with her lips. I didn't know her well enough to ask her to stop.

We were all disappointed in Roy. Roy, who had bloodied what I realized now was my favorite handkerchief, was dead silent, failing to explain or justify his conduct. He didn't even have the decency to apologize for creating such a spectacle and cutting our evening short. All of us in his company were now tainted as troublemakers.

We were a couple of blocks away from Clark and Division when Chiyo piped up, "You can drop Aki off first."

Ike signaled that he was going to change lanes, but I stopped him.

"Keep going," I said. "I went through nurse's aide training at Manzanar. I can help you with stitching him up."

Ike found an open space at the curb in front of the girls' apartment. Louise practically flew out of the back passenger's side, faintly thanking Ike for the ride. Kathryn tried to say something, but nothing came out of her mouth except for another pop. Only Chiyo lingered in the back seat. "I can help, too, if you need it. I've slaughtered animals on the farm before so I'm not scared of blood."

Roy's eyes widened and I had to stifle a giggle. Only Ike was the true gentleman, thanking Chiyo for her willingness to help but politely turning her down.

She slid over to the open door. "Well, bye," she said, and followed her roommates up the stoop steps.

I was going to make a snide comment but thought better of it. So what if she had a crush on Ike? When it came to romance, Chiyo seemed a straightforward person. My mother would call her *sunao*, lacking in any pretense. Only when it came to Rose, Chiyo didn't seem as forthcoming. At least Louise had shared some truth of what had been going on between the roommates.

As we passed the Mark Twain Hotel, the same gigantic person wearing a fancy cocktail dress I had seen before jaywalked in front of us. Ike had to swerve to avoid hitting her, causing him to murmur a curse word.

"I've seen her before," I said.

"Don't you mean him?" Roy had found his voice, although his speech was a bit affected by his split lip.

"What?"

He lowered the soiled handkerchief. "Yes, that's a man gussied up like a girl. There were even a few fellows like that in camp."

"No," I said. I couldn't imagine such a thing in the Japanese community.

"Yup."

"No, I can't believe that." Roy often played tricks on me, taking advantage of my gullibility.

"Look, you were spending most of your time behind a counter issuing overcoats and blankets to people. I was walking around our whole block, delivering mail and doing business. I was walking in and out of barracks. A guy is going to see things."

"Like who? Do I know them?" I wanted evidence.

Roy started to say something but then he stopped himself. "You know, Aki, sometimes you do remind me of Rose." He didn't say it as a compliment.

"What do you mean by that?"

"Rose was awful curious about things that were none of her business."

The admonishment stung.

"You know that you've ruined my handkerchief," I told him. "Rose gave me that handkerchief."

"Really?" he asked, his tone softening.

She hadn't, but I wanted to punish him, at least a little.

Roy and Ike shared a unit in what was called a four-flat, essentially a fourplex, owned by Ike's uncle. The uncle and aunt lived in two units on the left-hand side; I didn't ask why a married couple resided in two separate apartments. A Chinese family lived below the boys' apartment.

The building was old but relatively kept up. The gray paint on the wood structure seemed to look uniform under the moonlight. They had left a table light on inside their apartment, which glowed through bars in an open window.

Once we were inside, Ike turned on a standing antique light. The living room was well appointed with an Oriental rug on the hardwood floor, a fireplace, a couple of sitting chairs and a sofa with wooden feet shaped like bird talons. Their living room seemed absolutely normal, which made me feel both comforted and envious at the same time.

Roy immediately collapsed onto the sofa, which was also adorned with two fat cushions. He laid his head on one of them, still clutching the handkerchief to his split lip.

"I'll get my bag," Ike said, heading for one of the bedrooms. "I'll have to sterilize my needle."

I stood awkwardly in the living room. "Do you need my help?"

"No, no. Just keep the patient stabilized," he called out. I could hear his footsteps going back and forth in various rooms. I finally sat in one of the chairs, feeling the breeze through the window.

Roy was lying so still that I thought he may have fallen asleep.

"Are you awake?" I asked.

He moved his elbow and opened his eyes.

"I saw Tomi today," I said.

"Where?"

"I went to the house where she's working."

"In Evanston?" He propped himself up on his elbows. "How the hell did you get over there?"

I ignored his question. "What happened between her and Rose? And don't say 'nothing.' Louise verified that they had a fight about something."

Roy tried to avoid giving me a straight response, but I persisted. I didn't care that he was injured. In fact, I was committed to taking full advantage of his vulnerable physical state.

"Rose never shied away from a fight, and once she got into one, she usually got her way pretty easily. This Tomi must be something else. I got a taste of her today, that's for sure. Maybe I'll go back to Evanston first thing tomorrow morning."

I finally wore Roy down.

"Don't go back," he said. He lay back on the cushions and stared at the ceiling. "Rose thought that Tomi was certifiably nuts. You know, cuckoo-cuckoo. Camp and everything took a toll on her."

"She seems scared of something. You didn't date her, did you?"

"I went on one date. Nothing serious. We had dinner together. We didn't click."

"Or maybe she didn't click with you."

"I think that maybe her father had been a little rough on her. At least that's what Rose told me. That I should lay off her. So I took Rose at her word. I left Tomi alone."

Rough on her? Did that mean the father abused her? My mouth went dry. Pop had treasured both Rose and me; I couldn't imagine a father laying a hand on his own daughter. "She sure is beautiful." I didn't know what else to say.

"Well, looks aren't everything." Roy glanced at me as if to say I was living proof of his statement.

His comment stung and I quickly changed the subject. "Why were you fighting with Hammer tonight, anyway?"

"That guy has had it out for me even before camp."

I remembered that he got fired at the produce market. I needed to ask Pop if he'd had any run-ins with him. Before I could pursue the topic further, Ike had returned with a metal tray with a needle attached to surgical thread.

Roy's face turned absolutely green. I didn't know he was such a baby.

"Don't make me into a Frankenstein," Roy joked weakly.

"No worries. You'll be on the beauty-pageant circuit in no time."

While I held the tray, Ike first cleaned the wound and then applied some local anesthetic with a piece of gauze. Roy cringed several times throughout the procedure; I'm sure that he would have cried out if I wasn't there.

I hadn't noticed Ike's fingers before, but they were slender and beautiful. He kept his nails neat and manicured, and I was transfixed by his movements as he sewed up Roy's lip. He did two set of stitches, one outside of the lip and one inside. He was going to make a fine surgeon.

He gave Roy aspirin and a pill to help him sleep. Roy pulled himself up and said good night to me before he trudged to one of the back bedrooms.

While Ike put away his supplies, I wandered around the living room and stared at oval portraits of an impressive-looking Japanese man in a top hat and tie alongside a woman in a beautiful kimono. Ike was from a wealthy family, like Roy. They had much in common.

"Sorry that I wasn't more of a help," I said to Ike once we were back in the Oldsmobile.

"No, you were. You kept Roy calm and that was more than half the battle." He turned the key in the ignition to take me home. It was late, about midnight. Even my father would be asleep by now.

I looked out the window for a few blocks, not saying anything. I didn't know what to expect to see on the South Side of town, but the line of homes on the street all seemed impressive and well maintained.

When we stopped at an intersection, I finally spoke. "Has Roy been causing you many problems?"

"He's a good guy. I like him. He gets fired up sometimes. I can't say that I blame him. His father is still locked up in Santa Fe, his mother in Manzanar, and the family business is in shambles. The government froze all their money in Sumitomo Bank."

"How did you two meet?"

"It was actually because of your sister."

"Really?" I hadn't realized that Ike had even known Rose that well.

"It was at a dance at the YMCA earlier this year. The winter started off pretty warm, but then we had a snowstorm in February. All the Californians were dying with cold; they had never gone through below-zero weather. Roy was sure that he had frostbite on his toes, and Rose was telling him that he was being foolish. I guess he was insisting that it was true. She had heard that I was in med school, so she had me take a look."

"You got Roy as a roommate because of his toes?"

Ike began laughing and I saw that he had a gap in between his two front teeth.

"The timing was right. With my uncle's export-import business shot because of the war, my aunt needed some extra income from a lodger. I'm at the hospital most of the time, anyway. Roy keeps everything neat and tidy. And he's a hard worker, too."

That was definitely true.

"That was when Roy and Rose were still close. Tomi, too."

"You knew Tomi?"

"She was at the dance. She was giggling so much that ginger ale was coming out her nose. She's a funny one."

I was in disbelief. Tomi didn't strike me as a girl who had one silly bone in her body.

"How are you doing, anyway? Here in Chicago."

I didn't know how to answer that question. "It's better than being locked up."

"You'll get used to it. The Midwest has good people."

"I want to know what happened to my sister." To hear myself say it out loud in Ike's presence surprised even me.

"What do you mean?"

"She didn't kill herself. And she doesn't have two left feet or anything, so don't tell me she tripped onto the tracks."

The inside of the Oldsmobile became eerily quiet.

"Something happened to Rose."

Ike didn't ask me to explain myself. Maybe he was afraid of what I was going to say.

"Do you know Hammer that well?" I asked.

Ike shook his head. "All I know is that he came to Chicago from Boys Town in Omaha, Nebraska. He actually ran away from there."

"*The* Boys Town?" I remembered going to see the black-and-white movie about Father Flanagan, played by Spencer Tracy, and his rough-and-tumble charges in a home for troubled juveniles.

"Roy told me that Hammer got arrested for stealing in Manzanar."

Then it would make sense that he was sent away to a reform center. There was no way he was qualified for the leave program under normal channels.

"Hammer hates Roy. He thinks Roy was born with a silver spoon in his mouth. And then when Hammer got close to Rose, it drove Roy crazy."

I was too stunned to say anything. Hammer and Rose? I hoped that my silence would permit Ike to talk more, but we were now in front of my apartment.

"I've probably said too much," Ike said as the Oldsmobile's engine idled. "Don't mention anything to Roy, okay?"

"Thank you, Ike," I said before I pulled the lever up to open the door. "And thank you for being Roy's friend."

CHAPTER 12

Chicago is a lot like camp in that rumors spread like wildfire.

The lights were on when I went into the apartment. Pop was locked in the bathroom with horrible food poisoning, and Mom was trying to provide some kind of relief with cool water and wet compresses.

Pop, Mom explained when the worst was over, had eaten dinner at Aloha: a frightening affair of soup made from unmentionable parts of a chicken or pig. Once he was finally able to leave the bathroom, he collapsed on their bed. We gave him some privacy and sipped weak black tea at the living-room table. Mom was truly exhausted because she didn't even notice that I was wearing Rose's dress.

"Oh, by the way, how was it?" she asked in Japanese about the dance at the Aragon. "Did you meet any good persons there?" By good persons, I knew that she meant eligible bachelors.

I shrugged. I was starting to understand how Rose had felt when she was being interrogated about her love life.

The next morning, my parents were still in bed when I

woke up. Pop was hanging off one side of the bed, as if he were ready to retch into a basin on the floor. Poor Mom was flailed out as if she were floating on the deep sea, her cockatiel cowlick on display.

In spite of not getting much sleep, I was energized, adrenaline pumping through my body. I needed to locate Hammer and find out the truth about him and Rose.

I plucked my striped dress off the hanger, got dressed, and quietly left the apartment. It was Sunday morning, so the Christian church families, dressed in their finest, were on their way to worship. There had been talk of Buddhist priests coming to Chicago from a couple of concentration camps, but that hadn't happened yet. Being a Buddhist was harder in America.

I felt like a bit of a heathen, but in a way, I reveled in it. I may not have looked it, but I prided myself on being a rebel, at least that day. I even tried to saunter, but I was handicapped by my worn shoes again.

I walked past Rose's old apartment building, hoping not to run into the three girls from last night. There was only one person hunkered on the steps.

"Hey, Manju—" I said. A part of me felt a bit ridiculous calling a grown man by a nickname that meant "bean cake." "Have you seen Hammer?"

Manju, who had ditched his plaid suit for a plain white T-shirt and jeans, shook his head. "After the tussle last night, he took off. Haven't seen him since." He spoke in a disjointed fashion, as if he needed to take breaths of air in between every few words.

"Where does he live, anyway?"

"Anywhere someone will have him. My roommates said he couldn't stay with us anymore. This week I think he was staying with a girl in Chinatown." It amazed me that for a

Nisei with no prospects and a limited wardrobe, he seemed to be able to secure the affection of the opposite sex. My mother would say *moteru*, that Hammer could hold on to women, at least for a night. I couldn't deny that he had something, but to me, he oozed a kind of unwanted stickiness, like chewed gum that you unwittingly stepped on.

We both stared at the street in silence. I mustered up some courage and asked straight out, "Do you know if he was seeing my sister?"

Manju slowly turned his head, squinting from the sun's brightness. "You mean like dating?"

I nodded.

His body shook with laughter. "That's a good one, Aki. You have some kind of imagination."

I didn't like being seen as a fool and abandoned the stoop without even saying goodbye. It was obvious that Manju would not be of any help. I wasn't sure if he was being loyal to Hammer or really didn't know of them having any type of relationship.

I passed the barbershop where my mother cleaned. The two brothers were devout Catholics and closed business on Sundays. With all the news about the awful things the Japanese military had been doing in the Philippines, I sometimes wondered if they held a grudge against us Issei and Nisei. But they were able to separate us from the enemy in the Pacific. It probably didn't hurt that half of their customers were now Nisei either wanting buzz cuts to join the army or pompadours to complement their zoot suits.

After everything that had happened last night, I felt that I needed to treat myself and went into the diner and ice-cream parlor on Division Street. It must have been at least ninety degrees already, and the sun seemed to burn through my dress. I had been giving most of my paycheck to Mom, but she allowed me to keep a few dollars a week for incidentals. I should have been saving for a new pair of shoes, but the thought of ice cream was too enticing.

Ting-A-Ling was usually closed on Sundays, but for some reason, it was open today. The elderly Polish couple who operated the ice-cream shop and diner were absent; instead a pimply teenager sat me in one of the booths. Beside me in the next booth were other young heathens, high-school age. From the way the waiter was interacting with them, they were fellow classmates. The youths shared an easy camaraderie, teasing each other about incidents that had happened at school. The tone of their laughter was familiar, yet so distant.

A part of me wished that I was back in Manzanar, where at least I could spend time with Hisako. She had told me to write her as soon as we had settled, but I hadn't had the heart to tell her all that had happened. And with the Nisei moving around so much, who knows where she was now?

The strawberry ice cream I ordered finally appeared on my table. It was a perfect and generous mound, which I stabbed with my pointed spoon. As I swallowed the frozen delight, I felt a rush hit the back of my head. I wished I could bottle up the coldness to use against the heat I was going to encounter once I left the ice-cream parlor.

When I returned to the apartment after my fruitless search for Hammer, Mom was at the table, darning one of Pop's socks. "Your father is still under the weather. There's no way he can go to work today. Use the pay phone and call Papa's boss. Rocky Inukai."

"I'll go to the club and tell him."

Mom hesitated. "It's not a place for young women."

"I know where it is. I've passed it many times. I'm going to be twenty-one in a couple of months."

Mom examined her stitching on the heel of the sock. It was perfect as usual.

"That way I can make sure that he knows," I said. The people who answered Aloha's phone were not the most reliable, based on calls I'd attempted to make to Pop there in the past.

She couldn't argue with that. "Come straight back home afterward."

I nodded.

Aloha was on Clark Street, north of the subway station. It was a raucous neighborhood that I usually avoided. I occasionally saw fancy cars stopped at the curb with men dressed to the nines sitting in their back seats with well-endowed women. Drunks clutching cheap whiskey not quite hidden in paper bags staggered on the sidewalk. Prostitutes displayed their bare calves and thighs.

The club itself was in a nondescript three-story brownstone building next to a pawnshop. No sign outside identified the establishment. A big storefront window revealed men gathered around a large pool table. I took a deep breath and straightened my back. *You can do this, Aki*, I told myself.

I knew that Pop's boss was a Nisei from Hawaii. I walked through the side door, my eyes adjusting to the darkness. It wouldn't hurt if Aloha turned on a few more lights. It smelled as nasty as it looked, like raw chicken had been left out too long. A woman in a tight off-white dress revealing the outline of her *chichis* lounged in a chair beside a staircase that apparently led to a second floor.

"Looking for a job, honey?" she practically purred. "Playtime might be hiring."

I frowned. Playtime was notorious for hiring both *hakujin* and Nisei prostitutes for the GIs who frequented the place.

I tried not to look at her chest. "I'm here to see Rocky," I told her.

"Wait here." She teetered onto her high heels, almost losing her balance, and headed for another set of stairs that seemed to go down to a basement. I noticed that a lot of unsavory-looking men were going down those steps.

While she was fetching Pop's boss, I approached a small bar in the back that could only accommodate six stools. Seated on one of them was the Nisei man who had been in line behind me at the WRA office, reading the same magazine. On the far left was the man I had been searching for all morning. Hammer wore the same mustard-colored pants but was missing his jacket, and sweat stains were visible on the underarms of his white shirt.

"It looks like you haven't slept," I said as I climbed onto the stool next to him.

Hammer didn't acknowledge me. He attempted to finish his drink but the glass was empty.

I wasn't sure if he was on drugs; he seemed completely different than when I'd seen him on the streets of Clark and Division. No swagger or confidence. Something about his facial appearance reminded me of the frightening horned *oni* demon masks on the walls of Issei homes. One version of the *oni* mask looked downright evil, but another, with its downturned mouth agape, seemed tortured. I had asked my mother about it, and she explained that the *oni* were good demons that were supposed to scare the bad demons away.

"Stay away from me, Tropico. I'm no good." He banged his empty glass back onto the bar.

"I want to know why you were fighting with Roy."

Hammer finally turned his head toward me. "Didn't he tell you?" There were scratch marks on his cheek that I hadn't noticed the night before.

"What happened to your face?"

Hammer fingered the scratches as if he were acquainting

himself with his injury. My reminder did not sit well with him. "Aki, scram. This is no place for you."

I cut to the chase. "Rose was my sister. I deserve to know what you did to her."

"I didn't do anything that she didn't ask for."

"What does that mean?" My voice sounded shrill and unfamiliar.

The Nisei with the magazine narrowed his eyes, as if my presence was disturbing him.

"I mean that Roy's the one who should be explaining himself," he said before clamming up. I felt like a nincompoop sitting at the bar in between two men who didn't seem to want anything to do with me.

After a few minutes, Hammer broke his silence. "You're lucky, you know. You have family."

"I don't know if I would call me lucky."

"Well, Rose had a sister who cares about her. She was lucky, too."

I was now convinced that Hammer was on some kind of drug. This kind of philosophizing from him seemed totally out of character.

A hefty man in a flowered shirt with a pencil behind his ear and cash in his hands came barreling up the basement stairs and headed straight to us. "You asked for me? I'm Rocky."

I jumped down from the stool, and he gave me the once-over. "We only pay by the hour and you'll have to doll yourself up. Wear some heels."

"I'm not looking for a job."

Rocky seemed relieved.

"I'm Gitaro Ito's daughter."

"Oh, Geet's kid. What happened to him?"

"He's under the weather." *From your rotten food*, I didn't mention out loud.

"Oh, it's slow today, anyway. But we'll need him tomorrow for sure."

I nodded. His lack of compassion didn't surprise me. As far as I could tell, the Aloha was all about business, both legal and not. I did wonder exactly what Pop, who had erratic hours, did at the bar, because there didn't seem to be much to clean and what there was didn't seem that clean at all.

Rocky went behind the bar and poured Hammer a fresh drink as I scurried to the door. The half-naked woman in the chair had left her post. I turned the corner and faced a large *hakujin* man who blocked the exit. "Hello, little geisha."

I ignored him, looking down as I pressed forward. He didn't budge. "It's too early for you to leave," he said, pushing me against the wall. He attempted to kiss me, but I dug my chin down. His cheek felt like sandpaper and he reeked of beer.

"Let me go," I whispered. It was as if my voice were stuffed in my chest. *Find your voice, Aki,* I told myself. But the more I tried, the more futile it was. The fleshy man kept me trapped in the dingy corner of Aloha's, delighting in my lack of audible response.

I squirmed and turned back to the bar. Rocky was gone. Hammer was still hunched over his glass. The boy with the overgrown hair was still obsessed with his magazine. There was no one to save me.

Taking a deep breath, I somehow was able to cross my arms over my chest and barrel forward into a crack of space between him and the door. Bursting out into the street, I knocked into the ample *oshiri* of the scantily clad woman who was now standing in front of the entrance, smoking a cigarette.

"Hey, watch it!" she reprimanded, as a line of cigarette ash fell and scattered on the concrete.

I didn't make any excuses or apologies. All I knew was that I had to get out of there. I practically ran down Clark Street, leaping over trash on the sidewalk and almost crashing into a group of people walking in the opposite direction. In the center of the foursome was the tall man in the dress we had seen the night before. His friends were also garishly outfitted in tight, low-cut gowns. They were all laughing, not bothering to notice my wretched state. On Clark Street, it was every person for herself.

By Monday, all of us Itos had rebounded. I scrubbed my face extra hard until my skin glowed pink and tried to put the awful man at Aloha out of my mind. I couldn't tell Mom or especially Pop what happened. Pop might attempt to right the wrong in his own way, which might land him in jail.

Pop, although weakened, woke up for a simple breakfast of dry toast and coffee and announced that he was strong enough to report to work that day. Mom had left for the barbershop. I was grateful to be escaping to the Newberry. The tomes, the maps and the documents had become so familiar to me—they were the spine that held my days together. All three of us assistants found refuge in the library's holdings. Nancy, a shutterbug, was transfixed by the Newberry's collection of photographs of American Indians from the 1800s. Phillis, the art historian, could be found wandering around the stacks devoted to Renaissance painters.

Later that day I was working the desk when I saw a familiar person standing in front of me. Art's hair was combed to the side, making him look very collegiate and even more handsome than usual.

"Art—"

"I'm so glad that I was able to track you down."

"I've already taken my afternoon break."

"I had to see you."

I looked for our supervisor's gray head but she was nowhere to be found. Phillis, wearing a blue polka-dot dress, appeared from the stacks, her arms full of books.

"Have you seen Mrs. Cannon?" I asked her. "Art needs to talk to me about something and I wanted to get permission to take a small break."

She elbowed my ribs. "Go on," she said. "I'll cover for you. But don't take too long."

I led Art behind a huge fern in the corner. "What's going on?"

"I wanted to tell you to be careful," Art said.

"What are you talking about?" I felt my cheeks flush. Had he heard that I had gone over to Roy and Ike's place? Was my reputation already tarnished?

"A Nisei girl was attacked yesterday. In her own apartment." Art delivered the news with such solemnity that I knew I needed to take heed. And by the hushed tone of his voice, I suspected that she had been sexually assaulted.

"Where?"

"The South Side."

"Did you know her?"

"I can't say too much. Just be careful, okay?"

My mind raced. I found it difficult to process the shocking information. I could hardly say anything in response. Art said that he had to leave to meet his academic advisor, so we returned to the front desk. Waiting for us was Phillis, who had a funny look on her face that I had never seen before. She directly addressed Art: "Did you go to Hyde Park High School?"

"Yes."

"I thought so."

Art stood still for a moment, then pointed at her in recollection. "You're Reggie's little sister. Phillis, right? You live down the street from us."

Phillis coyly smiled, shocking me. She had a slight overbite that I had never noticed before.

Art's expression remained solemn. "I heard that Reggie is overseas."

"He's with the Ninety-third."

"The Pacific?"

She nodded and the three of us stood in silence for a moment. Her answer confirmed my suspicions. Her brother was fighting the Japanese.

"The army kept them stateside for the longest time. Almost like they didn't trust the Negro boys," she said.

I had been so fixated on the Nisei soldiers that I hadn't even considered the situation for black soldiers. They were also in segregated military units, and it seemed like they weren't receiving any respect.

"If you write him, let him know I said hello," Art told her.

"Oh, yes, yes. I will." Was Phillis stammering?

Art said his goodbyes and I walked him out of the reading room. Before we reached the stairs, he stopped and shoved his hands in his pants pockets. "Do you think that I can get your phone number?"

A lovely warmth spilled over my body. *Is this what it feels like to be desired and pursued?* "Ah, we don't have a phone. Except for the pay phone out in the hall. We've been using that one for now." Unfortunately I couldn't remember the number, but promised to relay it to him the next time I saw him. He said that he'd be in the area tomorrow around the same time.

"It's a date," I said and immediately blushed. I didn't mean it to sound like that, but Art grinned in response and headed down the stairs.

"Wait," I called after him. "What time did it happen?"

"What?" He seemed confused and then his face fell upon understanding. "In the morning. When her older sister was in church."

It was at the same time I had been wandering around Clark and Division by myself, eating strawberry ice cream at the Ting-A-Ling. I felt queasy as I returned to the front desk.

"He's a dreamboat," commented Nancy, who had not heard the conversation about Phillis's brother. Phillis smiled in agreement as she restacked some books the reference librarian had requested. Art's visit had put both of them in a better mood. Some of that elation spilled over to me, too, but I couldn't help but feel the darkness of his original message: a Nisei woman had been attacked.

When I went home, I casually disclosed the incident to my mother, not revealing how I had received the information. I was curious how she would respond.

"*Mah*, these Nisei girls are so ill-behaved. There's no wonder something like that would occur," my mother commented as she attached a new button to my father's shirt.

But how about me at Aloha? I had done nothing to provoke that stranger. I just happened to be in his vicinity. That in itself had been enough for him to think that he could have his way with me.

CHAPTER 13

The following morning I made sure that I was wearing one of Rose's dresses. Ever since I had donned the teal wraparound at the Aragon, I felt a new freedom to raid my sister's wardrobe. This dress was red gingham with ruffles, a bit flashy for me. I had been hoping to wear it for a special occasion, and meeting Art in a park seemed special enough.

The day started off with momentous news. ALLIES INVADE FRANCE was the headline, splashed in block letters across the front page of the *Chicago Daily Tribune*. Troops had converged on the northern beaches in Normandy. Some reporters referred to it as "D-Day," a code for a secret military invasion.

My stomach flip-flopped with both anticipation and dread. Did this mean that we were winning? But such an expansive invasion meant more fallen soldiers. Nancy and I exchanged glances as we silently arranged that day's newspapers for our patrons.

Phillis caught our silent exchange. "Reggie's not in Europe," she reminded us.

"That's right," Nancy said and breathed out a sigh of relief. Afterward, the three of us went to the bathroom to wash the newspaper ink off our hands.

The morning flew by. I made a deal with Phillis so I could skip my lunch break and take a late-afternoon break. When I mentioned that I was meeting Art, she couldn't help but smile.

I wrote my phone number with a short pencil on a piece of scratch paper that our library patrons used to write Dewey decimal call numbers. As soon as I saw Art at the gate, I gave it to him. During our conversation, I could see the outline of my name on that piece of paper through the fabric of his shirt pocket, which made me happy to no end.

We relaxed on a bench on the south side of the park underneath an elm tree. D-Day was at the top of our minds.

"I hope the war will soon be over," I said.

"Don't we all. But there will be much blood spilled before we get to that point."

I hope that you won't be drafted, I thought to myself.

It was as if Art had read my mind. "It's only a matter of time before I'll get my letter." He sounded like he was ready to serve. For a Midwestern Nisei like Art who had never spent time behind barbed wire, the decision to fight for our country wasn't so complicated.

We remained quiet for a moment. Art placed his arm behind me on the edge of the bench, and I felt my heart pounding. I'd never really dated before. I had gone to a few dances in high school and after graduation, but the boys always seemed to treat me like a sister and not a girlfriend.

"They say it's going to be hot this weekend," he said.

"It's hot every weekend."

"But no thunderstorms. How about we go to Lake Michigan?"

"Really?" I thought about all those sun-kissed *hakujin* I saw lying out on the white sands and playing volleyball. And then I remembered that I didn't have anything to wear.

"I've had bad experiences with swimsuits." I explained

briefly what had happened to me in eighth grade at Vivi Pelletier's house.

"Well, wear shorts and we'll walk along the beach. Barefoot."

"I can do that." I smiled, thinking of walking alongside Art, maybe his bare, sinewy legs brushing against mine. We spoke about silly things for a while, but my mind returned to my encounter with Hammer on Sunday. I tried to ask as casually as possible, "Have you heard anything more about the Nisei girl who was attacked? I imagine that it's quite awful for her and her family."

"She only has a sister here," Art said. From the strained expression on his face, I knew that he hadn't planned to share that bit of information.

For a moment, I felt as though my mind and heart were leaving my body. I wanted to escape and run away from the pain as usual, but I instead reined myself in. "I would like to talk to her," I murmured. "To lift her spirits, I mean."

"I don't think she'd feel comfortable with that. At least not now. She doesn't want anyone's company." Art hesitated. "She's been too afraid to leave her apartment."

"Has she gone to the police?"

"I told her to. I said I could even go with her and her sister. But she's scared."

"He could do it again, you know."

"I know," Art said. "Believe me, I know." He looked down at his fingernails. "Let's talk about something else for a while."

I readily agreed. Who would want to spoil a moment with Art Nakasone by talking about such darkness?

During the nights that followed my outing with Art in the park, I couldn't sleep well. I kept thinking about the girl who had been attacked. I tried to catch Harriet outside the apartment building to ask her what she knew, but she was always on her way to an appointment. I was starting to get the feeling that she was avoiding me.

I hadn't seen Hammer for days. It seemed as if he had completely disappeared from Clark and Division. Concerned enough about his whereabouts, I called out to Manju as he rambled through the neighborhood one evening.

"Have you seen Hammer?" I asked, a bit breathless from my run to catch up to him.

Manju exhaled some smoke, aiming it directly into my face. This man lacked manners, that was for sure. "Nope. Even went to his lady friend's apartment in Chinatown. She hasn't seen him, either."

Then where was he staying? And those terrible scratches on his face. I didn't think Roy had done that. They looked like the handiwork of someone with long nails.

"Does he do this often? I mean, disappear."

"He tries to, but I keep tabs on him. This time, though, is different." Manju's distress was palpable. I had no idea that a man could care so much for a friend. Maybe it was more about Hammer's general charisma. I was both repelled by and attracted to him at the same time. Had Rose succumbed to his *yogore* magnetism? Maybe Roy had suspected something wicked in Hammer all along. That would explain his outbursts of anger toward him.

"I'm sure that he'll turn up," I said, not convinced of it at all. Manju had not heard me. He was already trudging up Clark, leaving behind a plume of smoke.

The next few days I felt jumpy and unsettled, like pinballs were whizzing inside me. Being in Chicago was like riding a roller coaster at the Pike in Long Beach. There was the excitement of rising emotions, the anticipation of seeing Art, abruptly followed by a whiplash of panic over a rapist at large.

Phillis had also seemed distracted these past few days. She was the one we relied on to retrieve the more obscure books, the ones requested maybe once every ten years. Even during her breaks, she wandered around the deserted corners of the stacks, as if the most ignored books deserved some visitors now and then.

A new patron, a visiting history professor at Northwestern, had started coming to the library on a regular basis, sometimes making rush requests at the end of the day. He was studying military history, specifically the Gallic Wars under Julius Caesar. The Newberry had dozens upon dozens of editions of these accounts, and both Nancy and I deferred to Phillis's expertise to find the ones that he wanted.

Only this day, she kept bringing the wrong volumes.

The professor, a short man barely taller than me, snapped a little when she did it for the first time. But by the third time, he had lost all patience.

"Is she some kind of idiot?" he said, loud enough for everyone in the room to hear. Nancy would have given him an earful, but she had left for her break. I, meanwhile, froze. Something in his tone of voice sounded familiar. Like some of the so-called big-shot customers at the produce market, the ones who owned market chains. We, the Japanese, were below them. And now, Phillis, a young black woman, was being treated the same way by this professor.

Phillis didn't avert her gaze from this man like I would have done. Her mahogany eyes didn't even blink. "No, sir, I am not an idiot. I'd appreciate it if you spoke to me like a human being."

I was shocked by her answer. Her voice was steady and

calm, but I could feel the rage behind each word. The professor felt it as well, as he mumbled some kind of apology and slinked away.

"Are you all right, Phillis?" I said. Nancy had returned from her break and joined us at the front desk.

"Reggie is wounded," Phillis announced. "He got caught in a sniper nest. We received the telegram a few days ago."

"*Ohmygoodness*," Nancy exclaimed, immediately hugging Phillis, whose arms hung limp at her sides.

"Pacific Islands?" I almost whispered.

"A place called Bougainville."

The name made it sound like it was located in Europe rather than Asia.

"I'm so sorry," I said. The angle of the early-afternoon light coming through the windows temporarily blinded me, prompting me to take a few steps away from Phillis.

"It's not your fault. The army's been keeping the Negro boys from fighting on the frontlines because they didn't think they were up to it. And now this happens."

"Is he going to be all right?" I asked.

"He had surgery over there. I think that they have an underground bunker for that."

An underground surgery room? It sounded primitive and I feared for Reggie's recovery.

Before we could ask Phillis more questions, Mr. Geiger came down, asking if one of us could leave early to make a delivery to the law library at Northwestern's McKinlock campus on our way home. Still affected by Phillis's news about her brother, I wanted to leave the confines of the library immediately but waited for either Phillis or Nancy to volunteer. I was relieved that I was the only one available. Too much was happening—with both me and the people around me. I needed to get away and think.

Wrapped in brown paper and twine, the book was heavy and unwieldy. Even though the delivery location wasn't that far away, I took the streetcar and transferred once at the intersection of Lake Shore Drive and Chicago Avenue. As it was rush hour, I had to stand, and I planted my feet firmly to avoid accidentally thrusting the legal book into a neighboring passenger's stomach.

What will I do if someone tries to accost me? I wondered. I wanted to be a Rosie the Riveter type, my hair tied back in a red kerchief, my biceps toned and my will determined. But being trapped in that corner of Aloha had reconfirmed that I was really a weakling in many areas. I didn't want to be so handicapped. I did have a natural sense of curiosity, and I pledged that I would try to infuse such inclinations with more boldness.

The second streetcar stopped right in front of the campus. The grounds were compact yet impressive. It was easy for me to locate the multi-level law library, which was constructed of gray stone with an ornate façade that reminded me of structures that I've seen in photographs of British country estates. After leaving the package for the librarian at the front desk, I decided to explore this neighborhood, which was called Streeterville, before I went home.

The candy factory that had employed Rose and Roy was in this general area. I had looked it up once on a map and had seen that it was hemmed in by the mouth of the Chicago River, Lake Shore Drive, and a thin waterway called the Ogden Slip. Beyond Lake Shore Drive was the breakwater for the outer harbor. As I trekked, I could see Navy Pier in the distance, and I took a deep breath. Of course, no smell of salt water. Lake Michigan always had me fooled.

I was walking on Illinois Street when I spotted the letters BABY RUTH, as high as a one-story building, on top of a structure shaped like a giant shoe box. A sugary, chocolatey scent spilled out onto the street, but it had a slightly burnt edge to it, as if the candy had been expelled from a car's exhaust pipe. I had found the factory.

One of the working shifts had ended, as evident from the women exiting. They wore white uniforms, and a couple still hadn't pulled their white work caps from their heads. A group in street clothes was assembled outside the building, taking drags from cigarettes or chatting with one another. I recognized the brilliant red hair of one of the women and approached her. "You were at my sister's funeral."

Even though we didn't know each other well, she gave me a hug, her body feeling bony and sharp against mine. She reminded me that her name was Shirley. "How are you doing?"

"I'm okay."

"And your parents?"

"Doing the best that they can."

Her hazel eyes welled up with tears, and I realized that the woman was much older than I had previously thought. She had deep bags under her eyes that her makeup accentuated rather than camouflaged. Still, her face was kind and made me want to trust her.

"I've been beside myself ever since the funeral," she said.

Her emotional revelation seemed overblown. "I didn't realize that you were so close to Rose."

She fingered a cross that hung from her necklace. "I've had some sleepless nights, wondering if I could have helped her in any way."

I struggled between curiosity and resentment that this woman felt she could have saved Rose. "What in the world are you talking about?"

"I knew that she was upset about something."

How could she know? I was the only person who could sense Rose's more vulnerable side.

Shirley apparently read the skepticism on my face and offered more concrete evidence. "You see, I came across her crying in the restroom stall one afternoon. I did my best to console her."

"What?" I was starting to feel sick to my stomach.

"I thought maybe it was our supervisor, Mr. Schultz. He can be a bear sometimes."

"The one who was at her funeral?" I remembered the Teddy Roosevelt look-alike who overenunciated his words.

"Yes, I was surprised that he came out, frankly."

"So was he the one?" I balled up my hands.

"What?"

"Was he the reason my sister was so upset?"

"She wouldn't tell me what was wrong. To tell you the truth, she was very embarrassed. She wouldn't look me in the eye after that. I was afraid that I had offended her in some way."

I had never seen Rose shed a tear in front of me. For her to openly cry at work meant something was desperately amiss.

"About when did this happen?"

Shirley lifted her face toward the water. "It was cold, that's what I remembered. It was winter, definitely. She was wearing a heavy knit scarf around her neck. I helped wipe her tears with it."

A horn sounded and Shirley indicated that she needed to return to the factory. She took a few steps and then backtracked. "Are you here to see Roy?"

"Ah, is he around?"

"I think his shift is ending. I'll get him."

She squeezed my arm and went back in the building.

• • •

I moved to get out of the way of the next shift streaming into the factory. I debated whether I should force myself in and demand a meeting with this Mr. Schultz. But what would I say? *Did you make my sister cry that winter day?* I knew a simple reprimand from a supervisor wouldn't have caused such a breakdown. This time I needed real answers from Roy.

Hearing sharp words being exchanged, I turned my attention to the loading docks, where three Nisei women were having an intense conversation. I recognized two of them as the women I had briefly met at the Greek-owned restaurant where I ate pancakes with Roy. The third woman was bone thin; I feared that her loose skirt would fall down to her ankles.

"Somebody needs to go to the police. We can't let this man get away with it." The speaker was Marge, the short woman with the distinctive voice, scratchy like she had been yelling at someone for a while.

"Imagine if it happened to your sister, Marge. It's not an easy thing." The thin woman spoke in a quiet voice, but it still commanded the other women's attention. "She has to be not only Betty's big sister but her mother. And she doesn't want their parents to worry in camp. There's nothing they can do from there."

The tall bespectacled woman from the restaurant nodded.

"It's not right; that's all I'm saying," Marge said.

"Who's that?" The thin woman pointed at me.

Marge narrowed her eyes. She had a good memory because she recognized me. "Oh, she's Rose Ito's little sister." Her tall friend in the glasses confirmed my identity. They all stared at me as if I were a black cat, a bringer of bad luck.

Before I could respond, Roy came out of the factory in a gray uniform, his name embroidered over his chest pocket. He was still wearing a pair of work gloves, so I wondered if his shift was truly over. I strode over and greeted him. His lip had returned to almost normal. Ike was a wonder with a surgical needle.

"What's happened? Your dad?" he asked.

"No, no. I was in the neighborhood delivering a package for work. I saw the factory and thought I'd stop. I've never come here before."

"Impressed?" Roy said with an edge of sarcasm.

Actually, I was. I had never seen such a big manufacturing plant. Apparently the same company had other offices and even a farm in the country where a number of Japanese American families worked.

We swapped trivial stories until I finally got around to what I wanted to talk to him about. "I heard that a girl from the South Side was attacked."

Roy studied my face for a moment. He seemed both stunned and impressed that I had assimilated a bit of gossip without him. He shot a glance at the Nisei women by the loading dock. "Yeah, it's terrible." He took off his right glove and pressed down on his head by his ear.

"Did you ever think that's what happened to Rose?"

"I don't understand." Roy frowned, his thick eyebrows furrowed.

"Rose was pregnant." The words, raw and to the point, tumbled out of my mouth. In a way, it felt good to finally expel them.

"What?" I could tell that he was genuinely shocked.

"If it wasn't you, then who was it?" I didn't mention anything about the abortion. That was too scandalous to share, even with Roy.

Roy stood still for a long time before he spoke. "I always suspected that she might have had a secret boyfriend. Maybe he was married."

"Do you think that she could have been attacked?"

"No, I would have known."

"How would you?"

Roy's mouth closed, forming a straight line.

"Could it have been Hammer?"

His eyes flashed. "I'll kill him."

"Wait. I'm not saying that it was. But I heard that you were after him because he was getting too close to Rose."

"Who told you that?" Roy then shook his head. "Ike. He couldn't keep his mouth shut."

"Don't blame Ike. He's your friend."

The first shift continued to leave the plant. Some carrying lunch pails, kerchiefs around their hair or neck, slowly made their way toward the main street. "I noticed that Hammer and Rose were spending time together. A lot of time. During the last month that she was alive," he said.

The late-afternoon humidity pressed down, and being by the water didn't help. I felt like I couldn't breathe.

Roy gazed east, toward Lake Michigan. "The past three months, she cut me off like I had done something wrong. I couldn't figure it out."

I blotted the moisture on my forehead with my handkerchief, which was now stained with my pancake makeup.

"It makes perfect sense." Roy was not addressing me, but himself. "Someone had gotten her pregnant. That's why she didn't want to have anything to do with me. And that's why she threw herself at that train."

"I don't think Rose killed herself." I had to squelch that talk. If that was the common belief, no one would believe that someone had thrown her into the train's path. "Do you really think that she would?"

"Any Nisei girl who was pregnant out of wedlock would have considered it. Desperate people do desperate things."

Any girl? And specifically Rose?

"We were coming to Chicago. She had arranged the apartment and everything for us."

Roy had stopped listening to me. He had found his answer about why Rose was ignoring him, and that's all he wanted. He didn't want to know the truth behind her death.

A new crowd of Nisei, *hakujin* and black employees moved toward the entrance, energy in their step.

"I have to go in and get my things," Roy told me. "Wait for me?"

I shook my head and made an excuse that I was late for another appointment. I was so frustrated and disappointed in Roy. His thoughts were only on himself.

I stumbled out to the sidewalk, where the candy company employees seemed to be making their way to the train station. The neighborhood was industrial for a block or two before it became quite posh. A few blocks west the impressive Tribune building loomed ahead, which made me feel smaller and even more inconsequential than usual. My stride was brisk; I passed one group after another, darting in between people or sometimes walking on the other side of parked cars.

It took me a moment to realize that Marge was trudging in front of me with the thin woman she'd been talking to on the loading docks. They each carried the same kind of canvas bag.

I couldn't quite hear what Marge was saying. There were sighs of frustration and fragments of speech—"no one cares," "dangerous," and "police." After about a block of straining to listen, I tripped over a break in the sidewalk, causing both of them to turn around.

"What are you doing? Following us?" Marge rasped. I

was stunned by the intensity of her emotion more than her accusation. Lines of anger marked her forehead. "I don't know what's wrong with you Itos."

I was speechless. What had we done to provoke Marge like this?

"Your sister was an awful person. She was cavorting with that government worker, telling him all our stories. She was spying on us and I see that you've taken her place." The thin woman clutched Marge's arm. I thought at first that she was trying to restrain Marge, but then I saw that she was using Marge as a shield to protect herself from me.

Marge was not finished. "It's people like you Itos who sent my father to Santa Fe. An old man who has taught judo for thirty years. What kind of crime is that?"

I now had to respond. Being an *inu*, an informant, was the dirtiest accusation that an Issei or Nisei could make against another. "We would never do such a thing. Rose wouldn't and I wouldn't, either. Nothing like that would even cross our minds."

My words had no effect on Marge. Her ferocious anger needed to be released. "Some people say that Rose had it coming to her, the accident. I say it was *bachi*, plain and simple. What goes around, comes around." Marge pivoted, securing her arm around the other woman's waist, and together they headed down the street to the train station.

CHAPTER 14

When it first started snowing in Chicago, it seemed so beautiful and quiet. It was different than the occasional flurries at Manzanar, which lasted only a day or so. Lately, though, the snow feels like a slippery prison.

Marge's accusation—that Rose was a spy and that I was one as well—burned hot in my mind as I stood in the train, swaying as the car sped to the Clark and Division station. That such rumors would follow Rose to Chicago disturbed me, mostly because I had hoped that we could all start over from scratch. But the past dragged behind us, and deep down inside I knew that I had been overly optimistic, like my father had initially been.

Once the car arrived at my stop, I got off and headed southwest to our apartment. A familiar figure disappeared into our building. I only saw his profile, the thinning light-brown hair, the hunched shoulders from perhaps too much note-taking.

I went upstairs to Harriet's unit. I put my ear on the door. Again, muffled talking. I could have sworn that I recognized the monotone rhythm of Douglas's voice, the same tune played over and over.

I rapped on the door with my knuckle.

Whispers and then footsteps echoing away from the door. The hinges of an interior door squeaking.

Finally, Harriet's voice, a bit breathless. "Who is it?"

"It's Aki," I announced. "I know that he's in there, Harriet."

"What are you talking about?"

"I need to talk to Douglas."

A few moments of silence—probably only a few seconds, but it seemed like an interminable length of time. Harriet must have decided *shikataganai,* there was no use in trying to deflect me. She knew that I was stubborn, that I wouldn't give it up so she might as well open the door.

The apartment was tiny, one room with a kitchenette and a bathtub that took more space than the twin bed. Yellow cotton curtains had been hung on a rod above the large open window, allowing the setting sun to pour in. Somehow Harriet had made her miserable living conditions bright and cheery. I had to admit that I was impressed.

The bathroom door squeaked open and Douglas Reilly stepped out. "I'll let you two talk," Harriet said, escaping into the small bathroom, which seemed only to have room for a toilet.

Douglas stood awkwardly, his veined hands at his sides. Now that I was standing so close to him in such cramped quarters, I recognized the smell of Douglas's musky cologne. It was the same scent that had been on Rose's dress with the cranes.

"Did you spend time with my sister?" I asked him outright.

He shook his head. "Not much. Only through my interviews with her as part of my WRA work. Shared anonymously, of course."

Why would Rose do such a thing? Did she think that she was helping the war effort somehow?

"I'd like those stories."

"I can't give them to you. That would be a breach of ethics."

"Why is your cologne all over one of Rose's dresses? That doesn't seem too ethical."

"I gave her that dress. It was in appreciation. That's all." Dry flakes of skin were peeling off his top lip. I wondered if he had eczema or a related condition. I couldn't help but to examine his ring finger. It wasn't that well-defined, but I detected a slight indentation where a wedding ring might have been.

For a *hakujin* WRA staffer to give a Nisei female subject such an extravagant and personal gift was bad form. I feared that his relationship with Rose was much more intimate than he was letting on. I didn't want to hear any more denials, so I decided to shock him to see what he actually knew.

"Are you the reason that she had an abortion?"

Something hard clattered to the floor in the bathroom.

Douglas's legs seemed to buckle underneath him, because he staggered to sit down on Harriet's bed. "I knew nothing about that. She wasn't dating anyone, as far as I knew."

I didn't know why, but I felt anger rise to my throat. Someone had to be held accountable. Douglas was guilty of spying on us and giving Rose an inappropriate gift. Besides that, though, he seemed harmless. He was an easy target, someone I could overpower, at least emotionally.

I towered over him like that for a few moments. "You probably heard that a Nisei girl was attacked on the South Side."

"I heard the rumors." Douglas's green eyes revealed no emotion. "It hasn't been the only incident. There was a Peeping Tom, a flasher. Someone spoke about a sex maniac being on the loose."

I was astonished at how casually he tossed out that last term. "Was he arrested?"

"It was just talk. No one could tell me specifics. I don't know why you people don't go to the police."

"Why didn't you go to the police?"

"It's not my place. No one had firsthand information. It was more somebody who had heard it from somebody else."

I had little patience for observers who did nothing. Maybe in that sense I was becoming more like Rose.

The bathroom door opened and Harriet went to her small sink and began washing dishes as if we weren't even there. I figured this was a sign that my visit had come to an end. Douglas seemed even more defeated than I was, so I too decided that it was best that I go.

When I arrived at the apartment, my parents were fully dressed, a purse hanging from my mother's arm.

"*Nokorimono* in refrigerator," she said, referring to the leftovers from last night's dinner of fried rice.

"Where are you two going?"

"English lesson," my mother said, "over at YMCA."

As my father had worked as the manager of the produce market, his English was serviceable, but Mom had always had trouble with the language. When I wished her well, she glared like I was making fun of her.

I relished this time to be in the quiet apartment by myself. I took out the fried rice from the refrigerator. Mom had diced up Spam in perfect mini-cubes and added green peas for color. I turned on our electric burner, and with our only skillet, I warmed up the fried rice, enjoying the smoky scent of cooked Spam as it filled the room.

The pay phone rang. I quickly turned off the burner, unlocked the front door, and ran out to the hallway.

"Hello," I said, my voice breathless.

"Did I make you run?"

"No, I'm fine." It was so good to hear this voice. I was glad that Art couldn't see me because I was smiling so wide my cheeks were hurting.

"I'm looking forward to going to the lake," he said.

"I am, too."

"Pick you up at eleven."

"I can make some sandwiches for a picnic."

"Perfect. I'll bring some water."

The cord wasn't long enough for me to sit on the ground and talk, so I told him to wait a minute. I brought one of the dining-room chairs out to the hallway and sat right next to the pay phone. Twilight was moving into night, and through a shallow window I could see the top of some skyscraper as the sky turned from a pink spread to a hushed darkness. For a moment, in spite of all the shock, sadness and anger these past few years had brought, I felt my heart expand. Was it possible to be happy? Was it wrong?

Art had to work on a paper for a summer-session class, so we ended our conversation, and I returned to the apartment to eat my fried rice. It had gotten cold, but I didn't care. I sat with one of my legs up on my seat—a definite no-no if my mother was around—and brought spoonfuls of rice to my mouth.

I was washing my dish and the skillet when there was a knock on the door. *What now?*

I put my ear against the locked door. "Who is it?"

"Harriet Saito."

She had changed from her work clothes into pedal pushers and a white T-shirt. She looked about a decade younger.

I invited her in and we sat across from each other at the dining-room table. Harriet turned down my offer to get her something to drink, which was just as well since we only had our terrible tap water.

"You don't approve of me," she said.

I was stumped by her statement and it must have been apparent on my face.

"You don't approve that Douglas was in my room."

"You don't need my approval." *I hardly know you*, I thought.

"Douglas has been working for the WRA ever since I came to Chicago. He's a good man."

"Is he married?"

Harriet shifted in her seat. "He's separated. She's in New York City." She squeezed her hands together and extended her fingers. "Don't you feel that you can breathe here?"

The faucet needed a new washer and the water was dripping incessantly. We heard it now. *Kerplunk*, *kerplunk*, *kerplunk*.

I looked at her, confused.

"No one is saying Japanese can't act in a certain way. That we can't date or marry white men. We can be whoever we are."

I wasn't sure where Harriet was from. Probably Modesto or some farm town in the middle of California where it was murderously hot in the summer and the tule fog was thick in the winter. Perhaps she felt that her life had been too stifling in farm country, but the truth was that we were all being watched and evaluated in big cities like Los Angeles or Chicago.

"I want you to know that Douglas is working on behalf of us, the Japanese, to make life better."

"He's tattling to the government. And he made Rose look bad. The other girls think she was a spy or something."

Harriet pursed her lips. "Douglas gave me this to give to you." She handed me a manila folder.

"What is it?"

"You'll know," she said.

Inside were two pages typewritten in blue, a carbon

copy. One page was dated November 1943; the second one, March 1944.

I quickly closed the folder. I was going to wait until after Harriet had left the apartment to peruse it.

"I didn't read it," she said. I shrugged. "You know that he can get in trouble for releasing this report before turning it in to the government?"

I doubted that the repercussions were serious, especially in light of all that we had suffered. I fingered the edge of the folder. "Was he in love with Rose?"

Harriet's face lost its tightness. Her eyes looked rounder and shinier.

"I think he was," she said, as she got up from the table and headed for the door.

As soon as Harriet left, I opened up the manila folder and began to read.

> *NOVEMBER 1943*
> *Subject is a twenty-three-year-old Nisei woman. She comes from an area in between Glendale and downtown Los Angeles and worked as a produce clerk before war. She had been in Manzanar War Relocation Center from March 1942 to September 1943.*
>
> *She came to Chicago in advance of her family, her Issei father, a Los Angeles produce manager, Issei mother, and Nisei younger sister, who was in City College.*
>
> *She didn't have problems finding a place to live as she met another single woman her age from San Francisco at the WRA office. They were placed with another roommate from the Pasadena area who was in Gila River Relocation Center.*

While other subjects have expressed that they've enjoyed the freedom of being on their own, this woman says that she has missed her family more than she imagined. She finds the social activities lacking and says there are not enough efforts to support the Nisei soldiers in the 100th/442nd Regimental Combat Team.

She feels many men specifically seem dispirited and that the WRA needs to make efforts to ensure that Japanese Americans are compensated as much as other people in the same position.

MARCH 1944

It's been difficult to conduct a follow-up interview with this subject. She seems hostile and unwilling to cooperate with government officials. When observed in social settings, she appears quite unchanged but when approached by the WRA, she pointedly expressed that she feels completely abandoned by her country.

I read Douglas's report at least seven times in one sitting. I despised that he referred to Rose as a "subject," like she was a mouse in a scientific experiment. But I was also grateful that he provided a few glimpses into how she was really feeling. It made sense that she was still seeking ways to support Nisei men in uniform and advocating for equal pay for equal work; she had always been a champion for such issues. I choked back tears when I read that she missed us "more than she imagined." Most devastating was to learn that she had lost hope in America. Rose, more than any of us Itos, had been the most optimistic about the future. Now I feared that hope for our family was gone forever.

CHAPTER 15

I loved to go to the beach at White Point when I was a young girl. A smell reminiscent of rotten eggs let us know that we were getting close, and then before we knew it, we were jumping into a pool next to the ocean. The sulfuric properties made us more buoyant, like fishing lures floating on the surface of the sea. Fathers and mothers, in straw hats and cotton clothing, leaned against the white wooden railing to watch. At White Point, which was owned by Issei brothers, we could freely swim with *hakujin* men, women and children. Afterward our family and friends would all go to the shore and sit on blankets on the white sands and fill ourselves with a picnic of *onigiri, shoyu* chicken, sliced watermelon and *oden*, a type of Japanese stew.

I couldn't imagine that a body of water near Chicago could compare, but I had to admit that I felt happy when my bare feet reached the sand along Lake Michigan. I had not seen anything like this for more than two years. "It really looks like a beach!" I exclaimed as I turned to the skyscrapers. "In the middle of the city."

The air was hot and still, not a breeze in sight, and as a result, the water in Lake Michigan didn't move much either. Art maintained that sometimes there were waves, big ones fifteen feet in height. I had my doubts but I didn't care. I was away from my parents, the empty spot in my family where my sister once existed, Clark and Division and the war. I was walking along the water with a boy I liked and that's all I cared about.

Art went in farther and kicked some water and sand toward me. I shrieked and retaliated by splashing water on his crisp white shirt and khaki pants, which he had rolled up to his knees.

We finally called a truce and lay on a blanket on the sand, our shoes nearby. Art put on a pair of sunglasses while I lowered a bucket hat over my face to avoid getting sunburned.

"What do you like to do?" he asked. I was confused by his question, so he rephrased it. "What makes you happy?"

"I liked spending time with my dog." That sounded so pitiful, but it was true.

"You'll have to come over to my house."

I pulled off the hat to listen more carefully.

"We have two dogs, a cat and a parakeet. My mother is originally from a farm in Oregon."

I told Art about Rusty, how we got him as a puppy from a produce worker and how I had to bury him in our backyard a couple of months after Pearl Harbor. Surprisingly, I didn't cry. It felt good to talk about him and tell Art how much Rusty meant to me, even though he was only a dog.

"I've never met any girl like you, Aki."

I crinkled my forehead. "I'm an ordinary person."

"No, no you're not." He reached for my hand, and I felt an electric current go up my wrist and arm. He took off his sunglasses so he could look me straight in the eyes and then bent his face. His lips were soft and pillowy. I had never kissed a boy on the lips before. Kissing was wonderful. I felt that I could be kissing Art Nakasone for a very long time.

• • •

On the ride home, Art steered mostly with his left hand, reaching for my hand with his right as he slowed and stopped at major intersections. Our fingers entwined, and I didn't want to let go. When was I going to see Art next?

Unfortunately, the same Nisei girls were sitting on the stoop when Art was dropping me off. We didn't dare to kiss in front of them. Before I opened the passenger door, Art squeezed my hand. "I'll call you," he said, and I nodded.

I stepped out of the car, my head held high like Katharine Hepburn's. I carried my hat on the crook of my finger behind my back, and tossed my hair as I walked up the stairs. They gave me side-eyed glances but said nothing. I struggled a little with the front entrance door and then heard an explosion of comments about me and Art as the door closed behind me. Something had happened to me this afternoon. I had become the center of attention, the coveted one. I had taken Rose's place.

I tried to moderate my happiness when I walked into the apartment. My mother had returned from cleaning the Bello brothers' barbershop and was at the sink washing dishes, while my father was reading Sunday's issue of the *Chicago Daily Tribune* at our table. "*Baka*," he cursed the Japanese military for what he viewed as foolishness. "How can they imagine that they can beat America?"

While she was very opinionated about most other matters, my mother had nothing to say. Before the war, she had regularly sent letters to her parents and siblings in Kagoshima. That communication, of course, ceased as diplomatic relations between the US and Japan broke down. I sensed that she was worried about her relatives, but she never verbally expressed her concern. As I had never set foot in Japan and never met my grandparents on either my mother's or father's side, that world almost seemed imagined, like an old Japanese folktale.

"Ah, *yaketa*!" my mother exclaimed, seeing my sunburned cheeks. "Where did you go?"

I hadn't mentioned anything about my outing with Art to my parents. I needed to feel that something was 100 percent mine, separate from the Ito family. I mumbled about taking a walk around the lake. My parents started discussing whether they would be able to attend Chicago's first Buddhist service the next day at the South Parkway Community Hall on the South Side. I went into the bedroom and as I took off my old shoes, grains of sand fell onto the hardwood floor, filling my chest with a fleeting joy once again. I collected the sand and put it in one of my lockets, a reminder that no matter what happened in the future, I had had this perfect day.

That night, as I heard Pop snoring and Mom grinding her teeth—making an odd sound like the popping of popcorn—I fingered the locket, which I had strung on a chain around my neck. I felt such guilt over my elation about Art, and even more guilt over not telling Art about my efforts to find out what happened to Rose. Before he came into my life, Rose was all that I could think about, but now my head was filled with thoughts of Art. Of how his cheek, all prickly with his afternoon shadow, felt next to mine. The smell of his aftershave. I felt that he and Rose were on different sides of a balanced scale, and I was running from one side to another to make it even. But that, of course, was impossible. I had to eventually choose one side.

Two days later, I was in the stacks with Phillis retrieving some books on Celtic mythology and folklore. She had heard word that the surgery on Reggie's leg had gone well in the jungle of Bougainville. I had looked up Bougainville, which apparently had been named after a French explorer, and saw that it was a part of the Territory of New Guinea, located above Australia. I couldn't imagine a young man from the South Side of Chicago being relegated to such a place.

Ever since receiving the updated status on her brother, Phillis seemed more relaxed. I had heard that her mother was a schoolteacher and her father an insurance adjuster. She, like me, only had an older sibling, and his absence seemed to be keenly felt in the Davis household.

"Have you been seeing Art?" Phillis uncharacteristically asked me a personal question in the darkness of the stacks.

"You like him!" I declared.

She didn't deny it. "Everyone likes Art. He got along with everyone in high school. I wrote to Reggie about seeing him at the Newberry."

Before I could reply, Nancy came into the stacks and announced, "There's someone to see you, Aki. A woman."

I gently set down the Celtic books and made my way to the front desk.

It was strange to see Tomi here in the library, like a canary released from her Evanston cage. Little pink bumps had appeared along her hairline and she blinked rapidly. She was nervous about something.

"I'm off in ten minutes," I told her. "I can meet you in the park across the street."

Once I stepped into Bughouse Square, I couldn't spot her skinny frame and feared that she had run off. My eyes quickly scanned the long row of benches. I saw the regulars—a homeless man with an eye patch, a sandy-haired man who always came with a sketchbook, some young mothers with baby carriages—and then, in between a nun and a boy in a baseball cap, I spotted a very pale Tomi Kawamura with a carpetbag on her lap. I plucked her from her tight spot, and we moved to the south side where there were fewer people but more direct sunlight. Her skin looked almost translucent, like an underwater pearl.

She was struggling to speak. And even though we were sitting down, she was out of breath for a while. She used only words, not complete sentences. I could only make out, "The man. The knife. The man."

"Tomi, Tomi." I gave her shoulders a gentle shake. "Slow down. And breathe. And then start from the beginning."

She did what I instructed her to do and then began talking. "I ran into Ike at the hospital. I was there with Mrs. Peterson, my employer, for a routine checkup, and while I was waiting, he told me about the girl who was attacked a few weeks ago. A man with a knife."

She clasped her hands together, as if it was cold and not eighty-five degrees with 100 percent humidity. "I've also seen a man with a knife." Tears came to my eyes in anticipation of what she was going to share. "He was leaving our apartment."

Her whole delicate body rolled forward and she started crying so hard that she almost convulsed. I didn't know what to do and finally gently rubbed her back. I could feel the knots of her spine through the thin fabric of her dress. An elderly woman who was sitting near us eyed us suspiciously and moved to a bench on the other side of the park.

I let her cry like this for a good five minutes. I didn't care if I was late returning from my break.

When Tomi lifted her head, there were only two pink spots underneath her eyes. She looked even more beautiful than usual.

"Tell me, Tomi," I said. "Tell me everything."

She had been coming home after a shift at the candy company, ready to put her key in the lock, but she didn't have to. The unsecured apartment door should have been her first clue that something was wrong. As soon as she pushed it open, she was shoved to the wall and then the floor. She felt the force of someone heavy behind her, on top of her, whispering in her ear to count to one hundred and stay down. If she didn't do what he told her, he'd find her. And kill her. To make his point he flashed the sharp blade of a knife in her face. Her whole body shook. She began counting out loud because she felt that was her only protection. The man got up but she didn't know where he was. She kept counting. She reached one hundred once, then twice, then three times. Waited for a blow. A blade that would slice her ear off. But there was only an infinite hush. It had snowed that day and she was wearing gloves. The floor was wet underneath her. She thought it was melted snow, but she had soiled her pants.

She slowly got up, furtively looking to her right and then her left, inside the room. That's when she saw her. Rose on the floor, too. The bottom of her polka-dotted dress pulled up to her hips.

"I cried and cried," Tomi said. She had a hard time untying the bandanna around Rose's mouth. "'Undo my hands, Tomi,' Rose said. She was so calm. She was comforting me, not the other way around."

I stared at Tomi, noticing the faint bags underneath her eyes. In a split second, she looked so much older.

"He was waiting for her in our apartment when she was coming back from the ladies' room. We were all so careful about locking the door, even when we were going to the toilet, and Rose swore that she had done so. We don't know how he got in. Must have picked the lock. He was wearing a mask but Rose saw the hair on his arms. And the way he talked, he sounded like a Nisei."

I felt like vomiting right then and there. I had pictured a *hakujin* man, much like the one who had pinned me to the wall of Aloha. But a fellow Nisei? Had the world gone mad?

"Did she have any ideas of who it could be?"

Tomi shook her head. "The only thing he left behind was some scrap of paper. It looked like a movie ticket. It didn't mean anything. She told me not to tell anyone, not even Louise. She was working to get you all here, to Chicago. She didn't want anything to get in the way of that."

That's why this thing had been a secret. It finally made sense to me. Ordinarily Rose would not have hesitated to go straight to the police, no matter the shame or cost to her reputation. But if being a victim of such a sordid crime would jeopardize our arrival, Rose would have kept silent.

"Would it have been so easy for him to pick the lock?"

Tomi rubbed the knuckles on her left hand. "The lock was so old and decrepit, like one from the thirties that you open with a skeleton key. Rose got another lock, one that slides from the inside. Louise at first didn't understand why, but we told her that other places were experiencing break-ins."

As Tomi was telling me all of this, it seemed like the world was slowing down. I noticed every minor thing in the background, from a leaf falling from a eucalyptus tree to an old man adjusting his straw hat. I asked her for all the details that she could remember.

"Even though Rose had a new lock installed, I still didn't feel safe. I couldn't keep staying in that apartment. I couldn't sleep." Tears again. Tomi's hands were shaking. I sensed that something like this had happened to her before. She opened her bag to reveal a package in a pink *furoshiki*, the Japanese fabric wrap used for bentos. "Rose knew I was having a hard time. She told me that if we stuck together, we'd be okay. I told her that I couldn't stay there in the same apartment. We'd be sitting ducks; didn't she understand? We had an awful argument and I moved out. She came to Evanston to give this to me. She actually wanted it back in May. But I had refused to see her." She gestured that I take it. The package was rectangular and light.

"What's in it?"

"Don't look at it now. Take it home and look."

I had a bad feeling in the pit of my stomach. "You need to go to the police, Tomi."

"I can't. I'm sorry, but I can't." Tomi truly looked miserable. "Do you know that some of them are in cahoots with the mob?"

I shook my head in disbelief.

"Yes, it's true. Things are different here in Chicago. You don't know who to trust."

"What if the—" I couldn't bear to say the actual word, "it had something to do with Rose's death?"

Tomi gazed down at her emptied bag. "I wish I was a different kind of person. Strong, like you and Rose. Truly I do."

I felt like it would be useless and cruel to push her further. Already, Tomi seemed to have reached her breaking point. I glanced at my watch. I had stayed much too long. "I have to go, but we'll keep in touch."

Tomi nodded.

Placing the pink-wrapped bundle underneath my arm, I headed back to work.

"I thought that you may have been kidnapped," Nancy commented, eyeing my parcel. "Went shopping, huh?"

About an hour later, I couldn't stand it anymore and made some excuse about having to go into the stacks. I snuck

Tomi's bundle in with me and as soon as I was shielded by two high shelves, I stuffed it in an open space between two books and began to loosen the knot of the *furoshiki* to reveal a metal bento box, the kind that I used to see produce workers bring to work. I pulled off the lid. Nestled on balled-up pages of the *Chicago Daily Tribune* was a small gun.

When I returned to the front desk, my shock must have been written on my face because Phillis asked if I was feeling okay. I almost dropped the bento box, and imagined the gun going off and me ending up in jail. What was Tomi thinking, bringing that to me? And where did Rose get it in the first place?

I didn't know what to do with it. If I brought it home, my parents might discover it. There weren't that many hiding places in our bare apartment, and I wasn't about to stick it underneath my mattress. And then I remembered the mezzanine in the Clark and Division subway station. There was a row of lockers there. I left work without saying goodbye to anyone. The security guard with the snow-white hair and mustache called out, "Have a good night, Miss Ito." Usually I would reply, "Yes, I will, Mr. Fulgoni." But today I only nodded.

I walked down the stairs of the subway station, my whole body trembling as I clutched my pink package. I felt that everyone was staring at me, seeing through the *furoshiki* and bento box. Most of the lockers were full, except for one on the top. I slid the box in there and went through my purse for a coin—*darn it*, I couldn't find the right one at first. With much scrambling, I finally did. I attempted to slide the coin in the slot, but it fell to the ground, skipped, and then rolled in a circle to end up at the foot of a uniformed subway employee.

He bent over and handed me my coin. "You need some help, miss?" he asked.

I thanked him but told him I was quite all right, even though my hands were shaking. The coin went into the slot, the door secured and I was up the stairs and back on Clark Street again.

That evening, I couldn't eat dinner. Mom kept touching my forehead and cheeks to check if I had a fever. I told her that I was tired and went to bed early. I could hear the ringing of the hallway pay phone, but I didn't have the energy to get up and answer.

CHAPTER 16

"You did not sleep well," my mother declared as she got ready for work while Papa snored, his right leg occasionally jerking awkwardly.

I lay in bed and stared at a black spot on the ceiling. I wasn't sure if it was an old nail or a spider, taunting me. *What happened to you, Rose?* I had thought to myself all night. I hadn't been here to help her when she needed me the most. I was so angry at the government for keeping us apart. I should have been on that bus out of Manzanar with her—in fact, our whole family should have been.

She had been violated in the worst possible way and then maybe even killed because of it. I knew Tomi was too emotionally wounded to seek justice, but I couldn't pretend nothing had happened. Whoever hurt my sister was still out there. I couldn't let him get away with it.

Mom was in her slip, her brassiere holding up her breasts, which otherwise would have sagged like fresh soft New Year's mochi. While visiting our relatives in the countryside of Spokane years ago, the whole family had bobbed in a Japanese-style wooden bath. I remembered how I had marveled at my mother's body then, the sway of her large, heavy breasts and the curve of her buttocks. Her muscles now had atrophied and she had become a different type of woman, her body foreign to me yet foreshadowing who I might become. She quickly got into her cotton housedress and whispered goodbye before leaving the apartment.

I got up from my bed shortly thereafter and lifted the mattress. I pulled out Rose's diary and flipped to the back, where I had placed the ripped edge of what seemed like a movie or carnival ticket with the number twenty printed in red.

I toasted a slice of bread on a wire grill over our hot plate and dabbed some strawberry preserves on top. As I chewed my breakfast at our table, I was transfixed by that ticket stub. I knew that I couldn't report for work like it was an ordinary day.

I went to the hallway pay phone, dialed and made my voice as raspy as possible. "I came down with a cold," I told Nancy. "Can you let everyone know?"

"Good thing that you caught me before I was out the door. I'll leave a message for Mr. Geiger. Hope you get better quick. Summer colds are the worst."

I felt a pang of guilt about lying to Nancy. She had been nothing but kind to me. "Yes, hopefully I'll feel better by tomorrow."

There were at least three movie theaters in our neighborhood: the Windsor on Clark north of Division, the Newberry across the street from Bughouse Square, and the Surf at Dearborn and Division. I needed to start somewhere so I decided on the Surf because it seemed the most approachable. I slipped the ticket stub in one of the envelopes for the *koden* thank-you cards. Ever since my grammar-school years, I had been so careless with my belongings that my mother had dubbed me *Nakusu*

Musume, "Daughter Who Loses Things." I couldn't let anything happen to this item from my sister's diary.

The Surf was a ridiculous name for a theater near the Clark and Division neighborhood in Chicago. It was located on the first level of a gray multilevel walk-up. The large entrance was framed by light bulbs arranged in a half circle. Since it was late morning, the electricity was off. I feared that the ticket booth would also be closed, but someone was moving behind the glass window.

"Hello." I rapped my knuckle on the pane, where a sign, WAR BONDS AND STAMPS SOLD HERE, was on display.

A dark-haired woman looked up, startled by a customer this early in the morning. She was in the middle of transferring coins into the compartment of the cash register. "Our first matinee isn't until one-thirty," she said through the porthole of the ticket window. She was tall with bright red lips, a wad of gum visible on her tongue.

"Oh, I'm not here about that. I had a question for you. If you recognized this—" I carefully removed the ticket stub from the envelope. I took more time than the woman had patience for; she sighed deeply and rapped her manicured fingers on the counter by the register.

"Can't see it." She continued to vigorously chew her gum.

I slipped the torn ticket stub into the open slot of the window.

"This some kind of joke? Don't think you can get in with this." The cashier shoved the stub back through the slot. She showed me a roll of tickets, which were tan with a long row of numbers stamped on the end. "Did you want to buy a ticket or what?"

I shook my head and placed the stub back in the envelope. I retreated to the sidewalk and then returned. "Twenty-one ten-cent stamps," I ordered, pulling out some dollar bills from my purse. At least I could complete Rose's album of war bond stamps.

I didn't even have to refer to a map to reacquaint myself with the directions to the East Chicago Avenue Police Department. The mortuary, the War Relocation Authority office, the coroner's office and this police station were now all indelible parts of my Chicago life. The police station was a straight shot south on either LaSalle or Clark. I marched up the steps, into the lobby and straight for the front counter. "Sergeant Graves, please."

The police officer manning the desk appraised me. He was balding, with deep lines etched in his forehead. The few strands of long white hair he had were slicked back with grease. "Is he expecting you?"

"No, but it's very important. It's about Rose Ito's case. The woman who was killed on the subway tracks at Clark and Division."

The officer's face darkened a bit, his eyes blinking a tad out of rhythm. It was scarcely enough for anyone to notice, but I did. He told me to wait and then returned in a minute or so, too soon for him to have determined the sergeant's whereabouts, in my opinion.

"Sergeant Graves is unavailable right now. Would you like me to leave a message for him?"

"Yes, tell him to call this number." I recited the pay-phone number to him two times. "I have some information for him. He'll be very interested."

I remained in front of the counter until he finished writing the note. He looked up, annoyed to still see me there. "Miss, you'll have to move on. There are people waiting."

Sure enough, there was a shrunken old *hakujin* woman with a scarf around her head behind me and a young black man behind her.

The curt dismissal didn't make me feel that the Chicago Police Department was taking me seriously. I turned toward the exit and looked back for a moment, only to see the same officer ball up the note with my information and throw it into a wastepaper basket. *How dare he!* I wanted to protest, but who would hear me? My cheeks grew hot and I hung my head as I walked down the station steps.

What would I have done if I was in this same situation in Tropico? Would it have made a difference? Well, first I would have been on my home turf, where I knew the bend of the winding streets and the pitiful concrete bed of the Los Angeles River without looking. The familiar crunch of the wilted lettuce on the concrete floor of the produce market. I'd be standing on what I knew. Los Angeles. My birthplace. My father's American home since the early 1900s. The government had spit us out, but the land had not. Our Japanese-language newspapers—and there were many in Los Angeles before World War II—had been powerless against our wholesale expulsion from the West Coast. But a criminal case like this? The more sensational rags, not to mention the *hakujin* ones, would have featured an attack on a Nisei woman on their front page. Rose Ito's plight would not have been ignored.

The dread in my gut expanded. If the police weren't going to help me, was it up to me to figure out who Rose's assailant was? If he was indeed a serial sex maniac, odds were that he would strike again.

I felt that my world was spinning out of control, even more erratically than when I was in Manzanar. At least in camp, we had each other. There was some kind of structure to our lives—block managers like Roy ensured that there was some sort of representation and leadership in place. We had fighters and troublemakers who challenged WRA policies, although most of them were eventually shipped out to Tule Lake. Here in Chicago I didn't know where to turn. The government told us to stay away from one another yet we only had one another.

"Miss Ito?" In my preoccupation, I hadn't noticed that the authority figure that I was looking for was standing right in front of me.

"Sergeant Graves," I said, amazed that he remembered my name. "I was looking for you."

He looked down at me with compassion. Someone had heard my prayers.

We moved to the side of a nearby diner, where I relayed everything I had learned about Rose's rape. I didn't share Tomi's name, and of course he, being a law-enforcement officer, pressed me on it. "We'll need the witness's name."

"Uh—" I paused. "I do have a piece of evidence. The attacker left this behind." I opened up my purse and the war bond stamps fluttered to the ground. Graves bent down and retrieved them for me. "You'll want to keep those in a safe place," he said, and I nodded, flustered. I finally handed him the envelope with the ticket that had been in Rose's diary.

Grasping the corner of the ripped stub, Graves didn't seem impressed with the evidence. "Doesn't look like anything related to transportation. A movie is going to cost more than twenty cents. Maybe something in the red-light district." He returned it to the envelope and handed it back to me. "We'll really need the witness to come forward. That's the only way we can investigate this alleged crime." He added that he appreciated my coming forward. "I have a meeting at the station, but we'll continue this conversation."

I watched the sun bounce off of his golden head of hair as he walked down Chicago Avenue. I knew that Sergeant Graves was right. Tomi needed to talk, but she was so fragile.

I didn't want to push her too hard. In the meantime, I had to deal with the gun. I was convinced that there was only one place Rose could have gotten it.

Instead of walking up Clark and putting myself in danger of being spotted by my Newberry co-workers, I walked up LaSalle, past the Moody Bible Institute and our apartment, and made a right on Division. I turned at the Mark Twain Hotel and then north on Clark.

My palms became sweaty as I passed the pawnshop and neared Aloha. I pictured that lecherous *sukebe* man placing his fat, soft hands on my body. Would I be able to scream if I encountered him again?

The same blonde woman, this time in a bright-orange halter-top dress, stood in the doorway, her right hand bracing her against the doorframe. A few hairs were visible in her bare armpit. "Hello, doll," she called out to me. "Good to see you again."

I gestured that I wanted to enter, and she lowered her arm for me to pass. The small bar was empty. I proceeded down the stairs to the basement.

"Wait—" the woman called out, "you're not allowed—"

The basement was filled with a thick layer of cigarette smoke. Beneath the cloud, men of all races and ethnicities were eyeing their cards, throwing dice and jangling poker chips. I was shocked to see so many men involved in illegal activity in the middle of the day.

I scanned the room for anyone that I knew. A few of the gamblers were US soldiers in uniform. They must have been on furlough, seeking as much enjoyment as they could on leave. A few of them ogled me and I felt naked for a minute. Across the way was the large *hakujin* man I had dreaded to see. Apparently he had also noticed me, as he was making his way toward me.

I slid through the narrow space between the felt tables, searching the faces frantically. Finally I spotted him in a corner. Hammer looked like he had bathed. He was wearing a striped short-sleeve shirt and denim trousers, his zoot suit abandoned. He had a cigarette behind each ear.

"You shouldn't be here, Tropico," Hammer murmured. "I'm on a roll." He threw the dice again on the green felt table. "Dammit," he cursed. "You better have a good reason to ruin my luck."

I had no remorse. My rotund stalker stopped in his tracks when he saw that I was speaking to Hammer. "We need to talk. Now."

Hammer must have felt my sense of urgency. He pointed toward the stairs and we plowed through the crowd. At the makeshift first-floor bar we claimed a couple of stools.

The blonde woman served us. "You're not allowed down there," she scolded again.

"She's Geet Ito's kid," Hammer told the woman. "She knows to keep her mouth shut."

I ordered a beer because I thought that I might need some liquid courage to interrogate Hammer. I poured the can of lukewarm beer into a glass and took a long sip while Hammer downed half a glass of whiskey.

"You know there's a sex maniac loose here among the Nisei," I said, wiping a bit of beer foam from the corner of my mouth.

"Yeah, what of it?"

"Do you know who it could be?"

"Why would I know?"

"How about those scratches on your face that day after the Aragon dance?" Now they were only thin scabs, faintly visible.

"What are you—a cop or something?" Hammer recoiled from me. "It's none of your business. I don't owe you anything."

"You owe me everything, Hammer. Your whole life. Because of what you did to my sister."

Hammer darted his eyes across the surface of the bar. He looked at everything but me.

"You knew she was pregnant."

Hammer's whole body jerked. "I didn't do that to her. I'll kill the guy who did."

"So you suspected that she was . . . raped." To say it out loud devastated me and now I was crying. I covered my face because it was painful to be so public with my grief.

"She never really said what happened. I didn't know if it was Roy." Hammer's voice softened. "This winter, her face got this hardness to it. It never had that, even in camp." He played with the flap of a matchbook on the counter. "I remember her from camp. I used to watch her go back and forth from your barracks to the mess hall to the garden. It was like the wind was moving her."

My chest shook with more cries.

"She told me that she had to get rid of it."

I wiped my tears with the back of my hands. "Wait. Did you help her to get an abortion?"

Hammer didn't answer my question. He took a last sip of his whiskey. "She was most worried about you."

"About me?"

"That she would lose your respect. She talked about you all the time."

"You never told me that."

"She said that you were always trying to make her better. To get her to write her thoughts down. To think about things more."

I would never have tried to improve Rose. Why would I dare? "She was my hero. She still is."

"Well, then, live your life. That's what she wanted for you."

"I can't let whoever hurt her get away with it." To allow the culprit freedom would be disrespecting my sister's memory. Perhaps Hammer, being an orphan, was used to an impermanence of family relationships. I could not—would not—forget. "Did you give Rose a gun?"

"Why, did you find one?"

"Answer me, Hammer."

Hammer averted his gaze from my face. "She wanted one, but I told her that she was crazy."

I couldn't tell if Hammer was telling the truth or not. Before I could question him more, I felt the presence of someone next to me and turned to look.

"Pop—"

When Pop was mad, Mom used a Japanese expression to describe it: his eyes changed colors. Now they were the darkest black against his bloodshot whites. "What are you doin' with my daughta?"

"Nothing, old man." Still hunched over his empty glass, Hammer kept his back turned to my father.

"You good-for-nothing son-of-a-gun—" Pop was seething, his body erect and almost shaking, a stick of dynamite ready to explode.

"Pop, it's okay," I said, purposely keeping my voice as soothing as possible. "I came here to talk to him. He was trying to help Rose."

"I rememba you from Los Angeles. No-good worker back then."

Hammer slowly faced my father. Now his eyes were steely mad.

"No, stop." I jumped off the stool.

Hammer extended his chin, asserting his physical dominance over my father, who must have been at least six inches shorter. "I dare you to say that again."

"Lazy boy." Spit flew from Pop's lower lip and landed on Hammer's shirt.

I pushed my way in between the two, but I was too late and felt something smashing my head back. I don't know whose blow I interrupted, but I screamed and the two men immediately stepped back, releasing me to fall on the floor.

"Aki—" Hammer was on his knees, leaning over me.

"You get out!" my dad bellowed.

Rocky, who had been nowhere to be found, appeared then to pull Hammer out of the room.

My face stung, but a part of me had to laugh. It had taken this for Hammer to finally say my real name.

When Pop and I, holding a wet dish towel over my eyes, walked into the apartment, Mom dropped the colander she was using to strain pasta in the sink.

"What happened?" She rushed over to me while Pop locked the door. I sank into one of the chairs as she removed the stained towel and examined my eye, which was swollen shut. I'd be sporting a shiner tomorrow.

"What were you doing in Aloha?" My mother's voice was an octave higher than usual.

"Talking to that good-for-nothing Hammer boy," my father muttered, removing his shirt, which was missing at least one button.

"Hammer was trying to help Rose," I repeated. "He was there when we weren't there."

"*Yamenasai!*" my mother screamed. *Stop it!* She was tired of my shenanigans. She was tired of all the trouble I was causing. And then she burst into tears. She hadn't cried when we had to move out of Tropico. She hadn't cried when we arrived at Manzanar. She hadn't cried when we heard Rose had been killed. But now, on the day I got a black eye, she cried for hours.

CHAPTER 17

The next few days I stayed away from work at the Newberry because nobody would have believed me if I told them I got my black eye from walking into a door or falling in the bathroom. It was an ugly goose egg the color of a decomposing plum. When I looked at myself in the mirror, I couldn't help but think that I was split like this inside—one half battered and bruised, and the other half completely unblemished.

Art, I could only assume, was the one who kept calling me on the pay phone in the hallway. I was being watched carefully by both my parents. They seemed to have conspired to trade off shifts so I wouldn't be alone. I sat there on my bed, a Sears Roebuck catalogue on my lap, listening to the telephone ringing and ringing without anyone bothering to pick it up.

In two days, my eye had markedly improved. The bruise had turned from purple to green to now a putrid yellow. When I applied some makeup, you could hardly notice it, at least that's what I told my mother. She still barred me from going to work for another day.

I was going stir-crazy. There was hardly anything to do in our apartment, and I ended up writing pages and pages in a makeshift journal I made by binding together leftover paper from the funeral thank-you notes with some red thread. Pop brought in a copy of the *Chicago Daily Tribune* each day and I read every inch of it. In today's issue, there was a front-page story, complete with photos, about the cadet nurses at a local hospital. I studied the featured photo and the names of the women in the caption. They were all *hakujin*, but could I be one of them someday?

Only smears of Mom's *okazu*, fatty pork boiled with potato, remained on our dinner plates when somebody knocked on our door. We all exchanged looks. We never had visitors.

Pop went to the door. "Who is it?" he asked.

"Art. Art Nakasone. I'm Aki's friend."

I felt like dying.

Pop looked back at me and I nodded that I indeed knew him. Pop opened the door and there was Art, looking even taller than usual, in his crisp white shirt and khaki pants.

"Are you Mr. Ito? It's such a pleasure to meet you." He shook my father's hand with enthusiasm before handing him a thin package. "Here's some dried *ika*. My father has a grocery delivery service on the South Side."

Pop, I know, was at a loss on how to respond. Art was so clean cut, humble and affable. And dried squid was one of Pop's favorite snacks to eat while washing down a glass of beer.

Mom pushed down her cowlick and got to her feet. "Oh my goodness," she said. "Nice to meet you."

"I was worried about Aki. Your co-workers at the Newberry told me that you were sick."

"I'm fine now. Almost good as new." I angled my head so a strand of hair covered my left eye. I was relieved that I had applied makeup to my face this morning.

"Well, you talk," Mom said, shuffling Pop out of the

dining room into the bedroom. I knew that the two of them would have their ears pressed against the door.

I offered Art a seat and began to clear the table of our dinner dishes.

"So sorry to barge in like this. But I called you and nobody picked up. Some girls on the steps told me what floor you were living on."

"No, I'm glad you are here." I began to brew a fresh pot of coffee on our hot plate. "I wasn't feeling well enough to even answer the phone. I'm a lot better now."

Once the coffee was ready, I got out our good cup and saucer—the one without any chips—and poured Art some coffee. We were low on our sugar rations, but luckily Art preferred his coffee black.

We first talked of little, everyday things. How he was doing in his summer editorial-writing class. How his sister was hoping to try out for the cheer squad when school started in the fall.

"I want to invite you to my parents' house for dinner next Friday," he announced.

"Oh—" I said, a bit startled. A formal dinner invitation to the parents' house sounded so serious. Were we serious? I was inexperienced about such things and had virtually no one to talk to about it.

"It's nothing fancy. I think Mom has been saving our ration stamps for beef stroganoff."

I had never had stroganoff before; it sounded extravagant to me.

"Do you think you can come?" Art leaned forward in his chair. His face was only a few inches from mine, and I wanted to touch his cheeks and kiss him. I knew that he was feeling the same way about me because he started to gently stroke the back of my hand with his right index finger.

"Ah, yeah, I think I can."

Art grinned and rose. I felt giddy that saying yes made him so happy.

After he left, I heard the bedroom door slowly open into the hallway.

Mom emerged into our living area with a new bounce in her step. I realized then that she feared the incident at Aloha had ruined my future marital prospects. But then who should appear at the door but the handsome and polite Art Nakasone. All was not lost.

"His father owns a grocery store," she said to my father.

"It's actually a delivery service," I corrected my mother. He was preparing to open up his own grocery store, eventually. In my phone conversations with Art, I'd learned that his father had been a local truck driver before being diagnosed with debilitating arthritis. Before his physical limitation completely overwhelmed him, he was now attempting to launch his own business.

I appreciated Mr. Nakasone's openness to trying something new. Pop wasn't as flexible. Come to think of it, maybe all three of us were set in our ways. There had been no reason to change when we lived in Tropico.

Friday came before I knew it. I had wanted to stop by the Beauty Box for Peggy to set my hair, but there was no time for that. I needed to bring some kind of *omiyage* for the Nakasones, and Mom and I had spent many hours contemplating what would make the most appropriate impression. Chocolates would melt in this heat; besides, they were expensive during the war. Mr. Nakasone, being in the grocery business, would already have access to choice produce. We finally decided on a set of doilies that Mom had crocheted in the evenings. I had even tried making one myself, but it was subpar and I discarded it. I wrapped the doilies Mom made in a blue handkerchief and tied a red ribbon around it.

I also wasn't sure what I should wear—I didn't want to seem too eager and wear my fanciest dress, a black one I had worn to Rose's funeral. Signaling that she meant business, Mom pulled Rose's suitcase out from underneath their bed. She unlatched it to display the riches of my older sister's wardrobe. I had returned the crane dress—albeit a bit soiled. But there were many other dresses that were less flashy that I could wear. By this time, Roy had delivered a used dresser to our apartment building—oh, what an ordeal it had been for him and Pop to haul it up to the fourth floor. Mom had assigned the second drawer to me. As a sign that I was taking my sister's place, Mom started moving the dresses to my second drawer as we went through Rose's clothing in the suitcase.

I chose a gray one with a zipper on the back. It was demure but there was something in the cut that also made it alluring. I wanted to impress his family, yes, but Art was going to be at that dinner, too, and I didn't want to look like a nun.

Art picked me up promptly at six. This time he brought some fresh flowers for my mother, and she nearly melted onto the floor. It was quite embarrassing how she carried on about some simple posies in tissue paper. He also brought another package of dried *ika* for my father, which would no doubt completely win him over once he returned from work.

Lodged between two brick buildings on a street of the brownstones that were all over Chicago, the Nakasone home was a wood-framed two-story building, a little worn.

I noticed that there was no sense of open space like there was in Los Angeles. If you looked through your window in Chicago, your view was most likely either your neighbor's wall or right into their window.

Art parked the truck in the driveway and we walked up to a screened porch. As soon as he opened the front door, it was pandemonium. A mutt, which must have been at least one hundred pounds, leapt on top of him and then moved over to me, furiously licking my face. "Down, Duke," Art called out, pulling at his collar, which only made the giant dog more determined to welcome me. I couldn't help but collapse in laughter. A few seconds later, a tiny white poodle, apparently not wanting to miss out on the excitement, came bounding toward us. In the background, I could hear the twittering of a bird.

A girl with the same open face as Art walked in carrying a kitten on her shoulder like it was a newborn baby. "Hello, I'm Lois," Art's sister introduced herself. "Ah, this is Crockett."

"Awww—" As I stroked his back, the black-and-white kitten mewed and greeted me with a swat of his paw.

The Nakasone house was large and comfortably cluttered, with bright colors everywhere. Whereas our apartment seemed so drab and dreary, Art's house was full of life. This was a reminder of what we had in Tropico.

Art's mother, wiping her hands on a full-length flowered apron, came out to the front room to greet me. Her wavy salt-and-pepper hair was pulled back from her face. She wore glasses and when she smiled, deep dimples cut into her cheeks. "Oh, so nice to finally meet you," she said with no detectible accent—maybe because the Nakasones were surrounded by *hakujin* and blacks? "All Art talks about is Aki, Aki, Aki."

"He does?"

Art's face was visibly flushed; even the tops of his ears were turning red.

"Thank you for having me. Here's a little something." I handed the wrapped doilies to her.

She thanked me for the gift and then ushered me into the long dining room, which was separated from the sitting room by a paneled wall. In the sitting room were stacks of foodstuffs, boxes with print identifying their contents—dried noodles, rice crackers, and dried squid. Somewhere in there was a couch, where an older man with a bald pate and tufts of white hair sat with a clipboard and abacus in his lap.

"Dad, say hi to Art's friend," Mrs. Nakasone said, before disappearing into the far room, probably the kitchen.

"Oh, hallo." He looked at me above his reading glasses.

I smiled and waved. It was obvious that he was in the middle of his work.

Art had me sit at the dining-room table, which was set for six. The tablecloth reminded me of Thanksgiving, as it sported orange pumpkins, green squash and maple leaves. There was a white plate at each of the settings, along with a crystal glass. It felt luxurious to use matching dishes.

"Dad, dinner!" Mrs. Nakasone called out to her husband.

Art poured water in my glass, then gestured to someone behind me.

"This is my Aunt Eunice."

I turned and was surprised to see a wrinkled old white woman.

"Aki—" Standing up, I introduced myself and extended my hand. She disregarded my hand and gave me a quick hug. "You are so beautiful," she said to me, and I was speechless for a moment.

Mrs. Nakasone brought rolls in a ceramic bowl to the

table. "Eunice, you are embarrassing her. But she is pretty darn cute."

Beautiful and cute. I had never heard anyone describe me like that.

Dinner was a mishmash of stroganoff—delicious—and Japanese foods like rice and even *tsukemono*—pickled cabbage. This generous offering of food reminded me of my Tropico days when the table was covered with endless dishes created from the freshest produce and fish from the market. The evening was filled with flashbacks of my old life. Could we ever return to that way of existence? Would we ever have a meal with our own matching china on a table that was not a hand-me-down?

"Does the stroganoff not agree with you?" Mrs. Nakasone broke my reverie.

Sure enough, half of my dinner was still on my plate, while Mr. Nakasone was scooping another serving of noodles.

"Oh, no, it's quite wonderful. It just made me think of home. *Home* home, Los Angeles."

"You must have had beautiful produce in California," Mrs. Nakasone commented.

To prove that I was enjoying dinner, I shoveled an extra-large portion of the stroganoff into my mouth.

"The Japanese dominated farming on the West Coast. It's no wonder that the government wanted to take that from them." Art had never been that political around me, but I was grateful to hear that he was sympathetic to our position.

The military exclusion line did seem most arbitrary, going down the Pacific Coast and even splitting cities like Phoenix, Arizona, in half. What made an Issei or Nisei more loyal on one side of that line than the other? Pop would often say that it was no coincidence that we who had developed bountiful farm and fishing operations would be the ones forced to leave behind our lucrative businesses.

Aunt Eunice placed some of the *tsukemono* on her plate.

"You can use chopsticks?" I didn't mean to sound so rude, but I was honestly amazed.

"Because I'm a *hakujin*?" she said and laughed, the mushed-up cabbage visible in her mouth.

She told me a condensed version of her life. Aunt Eunice was born in America to Greek immigrants. Because she had married an Issei man, Mr. Nakasone's brother, Ren, she'd lost her American citizenship for several years.

"I can't believe it," I said.

Eunice nodded. "We fought for women's suffrage but I couldn't even vote. It took a special act and some amendments until I finally got my citizenship back earlier this year. I wish Ren was alive to have seen it."

As I accepted another helping of the stroganoff, I felt something press down on my foot. It was the white poodle, begging for a handout.

"Polly, bad girl! I'm so sorry," said Lois, who was seated to my right.

"Oh, I like animals," I told her. "We even had some pets in camp. The guards weren't going to do anything about it because they liked them, too."

"What did your father do in California?" Mrs. Nakasone asked.

"He managed a produce market in Los Angeles. One of the biggest ones in the city." I immediately felt embarrassed because my parents told me not to *ebaru* in front of strangers, although Mom did it quite often within the confines of our house. "But that was before. He's not doing anything like that now."

The Nakasones were sensitive enough not to ask me for

more details. "I suppose we do what we have to during these times," Mrs. Nakasone commented.

"*Shikataganai*," added Art's father, who up to now had said nothing.

"Aki works at the Newberry Library." Art smiled at me from across the table.

"Yes, we heard." Mrs. Nakasone put a scoopful of peas on her plate. "What a marvelous place."

"I can't believe my luck."

"Do you think that's what you might want to do, be a librarian?"

"I want to go to nursing school." I startled myself by saying it out loud. Once I did, I realized that it had been on my mind.

"I didn't know that." Art creased his brow.

"Yeah, I've been thinking about it."

"That's wonderful," Mrs. Nakasone said. "Mr. Yoshizaki's niece is going to Mother Cabrini Hospital School of Nursing in Little Italy. It's even all paid for by the cadet nursing program."

"Really." I felt a pang of hope, such a rare, desperate feeling that I was almost afraid to entertain it.

Eunice swallowed a bite of food and asked, "So, what was it like in those camps?"

"Auntie!" Lois cried out, her fork of carefully wrapped noodles a couple of inches from her mouth.

Eunice seemed impervious to her niece's protests. "I'm curious. I mean, Betty across the street helps Kiichiro organize his foodstuffs, but she's too young to know anything. And the government puts out this propaganda where everyone is smiling."

A dull pain began to weigh on my chest.

"You don't have to say anything," Art said.

"No, it's all right. It was really bad in the beginning," I said. "The barracks were just built. Nothing in them. We had to stuff our own mattresses with straw."

"And no privacy in the lavatories, I heard," Eunice added.

I shook my head. "But over time, we could order things from Sears Roebuck. Or some friends and old neighbors would bring up our things from storage." I didn't say what a poor imitation of our former life it had been. The outdoor basketball courts and the gardens were supposed to make our captivity as normal as possible, but in some ways, they made me more acutely aware that we were all locked up.

"The worst was not knowing what was going to happen. We were separated from our homes, taken away from everything we knew before. It was hard to adjust. I mean, I've seen those WRA photos—my sister was even in one of them. They don't show how we felt inside. We didn't even know how we felt most of the time."

None of us were going to give other Americans the satisfaction of seeing us look miserable. We were going to look our best, with our lipstick freshly applied, our hair styled and our clothing neat and unstained.

Rose had been photographed outside after lunch in the mess hall. The wind of the Owens Valley was blowing through her hair, revealing her long forehead and well-shaped eyebrows.

"We heard about your sister. I'm so sorry, dear," Mrs. Nakasone said as Lois rose to help her clear the table.

I swallowed hard. *I'm not going to cry*, I told myself.

Art looked distressed that his mother had referred to Rose's demise in front of his family. I didn't mind, however. It was a relief that her death was out in the open. I was tired of pretending it had never happened.

• • •

After dinner, Mrs. Nakasone suggested that we "young people" sit out on the porch with some fresh-squeezed lemonade.

The porch was screened, barring the bugs from invading our space. I already had plenty of marks on my legs from random insect bites. I wasn't that self-conscious, because every Nisei with bare legs seemed to be similarly branded.

"Your mother seems so young. A lot younger than my mother," I said. Art and I both sat on a rattan love seat while Lois made herself comfortable in a chair with the cat on her lap.

"That's because she's a Nisei."

"She is?" I was surprised. Most of my Japanese American friends had parents who were straight from Japan like Mr. Nakasone, who was from Yamaguchi Prefecture.

"Because she was American-born, her citizenship was taken away when she got married, just like Aunt Eunice's was. Only my mother got hers back earlier."

"Why's that?"

"The Nisei women made a fuss. They were able to amend the act to exclude them about five years before it was done away for good." Art held up his glass as if he was toasting me. "Never cross a Nisei woman."

We both took swigs of our lemonade. It was refreshingly tart with a sweet aftertaste from the sugar that had accumulated on the bottom.

"Wait a minute," I said. "If your father is Issei and your mother is Nisei, what does that make you?"

"I don't know. Nisei and a half? I never was into labels."

I decided that I wasn't going to be into labels, either.

As we sat and finished our lemonade with Crockett purring in Lois's lap and the bugs safely buzzing away on the other side of the screen, I felt more relaxed than I had felt in almost three years. "I like where you live," I told Art.

"That's a first. I don't hear that often."

"It's like a neighborhood. A real one. Clark and Division seems more like a way station. People are always moving."

"That's true. I guess that's one of the few places where you camp people can move in." Art gestured down the road. "Phillis and her family live on the other end of the street in that brownstone with the yard."

I squinted in the setting sun. A number of brownstones were lined up against each other like soldiers. I thought I spotted a chain-link fence around a square of green.

Mrs. Nakasone came out on the porch with a message for Art. "Yoshizaki-*san* called. His car battery is dead so he can't give Dad a ride to the Mutual Aid Society meeting tonight. Can you take both of them to the meeting?"

I got up from the love seat. "Maybe I should leave then, too."

"No, no, I'll be gone only a half hour or so," Art said.

Mrs. Nakasone also insisted that I stay. "Lois can keep you company."

I remembered that Art had told me that the society meetings had been banned, so this gathering must be clandestine. It was a bit exciting to be part of a type of Issei secret organization that helped families like mine resettle in the "free" area of the Midwest.

Lois continued to stroke Crockett in her rocking chair as Art and Mr. Nakasone piled into the pickup and drove away. She was like Art in that she was perfectly fine to sit in silence, so we did that for a while.

As twilight descended, black men wearing work uniforms trudged home with their lunch pails while younger ones riding on bikes called out to each other. Two Nisei girls, one obviously older than the other, strode down the sidewalk toward the house.

Lois began to wave at the women. The younger and smaller one only offered a weak wave back.

"She's one of my classmates, Betty, and that's her older sister, Elaine. They live in that green apartment building." We watched them cross the street. "Betty was helping Daddy with his grocery business this summer, but she hasn't been coming around lately. She hasn't been feeling well."

My mind whirled. Could this be the girl that Art had mentioned? Marge and the other Nisei women gathered outside the loading dock of the candy company had revealed that the attack victim was the younger of two sisters. And the name Betty sounded familiar.

"Was she the one who was—" I felt bad bringing this up to Lois, who was only a teenager. She was mature enough to understand and nodded.

"Maybe she'll want to see your new kitty cat," I suggested.

"Ah, no. I don't think so. Art says not to bother her."

"But think how Crockett could cheer her up. I know my dog, Rusty, could make the darkest day brighter." At least that last statement was true. "We should go over there, even if it's only for a minute. I know that I'd want to help a neighbor and classmate." I fixated on getting into their apartment. *Surely there may be a clue that would tie this girl to Rose?*

Lois reluctantly agreed. I felt a pang of guilt but pushed it away.

The sisters lived on the bottom floor, Lois explained to me, as we approached their weathered door. The paint was peeling and a pie pan was hammered on the wall to hold mail.

Lois gently knocked. "It's me, Lois Nakasone. I've brought over my new kitten that Betty might want to see."

The door cracked open. "Oh, Lois," said the older one, Elaine. "I don't think this is good time—"

"I want to see the kitten." Betty's voice from within the apartment sounded high-pitched and frail.

"Well, only for a minute." The door was opened to us. We walked into a one-room apartment with faded pink wallpaper. Clothes were hung on hooks on doors, pipes and walls. The kitchenette consisted of one gas burner and a small, dingy icebox. A couple of plates, utensils, one pot and a pan were stored on a low table. I didn't see a sink or bathroom, so I figured that they had to share with other people in the building.

Betty's pale face brightened when she saw the kitten. Her dark-brown hair looked like it had been cut at home; her bangs hung unevenly over her forehead. She was a child, nothing like the force of nature that Rose had been. The only thing they seemed to have in common was that they were Nisei women, so far from home.

The two girls sat atop the bed—there was only one—and teased Crockett with a piece of loose yarn.

"I'm Aki," I introduced myself. "I'm Art's friend."

Elaine, whose wavy hair was up in a loose ponytail, introduced herself, too. Since there was literally no place to sit, we stood and talked.

"What camp were you two in?" I asked.

"Minidoka. In Idaho. Before that we were in Camp Harmony."

"Where's that?" Camp Harmony sounded like a more pleasant place than the other ten camps.

"Oh, it was actually the fairgrounds in Puyallup near Seattle. That's the assembly center where they first sent us."

Fairgrounds and racetracks—those were the temporary holding centers that our family had been able to bypass by going straight to Manzanar.

I learned the sisters came from Seattle. "We have relatives in Spokane," I said. "That's nowhere near Seattle, is it?"

"It's on the other side of Washington," Elaine said, but not in a disparaging way. She seemed to enjoy talking about her home state, the difference between the wet Pacific coastline and the middle of the state, which was full of cornfields.

"You're Rose Ito's sister?" Elaine studied my face as if to find any resemblance. "I'm so sorry."

"Yes, it's been terribly hard."

"I can imagine."

"She didn't kill herself," I added. "I know that's what people are saying." I balled up my hands into fists, as if I were preparing myself to jump from a diving board into a deep, dark pool. "Someone hurt her. Even before she was killed by that subway car."

Elaine's eyes widened. Her irises were a light brown, the color of amber.

Now that I had jumped, there was no going back. "He's hurt other girls, too." I glanced at Betty.

Elaine recoiled, as if she were too close to the heat of a flame. She knew exactly what I was insinuating. "I think that you better leave." Her voice was not shrill, but unyielding. She locked eyes with me and I could feel that she was dead serious.

"Lois, we need to go," I said.

"Already?" Betty seemed disappointed and I was relieved that our visit had been a welcome one, at least for the younger sister. Lois fumbled to catch the wriggling Crockett and then stood up, pressing the kitten to her chest.

"We've overstayed our visit. Art should be back by now, right, Lois?"

Lois seemed to sense that something was amiss and headed for the door.

Elaine didn't bother to say goodbye and as soon as we crossed the threshold, she pushed the door closed.

Outside, a kickball game was in full swing in the street. The Nakasones' pickup truck was back in the driveway, and Art was waiting for us on the sidewalk.

"We were at Betty's house," said Lois, holding Crockett firmly by his middle.

"Betty's?" Art frowned.

"Aki thought Crockett would cheer Betty up, and you know what, she was right."

Looking confused, Art was about to say something but stopped himself. For the first time, he seemed doubtful about me; but like the gray clouds of Chicago, the uncertainty had quickly disappeared, at least for the moment.

CHAPTER 18

Over the next few weeks, I began my new life as part of a couple. On Saturday nights, Art and I would attend dances at different locations, where we'd usually run into Ike, Kathryn, Chiyo and the rest of the gang. Louise started dating the tall, gawky Nisei, Joey Suzuki, whom she first met at the Aragon. Bespectacled Joey had long sideburns and an anemic mustache that didn't show any signs of having a successful future. A nephew of Reverend Suzuki, he was also originally from Los Angeles and even attended the same junior college that I had, but he had graduated with a degree in recreational studies a year before I started.

All of us were sitting at the same table one Saturday, drinking pop during the band's break. Ike always gave me updates about Roy whenever I saw him. The latest was that Roy was hot and heavy with an Italian woman, which was causing all sorts of chaos within the Tonai family.

"I can't believe that Roy told his mother," I said. Roy's parents were very conservative, even more so than mine.

"He's serious about her. Like marriage."

Our intimate group gasped in response.

"His family keeps sending him telegrams. Western Union is constantly knocking on our door."

"What do these telegrams say?" I asked.

"Do not marry STOP," Ike responded, and we all exploded into laughter. I felt a little guilty because Roy was almost like an older brother to me. But ever since our last encounter at the candy factory, I got the sense that Rose had been only a prize to him, not a full-blooded person.

"Oh, guess who we saw at church last Sunday," Louise said. "Hammer Ishimine."

"You can't be serious," Ike said.

I was also dumbfounded.

"He's even a member of the choir," Joey interjected.

"You mean he's a regular?" I asked.

"That's what my uncle was saying. He's working as a house boy for a *hakujin* lady in Lakeview."

I realized I hadn't seen Hammer since the altercation at Aloha. I was so distracted by my relationship with Art that I hadn't even noticed.

There was a break in the conversation, and both Chiyo and I excused ourselves to go to the ladies' room. Chiyo had transformed over these past few months. Now a regular at dances, she had plucked her heavy, natural eyebrows into two perfect arches and was always reapplying her red lipstick. She and Kathryn were still competing for Ike's attention, and it was obvious that Kathryn was in the lead.

The hall had only one bathroom stall for women, and we talked while we waited outside the locked door.

"Art's nice," she said.

"He is." I couldn't help but smile.

"How did you two meet?"

I told her the story about going to the Montrose Cemetery, where Rose's ashes were being stored.

"How long has it been now since then?"

"Two months," I said. Actually, two months exactly. Art

had pointed it out to me because he was more of a romantic than I was.

"My parents are going to be moving to Chicago. I've found us an apartment on the South Side."

"That's wonderful, Chiyo. You must be so happy."

Chiyo shrugged. "I'm sure I won't be going out like this when they arrive."

"Yeah, it'll be an adjustment." I spoke in general terms of the struggles I had been having with my own parents.

"You know, I regret that I never really told you everything that was happening with Rose."

Chiyo's words shook me. They cut through the din of voices in the dance hall and workers wheeling wooden crates of pop to the concession stand. "Tell me now." Another woman joined us in line and began examining her face in her compact mirror. "Tell me, Chiyo," I said more urgently. I didn't know when I would have another opportunity to speak to her alone.

She lowered her voice. "I think that she went somewhere and got *something* done. *Something* that caused her a lot of pain." Both of us knew what that something was.

My heart literally hurt and I found it difficult to breathe.

"In late April I had come home early from my job at the factory and there she was, in bed already. I thought that she had fainted, or even worse. I had never seen her face so pale."

The woman who had been in the bathroom emerged, but we let the woman waiting behind us go in.

"What, Chiyo, what." I couldn't stand another second.

"Her bed was soaked with blood."

I became slack-jawed, almost losing my footing. Would I collapse right there on the floor?

"I told her that I was going to call an ambulance, but she said no. She said that she'd be okay. She had some medicine.

She did ask for my help to wash the sheets." Chiyo tightened her grip on her purse. "We never talked about it afterward. I may be from the *inaka,* but I can put two and two together."

When the next woman came out of the bathroom, I told Chiyo to go before me. After she closed the bathroom door, I bent down, my hands on my knees. My heart seemed to be pounding out of my chest and it was hard to catch my breath. Who had done this procedure on my sister? Had they known what they were doing?

When I finally returned to the group, only Art seemed to notice that something was amiss. "You all right?" Art asked me, gently rubbing my back for a brief moment.

"Fine," I said, forcing a smile.

Luckily, Ike was telling one of his stories and I could remain quiet and listen. I finally joined the laughter about a minute too late, when it wasn't that funny anymore.

After Chiyo's revelation that Rose had suffered excessive bleeding from her abortion procedure, the nights were the worst. In the morning the blinding sun was out, forcing me to get up for either work or an excursion with Art. When I was home at night, my parents snoring in their beds, I'd lie down on my pillow and try to will myself to sleep, but sleep would not come. I'd hear the cockroaches skittering on the floor, the faucet dripping in our sink or the rats running through the space between our walls. I'd imagine Rose moaning in blood-soaked sheets, calling out for someone to help her.

I was consumed with anger. It soaked through my skin and flowed through my body. I sometimes snapped at my parents for asking one too many questions about Art's family. I was cross with Professor Rip Van Winkle for making too many requests for books he would never peruse.

Only Art seemed to take the edge off of my worries. When we found ourselves alone in the truck, we would escape to the Thirty-First Street Beach and find a secluded place to park. He'd kiss my lips and then my neck. My blouse would end up pulled from my skirt and his hands would caress my breasts. I wanted to get lost in him. Anything to get my mind off of Rose.

I should have told Art what I was going through, but I didn't want my two worlds to mix. By keeping our relationship separate from Rose, I created a place that was pure and maybe could end happily ever after. But the weight of my torment pressed against that dividing line.

One afternoon we had collapsed on the rattan love seat in the Nakasones' screened porch after a long walk around Lake Michigan, when Mrs. Nakasone returned to the house with a towel wrapped around a casserole dish. She was still wearing an apron and wasn't carrying a purse, so I guessed she had come from visiting the neighbors.

Art sat up, his balled hands on his thighs. "They didn't accept it again?"

Mrs. Nakasone shook her head. Her usually jovial face was drawn. "It's good to see you, dear." She managed a faint smile my way, but the Nakasones, in general, weren't good at hiding their true feelings. Balancing the casserole in her left hand, she pushed the front door open with the side of her right hip.

"I'll be right back." Art followed after his mother while I straightened the wrinkles on my pedal pushers. *What had happened?*

After quite some time, Art returned with two glasses of water. It was obvious that the breeziness of our lazy, relaxed day had ended. I accepted a glass from him. "Is something wrong?"

"The casserole was for Elaine and Betty across the street. Betty hasn't been well. But Elaine won't accept any help from anyone. She's pretty much demanded that my mother stop leaving food for them."

I grasped hold of my glass with two hands. "They should go to the police," I said without thinking.

"Why, how . . ." Art's face turned a ghostly white. "How did you know?"

"I'm not a dummy," I said. I wasn't going to reveal that Lois had confirmed my suspicions the first time I had visited.

"Elaine's not going to let Betty go through that. In some ways, I can't blame them." Art chugged down some water, an excess drop hanging from his lip. "They are thinking about moving on. I don't think that's a bad idea. A fresh start somewhere else."

I narrowed my eyes. I knew first-hand what it was like to make a new life. The ghosts of the past never completely left.

August was blazing hot in Chicago—in fact, record highs according to the reports in the *Chicago Daily Tribune*. Even the short walk from the LaSalle apartments to the Newberry left my dress moist with perspiration. Going from that heat into the coolness of the library gave me the chills, and I thought that I was coming down with a cold.

I had finished gathering some books on the American Revolutionary War when Tomi walked up to the reference counter. She was wearing a soft pink dress and hat, as if she was going to attend a garden party. I thought she looked gorgeous, but I didn't bother to tell her so. As no one else was in the reading room, we were able to speak freely.

"I'm going to be moving out of the Chicago area," she

announced. "I'm planning to meet my old neighbor from San Francisco in Detroit."

This was not the news that I expected. "Don't leave," I told her. "I need you here."

Tomi looked confused for a moment, and a crease appeared on her forehead. "If this is about Rose, forget about her. Nothing you do will bring her back."

"You can't do this," I said to Tomi. I knew that was a ridiculous thing to say as soon as I said it. Tomi was my closest link to Rose in Chicago. If she left, another piece of my sister would break away and dissolve into the ether.

"I can get an office job instead of working in someone's house."

That made no sense. Tomi could easily get an office job in Chicago, but it would mean that she'd be back in the city where Rose had been assaulted.

Nancy walked into the reading room and I gestured for her to relieve me at the desk. At first she seemed annoyed but, absorbing the disturbed look on my face, she agreed to fill in.

I walked with Tomi to the ladies' room. As usual, it was empty, allowing us a bit of privacy.

"When are you planning to leave?"

"Later this month. I just bought my ticket." Tomi unfastened the clip on her pocketbook and waved the ticket in front of my face to prove that she had made up her mind.

"Let me see that." I snatched it away from her delicate fingers.

"Don't you do anything with that!"

What? Did she think that I would flush it down the toilet? She seized it back like it was her lifeline.

I planted myself squarely in front of her, my hip pressed against one of the bathroom sinks. "If you're going to leave anyway, at least go to the police and tell them what you witnessed. Do it for Rose's sake."

"Nothing I say will help. I didn't see his face."

"You heard his voice. You saw what he had done to Rose."

Tomi lowered her head, a pink silk flower visible on the headband of her hat. "Don't you understand?" she said. "I can't get his voice out of my head. As long as I'm here, he'll be haunting me."

I was convinced that she wouldn't escape that voice, no matter how far she traveled. "You'll regret running away," I said.

She pursed her lips, considering my prediction. "No," she said, "I will never regret leaving Chicago."

I couldn't go straight home that evening. I walked a block up to one of the two local Japanese grocery stores where we bought tofu, *shoyu*, miso and our splendid rice, not to mention regular American foodstuffs like mayonnaise and spaghetti. I loved how neat and orderly the store was. Rows of soup cans stacked on one shelf; canned tomatoes on another.

"Can I help you with anything, Aki?" The proprietor, Fred Toguri, had a full-length white apron hanging from his neck. I knew that it was almost closing time and I didn't want to cause any inconvenience, especially since I was there to be distracted and not to buy any groceries.

"Nope, but thank you," I called out, scurrying to the exit.

Fake-shopping in the pristine store would not erase my predicament. I had hung on to the hope that the truth would eventually be revealed, but now the two women who could testify to the crimes they experienced and witnessed were leaving Chicago. Art had told me that it was not my business. He was wrong.

I stood in front of the Chicago Avenue police station; my body had brought me there before I had decided where I was going. My legs took me up the steps and then to the counter, where there was no line.

"Sergeant Graves, please," I said to the officer manning the desk. He was a younger man I had never seen before. After asking for my name, he got on the phone without giving me any grief.

Within a few minutes, the trim figure of Sergeant Graves appeared in the hallway. He was one person of authority in Chicago who seemed both capable and compassionate. "Miss Ito. Are you here to give me the name of the witness?"

My chest tightened. "I wanted to let you know that there's been another rape."

The sergeant's face softened. "When did this happen?"

"This was on the South Side. She's only a high-school student."

"The South Side is out of my jurisdiction."

"But you can still help." My voice assumed a pleading tone. At this point, I didn't have any more energy to mask my desperation.

"Of course." He took out a notebook. "What's her name and address?"

"Uh—" I hesitated. I didn't know Betty and Elaine's last name. Or their exact street address. And even if I did, I would be substantiating Marge's accusation that we Ito sisters were spies. "I don't know if they will cooperate with the police. And they may leave town."

Sergeant Graves flipped his notebook closed. "That's quite unfortunate. But not unusual in cases like these. We can't do anything based on hearsay or rumors."

"Yes, of course." I felt so foolish. I was like the little boy who cried wolf. One day the wolf would arrive on my doorstep and there wouldn't be anyone to help me.

That Saturday, Art and I were to meet for lunch at the same diner near the candy company where I'd first met Roy back in May. Everything that had once seemed new and quaint was now routine. I pocketed the Milk Duds that were given to me at the door, ordered a cup of coffee, and without even looking at the menu, asked for the meatloaf.

Art was especially quiet during our meal and I immediately knew that something was wrong. Afterward, we drove out to Thirty-First Street Beach, like usual. But after he parked, Art didn't hold me close to him. He even had a hard time looking at me. "Listen, Aki, I didn't know how to tell you—"

My heart pounded. *He's going to break it off*, I thought. I didn't know what had gone wrong, but something obviously had. *Maybe he found out about my visit to the police station?*

"I can explain—" I said.

"I got my draft papers."

I felt like I had fallen in a deep and dark well. I was completely blindsided by Art's announcement and it took me a moment to regain my voice.

"When do you have to go?"

"I have basic training in two weeks in Camp Shelby."

I had been around enough Nisei men to know that the army gave more advance notice than that.

"How long have you known?" Hot tears came to my eyes and I folded my arms tight to my chest.

Art didn't answer my question. "I wanted to spend as much time with you as I could without this hanging over our heads," he explained.

"I bet you did." All those romantic evenings by the lake. He wanted to see how far he could get and then toodle-oo.

"No, no, it's not that."

I felt like a fool. Deceived, like Roy's discarded girlfriends. I looked in my purse for a handkerchief or tissue to wipe my tears, but there was nothing.

"No, Aki. I'm head over heels for you, don't you know? I'm a goner." He struggled with his pants pocket and brought out a small box. "I'm in love with you. I want to marry you."

CHAPTER 19

I didn't say yes or no.

I sat there, my mouth wide open, staring at the engagement ring stuck in a white velvet insert in a blue ring box. As it was still late afternoon, the sunlight flickered through the truck windows, spreading a kaleidoscope of colors from the diamond. I didn't know what to say.

"Well, Aki, what do you think?"

A part of me felt that we barely knew each other. That I didn't think I was ready to get married. But on the other hand, I knew that I had never met anyone like Art Nakasone and if I didn't say yes, I would lose him forever.

"Yes, I'll marry you."

His whole body relaxed and I heard a rush of air being released from his lungs. Had he doubted what my answer would be?

I told him, though, I couldn't run off and get married tomorrow at the county courthouse. "It wouldn't be right," I said, knowing full well that Nisei women were doing it all the time.

I was able to convince him to keep our engagement a secret, which was a great relief. I still needed to wrap my own mind around it, never mind dealing with other people's opinions. His parents, our friends, Nancy and Phillis, and especially my parents—they all would be over the moon. I didn't want their predictable excitement to eclipse my own.

I had to tell Pop and Mom that Art was drafted, of course—news that crushed my mother. "What a shame. Just when everything is going so well for you two." Mom washed rice in a pot in the sink before cooking it. Pop, who sat at our table, didn't seem that concerned. In fact, lately he seemed so disconnected from us that I could barely recognize him as the same father I knew in Tropico.

I was happiest when I was by myself in the apartment, wearing the ring and admiring its sparkle. Art and I would be a married couple someday. We would build a future together and have children. I didn't let my mind wander to the darkest possibility: that he might not return alive. That prospect was too unbearable to consider.

Understanding that we were entering into a serious commitment and that our time together was limited, we stopped going to Nisei socials and dances. Why waste time listening to other people's silly stories? We wanted to spend every moment together when I wasn't working. We had more rendezvous in the truck late at night. One evening, with his trousers unzipped and my bra unfastened, we were interrupted by a police officer tapping the car window with the end of his billy club. Flushed by both lust and embarrassment, we immediately released each other, flinging ourselves into opposite ends of the truck's cab. After pulling up his zipper, Art started the engine and drove me home.

I made an appointment at the Beauty Box for the day before Art was going to leave. Later that evening we were going to stay in a hotel room on Wabash Avenue in the South Loop, and I wanted to look my best for our encounter. The last time Peggy had cut my hair in a simple bob for a Fourth of July picnic. This time I mentioned that I wanted a look like Lana Turner's.

"Ooooh, Lana." The tall man wearing a dress had walked into the Beauty Box and bent down to study my face in the mirror on the wall. "I can see it, definitely."

"Georgina, I'll get to you in a minute," Peggy said. I was mystified by how casually they spoke to each other. I wasn't quite sure how to respond and remained quiet in my shampoo smock.

Georgina sat in the chair right next to me. "I've seen you all around Clark and Division. All those Nisei boys going gaga over you."

I was confused. Georgina had never acknowledged me before, and I certainly hadn't had anyone—well, outside of Art—show any interest in me. I tried to compose a witty retort, but my tongue was tied up in knots. And I wasn't quite sure whether to refer to Georgina as a "he" or a "she." Peggy cleared it up by saying, "Don't take her seriously, Aki."

"Aki? What a perfectly charming name. Does it have a special meaning?"

I could hardly get the word out. "Autumn."

"Excuse me?"

"Autumn," I said louder.

"Autumn! And look, here we are in September. It's your season."

"Stop teasing her," Peggy said as she finished putting the last large roller in my hair. "She's a good Nisei girl."

If only Peggy knew the truth.

"Georgina is an entertainer up on Clark Street."

"I'm a dancer." Georgina stretched out her long legs,

which were meticulously shaven. "And Miss Peggy makes sure I'm pretty."

As Peggy led me to one of her two domed hair dryers, the Nisei man who worked at the hotel registration desk entered the beauty shop wheeling a large box on a dolly.

"Oh, Keizo, thank you for bringing that in. I've been waiting for this delivery," Peggy said. She told Keizo to leave the box in the corner and as he lifted it from the dolly, the muscles in his forearms bulged.

"Grrrr." Georgina practically growled, apparently responding to Keizo's fit build. He had a wide chest like a football player's and curly hair—probably natural—that put my hair to shame. Keizo didn't seem to appreciate Georgina's attention and visibly scowled, delighting the dancer to no end.

I enjoyed watching this interplay under the safety of the hair dryer. The hum of the fan insulated me. I liked feeling invisible at times, but before he left, Keizo gave me a second look. Perhaps I was on my way to looking like Lana Turner?

When I walked to our meeting place outside of the Hotel Roosevelt, Art was already there and let out a low whistle. Not only was my hair newly styled but I had purchased a tight red dress from Goldblatt's. The cost of the hotel room came out of my paycheck since Art didn't have a job outside of his father's business, but Art was the one who went in and gave the money to the hotel clerk. I sat in the lobby and when Art entered the elevator, I followed but stood on the other side. It was exciting to pretend that we were strangers. We exchanged sly looks behind the elevator operator, but I had a feeling that he knew exactly what was going on.

Art unlocked the hotel room door and I quickly went in behind him. I didn't have a chance to look around because he lifted me up in his arms and took me over to the bed. "Close the curtains," I told Art, and as he darkened the room, I stripped down to my slip, carelessly throwing my new dress onto the ground. I wanted Art now. I wanted him inside of me and for us to be together like we had never been before.

We had sex twice. The first time was awkward and somewhat painful, but the second time was slow and rhythmic. I felt that we were speaking without words. He had brought condoms and knew how to put them on, so he had obviously done it before. I didn't want to ask for any details because he was leaving tomorrow, and I didn't want our final conversation to be marked with any kind of conflict or misunderstanding.

As we both lay on the bed naked, I put my head on his shoulder and he grasped my arm and then hand. "Hey, you're wearing the ring," he exclaimed. "When did you put that on?"

"I put it on in the lobby," I told him. "Because I was going to meet my husband."

I hated to have to go to the train station the next morning to say goodbye. There were too many farewells in my life and I was starting to feel superstitious. If I showed up for Art, would I be the albatross that he would carry overseas?

"We'll get married as soon as I'm on leave," he whispered in my ear. "But you'll write to me, right?" We embraced and kissed in front of Art's parents, Lois and Aunt Eunice. His family was crying, as was I. After he got into his train car, I blew my nose in my handkerchief. Eunice was doing the same in hers, making a loud honk like a goose's. Our eyes met and we laughed in spite of the sad situation. She linked arms with me as we walked away from the platform. "He'll be okay," she assured me. "Make sure you take care of that ring."

I stopped, amazed. Eunice knew about our engagement. I thought we had promised not to tell anyone else.

"Don't worry. I'll keep my mouth shut." Eunice pressed her index finger to her closed lips. She then said, "Where do you think he got the ring?"

The ring had been hers. Ren Nakasone had proposed to her with that ring thirty years ago. It was hard for me to imagine an Issei man marrying a *hakujin* woman in 1914. That was during World War I and Ren had been drafted, too, into the US Army even though he was a Japanese immigrant. He was supposed to gain American citizenship for his military service, but because of some bureaucratic bungling, that promise hadn't come through.

"I'll treasure it," I told Eunice, and she ruffled my hair as we went our separate ways.

When I arrived home, my mother had already completed her cleaning job at the barbershop. She now had three other customers, all conveniently located around Clark and Division, so she had purchased her own cleaning equipment—a bucket with wheels, mop, and broom. Sometimes when I walked in the neighborhood, I'd see her coming my way, her hair tied back in a kerchief and an apron over her dress. I'd feel so distressed that it had come to this—my proud mother, wife to a former produce market manager, had been reduced to being a house cleaner. Her acceptance of her new lot in life was as heroic as it could get. Years later, I would finally understand she had done it without complaint for the sake of our family. Today, however, I was only feeling annoyed by her inquiries.

"Did he talk about marriage?" my mother asked in Japanese.

"Mom, he's getting ready to put his life on the line for our country. It's not the time to talk about that."

Mom looked wounded by my harsh reaction. Feeling bad, I offered to make her some coffee and pancakes. Pancakes had the power to improve almost every situation, if only for a few hours.

With Art gone and Tomi preparing to leave, I felt rootless again. Every time I seemed to regain footing, the ground below me moved. Both Nancy and Phillis were extra accommodating at work, bringing me treats from home like oranges and peanut drop cookies.

I sent letters to Art every other day at first. I could pour my heart out in those letters, tell him how much I missed him. But since I had stopped going to dances, there wasn't much else to report on my end. Several days had passed when Nancy cornered me before I left work.

"I'm having a birthday party at my house this Sunday afternoon after Mass. It's not a big deal, so don't bring a present or anything. I talk about you all the time at home, so my family wants to meet you."

I was both curious and anxious to consider what stories Nancy was telling her household. I was sure that my being Japanese was one of the talking points, but what else? I agreed to attend because, at the very least, I would have something new and interesting to share in my letters to Art.

A phone message was waiting for me when I got home. My father rarely answered the pay phone but he had that day. In his beautiful script, he had written Tomi Kawamura's name, tomorrow's date and a time. Tomi was leaving on the first train out to Detroit and I had almost forgotten. I hadn't known that Tomi had my phone number and was touched to have received the reminder.

The next morning, I was late in getting out the door and didn't have any *omiyage* to give her for her journey. By the time I arrived, the porters were rushing back and forth with the last suitcases and train conductors signaled that everyone but ticketed passengers should back away from the car.

"Aki, Aki!"

I spotted Tomi's slender figure on the steps of the last car. She wore gloves and as she waved, she reminded me of a Japanese diplomat's wife, all *chanto* and well coiffed. I barged by a conductor, earning his wrath, but I didn't care. She held out her gloved hand and I thought that she wanted to shake mine, but as I got closer, I saw that she was trying to pass me an envelope.

"Bye, Aki," she called out as the car moved forward. I stepped back and watched the train leave the station.

Once it was gone, I took a closer look at what she had handed me. *To Aki*, the outside of the envelope read. *I should have given this to you sooner.*

Inside was a ripped page from Rose's journal. There were only three sentences written on it in my sister's distinctive handwriting:

> *I wish Tomi would believe me when I tell her that everything will be okay. I'll make it right. She has nothing to worry about.*

Was my sister referring to the aftermath of the attack? Tomi must have interpreted it that way. Why else would she have taken it from Rose's personal diary? She had clung to my sister's words throughout her stay in Chicago. And now that Rose was gone, there was no one who could honor that promise.

CHAPTER 20

Nancy had mentioned going to Catholic Mass before her birthday get-together, so church was on my mind. Both Art and I had an open invitation from Joey and Louise to go to Reverend Suzuki's church service at the Moody Bible Institute. I wasn't quite sure why because none of us were particularly religious; I got the feeling that their motivations were more social than spiritual. Without telling either one of them, I decided to check out the Moody Bible Institute that Sunday morning.

The campus was large, with towering dormitories to house male students and a smaller one for women. Joey had told me that the service designed for Japanese Americans was held in Moody's social hall next to its coffee shop. There was no sense in having such a small Christian gathering in Moody's main auditorium, which could fit probably a thousand people.

I hadn't been sure what to wear. I had opted for my simple striped dress but, inspired by Tomi's example, I wore a pair of my mother's gloves to look more dignified.

I knew the social hall's approximate location and searched for some Nisei dressed in their Sunday best to follow. I spotted a Nisei couple in their thirties with two children, walking with their hands linked. The man wore a light-colored suit and hat; his wife, a dress made of white eyelet. The boys, their hair freshly combed to reveal their shiny, spotless foreheads, wore matching outfits of baby-blue shirts and shorts. They were perfect, all-American, and probably came from one of the ten concentration camps in California, Arizona, Utah, Wyoming, Idaho, Colorado or Arkansas.

"Tropico, what are you doing here?" I heard Hammer's familiar voice behind me. I stopped and turned around. Hammer's hair was still in a pompadour, but it was less outrageous—shorter and more controlled. Instead of a zoot suit, he wore a conservative dark suit that flattered his lean physique.

"Shouldn't I be asking you that?" I grinned. I had missed him. We were now walking side by side, and I saw the black Bible that he had tucked under his arm.

"It's all healed up," Hammer said.

"What, you mean my face? You gave me a good shiner, I'll tell you that."

"I've been meaning to talk to you. I even tried to go by your place to give you my mea culpas in person, but your parents didn't seem like they were leaving your side."

I gave him a sideways glance. "You were spying on me?"

"Just for a few days. Then I decided to leave Clark and Division."

"I heard that you're at some *okanemochi hakujin* woman's house in Lakeview."

"Yeah, she's a church person. She's helping Reverend Suzuki set up this place."

"Oh, I get it now," I said.

"Whaddaya mean?"

"This whole church business. Your latest scheme?"

Hammer looked wounded. "I'm trying to turn my life around, Tropico. Things were spinning out of control. *Kuru-kuru-pa.*" What in the world was he referring to?

We walked into a two-story building made of dark-brown brick, in contrast to the taller reddish ones. Folding chairs were set up across the wider axis of the room with an aisle in the middle, all facing a podium with a large cross on the front.

I was amazed that Hammer knew the other parishioners and they seemed genuinely happy to see him. About half were *hakujin*, probably do-gooders like his patron, while the rest were Issei and Nisei. I scanned the small-yet-animated crowd for familiar faces, but I recognized no one, not even Joey and Louise. While Hammer disappeared into the choir room, I sat in the back row, feeling a bit out of place. I was so bored that I even opened up the hymnal that had been placed on my chair and tried to find songs I had heard before.

"Miss Ito?"

I was surprised Reverend Suzuki had recognized me. He was in the same robe that he had worn for Rose's funeral.

"Hello, Reverend."

"I'm so glad to see you. I've been meaning to call you, but I had no phone number for you on file." He asked me the perfunctory minister questions: How were my parents doing? Where was I working? How was I finding Chicago?

I could not answer any of his inquiries honestly. I surely could not have told him that I was no longer a virgin and I was secretly engaged. Or that my parents and I were not getting along. Or, most importantly, that my sister had been assaulted and I was determined to find and punish whoever had done this awful thing to her.

Instead, I sat in my folding chair with the hymnal on my lap, said some pleasantries, nodded and smiled. Thankfully, an older couple approached Reverend Suzuki, releasing me from my charade.

I took no comfort from Reverend Suzuki's homily, which was about forgiveness, but I was moved by the choir. There were only about ten of them, Japanese, *hakujin*, and one black woman. Hammer stood in the back row and I cringed a little because it was such an incongruous sight. But he behaved himself and moved his lips along with everyone else's. They sang a hymn that I had heard maybe once before, "Be Still, My Soul."

When disappointment, grief and fear are gone
Sorrow forgot, love's purest joys restored
Be still, my soul: when change and tears are past
All safe and blessed, we shall meet at last

A *hakujin* male soloist belted the refrain and I was overcome with tears. I wiped them away with the tips of my fingers. What was happening to me?

At the end, Reverend Suzuki gave the benediction and marched down an aisle between the rows of folding chairs. I didn't want to talk to him again but had to if I wanted to leave.

"I hope we see you again, Miss Ito. And give my regards to your parents." He covered our handshake with his left hand as if to secure some sort of promise. I wasn't going to give it to him.

According to my watch, it was twelve-thirty, a good time to head to Nancy's house in Polonia Triangle.

As I walked up Clark to catch the bus, I heard a burst of footsteps behind me. His Bible in his right hand, Hammer had caught up with me. "What did you think of it?" he asked.

"Church? It was all right. I did like your singing. It made me cry."

Hammer seemed genuinely moved by my comment and he started to blink more rapidly. He said that joining the choir had been Reverend Suzuki's idea. I smiled, remembering that

Hammer had been the one to tell me that the minister had "screwed up" Rose's funeral.

Maybe being here with Hammer was a sign. When would I have this opportunity again? I tried to recall the details of the sermon. "Reverend Suzuki spoke a lot about forgiveness. 'As long as you confess, your sins will be wiped clean.'"

Hammer readjusted his grip on his Bible. From the tone of my voice, he sensed that I was going to engage him in a serious discussion. We had stopped walking and stood outside some buildings in front of the Henrotin Hospital.

"Did you know where Rose got her abortion?"

Hammer flinched, as if the word caused him pain. "Why? Why would you want to know something like that?" His voice became rough; he sounded like the old Hammer. "Are you planning to go to the cops?"

I already tried that, I thought. "No, no. I need to know, Hammer. It may not make sense to you, but I can't rest if I don't find out everything that happened to Rose while she was in Chicago."

Hammer took a deep breath. "There's a doctor's office on State Street near Marshall Field's. His name is Thomas McGrath. He delivers babies but he also has this side business on Sundays."

Side business. That sounded hideous.

"I found out about him through his driver who is a regular at Aloha." We both resumed walking but Hammer slowed as he saw some Nisei women from my apartment building coming our way. He waited until they passed by before he continued. "Rose was so desperate; I said that I'd help her. At least with finding someone."

"Do you think that this Dr. McGrath is legitimate?"

"Whaddaya mean?"

"Rose was bleeding a lot afterward."

Hammer looked truly pained. "I was worried about that from the get-go. I told Rose not to do it. I said we could get married, at least in the short run."

I was amazed by Hammer's offer.

"She laughed about that one. Not at me, though. She thanked me but said that she had to handle it her way."

I started to head up Clark but Hammer didn't follow.

"I'm staying away from Clark these days."

I fanned my face with the church bulletin. "Why?"

"I can't get into it with you." Hammer's voice dropped an octave.

"Does it involve Aloha?"

"No, no."

"How about Manju? You aren't spending any time with him these days?"

"Tropico, stop. Believe me, some things are best unsaid." The demon face returned, only this time Hammer seemed more afraid than tortured.

I said goodbye and left him on the corner. When I was halfway up the block, I turned back, surprised to see that he was still there, unable to decide what his next move would be.

CHAPTER 21

From Clark and Division, the bus ride to Polonia Triangle was easy, a straight shot two miles west. The bus was relatively open and I had a seat to myself. I was still a bit shaken by my conversation with Hammer. I had written Dr. Thomas McGrath's name in my notebook as soon we separated so I wouldn't forget. I planned on stopping by his office after Nancy's birthday party. I wasn't sure if I would be allowed in because they were engaged in an illicit activity. Going to the office at least would give me some idea of what kind of doctor he was.

Getting off at the stop for Polonia Triangle, I tried to readjust my mood. Luckily, the neighborhood was bright and lively, with a large fountain in its square and red awnings on storefronts. The area's gigantic churches were impressive, with twin spires and columns like I'd seen in photos of the Supreme Court. I followed Nancy's directions and found myself in front of a two-story concrete building with a balcony that faced the street. I went through the gate and up the stairs, but before I could ring the bell, the front door flew open. I looked down to see a girl who was about nine, with wavy blonde hair and an impish grin like Nancy's.

"Hello, I'm Aki. I work with Nancy."

The girl didn't bother to say anything and opened the door wider to let me in.

The house was filled with people—balding men wearing short-sleeved shirts and suspenders, women in aprons running from the kitchen to the living room with steaming dishes, skinny teenagers with terrible skin. They were all *hakujin* and some of them did a double take when they saw me. As I walked in, I was enveloped by smells of starchy potatoes, fragrant dill and acidic vinegar.

"Aki, you came!" Nancy was dressed in a marigold-colored dress that complemented her eyes. She had her Brownie camera and took a quick snapshot of me before I could fix my makeup. "Come here, Mama, here's one of the girls I work with, Aki."

"My, you're a beauty. Nancy wasn't wrong about that."

Two other women added their agreement, nodding and murmuring in a foreign language, probably Polish.

I was mystified about why all these women were paying me such compliments. Maybe it was a Midwestern practice, I figured.

Nancy's mother sat me down at a table and a plate full of food was placed in front of me. Nancy recited the menu: pierogi, a type of dumpling filled with potatoes and cheese; kielbasa sausage; cabbage roll; and a pile of sauerkraut. "Oh, and here's some pickle soup," Nancy said, leaving her camera on the table to carefully place a cup of yellow broth by my plate.

I thought that maybe Nancy was joking, but I looked into the cup and, lo and behold, bits of green pickle were floating on the surface. The women watched as I took a sip. Delicious! So was everything else on my plate. They were astonished and delighted by my appetite.

I was finishing off some strudel when Phillis appeared at

our table, her hair curled around her face instead of pinned into victory rolls.

"I ate already," she said, a gift in her hand.

Before Phillis could object, Nancy took a quick photo of her, too. I was impressed by Nancy's speed in capturing her guests on film.

"Oh, I brought you something, too," I said, wiping my mouth with my handkerchief, while one of Nancy's older female relatives whisked away my dirty plate. It was like musical chairs, and someone new needed to take my place.

Gesturing that we should follow her with our presents, Nancy wound past the tables crammed with food. Bumping shoulders and elbows with different generations of Kowalskis, we walked up a staircase to the second-floor hallway. Framed photos were plastered on every inch of the walls. It was a bit overwhelming to see so many Kowalskis in one place, not only live on the first floor, but also captured in photos here.

Phillis and I followed Nancy out a set of French doors leading to the balcony.

Nancy moved a loose brick on the edge of the balcony connected to the outer wall and pulled out a pack of cigarettes and a plastic ashtray.

She offered us a cigarette and we each declined. "I didn't know that you smoked," I said as she took one out for herself.

"Only on special occasions." She grinned, pulling a match against the matchbook and lighting the cigarette. Both Phillis and I laughed. We figured that every weekend was a special occasion for Nancy.

We presented her gifts. Phillis had given her a small photo album, which Nancy cooed over. I pulled out my present, a Red Majesty lipstick in a paper tube. I hadn't bothered to wrap it.

Nancy seized upon it, immediately twisting off the top and checking the shade. "This is the color you wear. I adore it."

"It was actually my older sister's favorite color lipstick. That is, when she was alive."

Both of them stared at me.

"I thought she was maybe stuck in one those camps," Nancy said.

I shook my head. A welcome breeze blew through the ash trees and reached up to the balcony.

I told them everything that had happened. How we were forced out of our homes and how the Tonai produce market was taken over by a neighboring market run by whites. The frightening drive to Manzanar with a military escort. The whip of the Owens Valley winds and loneliness of the desolate basin held in place by the majestic Sierra Nevadas. The line of freshly constructed barracks that were to be our homes—for more than two years in my case. And then, a thread of hope—the good ones, the American-born, would be released into America's interior, to places we had never been before. My sister was one of those early chosen ones. We were to follow her to Chicago, but as it turned out, we never saw her alive again.

Phillis's eyes took on a fierce glare. "That's not right," she said and shook her head.

Nancy had snuffed out her first cigarette in the ashtray and was already working on her second one. "What happened to your sister?"

"She was killed by a subway car on Clark and Division. But before that, she was sexually assaulted. She got pregnant and went through an abortion in Chicago."

Nancy was horrified. I wasn't sure which part of it angered her the most.

"I don't think the procedure went well. I found out that it

was done at a doctor's office on State Street. I'm planning to go over there after the party to see what kind of place it is."

"Well, you can't go alone. I'll go with you," Nancy quickly volunteered.

"I don't think that's a good idea," Phillis said.

"No, no," I added. "It's your birthday. You can't leave your guests."

"My guests? They are family. They don't even know or care where I am. My birthday is an excuse for them to have a get-together."

"Don't do it," Phillis said. "You could get into some trouble."

"I'm good at talking to people, right? Aki's not going to get anything out of anyone, especially a stranger."

Phillis pursed her lips in agreement. My co-workers had me pegged.

Nancy asked for the doctor's name and I showed her my notebook. "I'll check the phone book for his address." Nancy mouthed his name silently as she went into the house.

Phillis and I stood in awkward silence on the balcony. I pretended that I was intensely interested in a bluebird resting on a branch of the ash tree.

"You know I can't be any part of this," Phillis said. She had a family supper to go to, but I knew that it was more than that. Being black, she was more vulnerable to scrutiny by authorities than Nancy and even me.

"I don't expect you to. Rose was *my* sister. This has nothing to do with either one of you." I sounded extraordinarily harsh and immediately regretted it. I realized that I hadn't asked about her brother for a few weeks. "How's Reggie doing, by the way?"

"The army is sending him to Hawaii for rehab. I wish that they would bring him home."

I felt the weight of her worries. Each of us had our own problems and it was selfish for me to expect them to be roped into mine.

When Nancy returned to the balcony, her face flushed with the discovery of the doctor's address, I tried to make my stance clear. "Listen, I can't involve you in this."

"This awful thing happened to you and your family. You don't know a soul in Chicago. We can't let you go through this alone. Right, Phillis?"

"We're friends." Phillis's simple declaration moved me deeply.

"See, we're friends. We have to look out for each other. Besides, truth be told, I'm bored stiff by this party. I need some excitement."

Nancy's unbridled enthusiasm lifted my spirits. My whole life I'd searched for true female friends, and it felt both glorious and odd to find them here.

CHAPTER 22

The office was in a ritzy area in the east Loop, across the street from the Marshall Field's building, a few blocks from Lake Michigan, and not far from Grant Park and the candy factory. As Nancy and I rode the train, I started to get a knot in my stomach. It wasn't right to involve Nancy. Why had I even mentioned anything to her on her birthday of all days? Nancy, however, was electrified by this mission. She stood straight as a rail as she held on to the pole in the train car, her camera in a bag that she wore across her body. I had sometimes dismissed Nancy because she felt compelled to chatter during gaps in conversation. I realized now it was more a nervous habit than a reflection of her character. She was a deeper person than I had made her out to be.

Since it was Sunday, the neighborhood wasn't that crowded with commuters or office workers. As we neared the multistory building, I started to have second thoughts. There was no way that an abortionist would open his door to us, not without a prior appointment. "Look, I've changed my mind," I whispered to Nancy. "I'm sure they will just throw us out on our ears."

"We've come this far," Nancy argued. She had a stubborn

streak and wanted to see this through. "Maybe we can talk to some of the patients."

We stood under the balcony of one of the high-rises and observed as the occasional pedestrian passed on the sidewalk. After about thirty minutes, two *hakujin* women around our age slowly approached the doctor's office. There was something unusual about the smaller women's gait. She would take a few steps and then halt, fidgeting with the cardigan she wore over her shoulders. She seemed afraid. Before I could deter her, Nancy ran after them.

"Excuse me, excuse me," she called out. They stopped and the one who had seemed fearful now looked terrified. The other woman spoke to Nancy and, based on the look on the woman's face, she wasn't pleased. The cardigan girl clutched her stomach and strode the other way, her companion following after her.

"What did you say to them?" I asked Nancy when she returned to our spot underneath the balcony.

"I told them that I was looking for Dr. McGrath's office and wondered if they knew where it was."

"Nancy, you scared that one girl half to death."

"I know. I think that I have to find another way to approach them."

On our side of the street a middle-aged woman approached with someone who looked like she could be her daughter. They both had honey blonde hair, broad cheeks and thin necks. Nancy started to walk alongside them and the women at first seemed startled and then confused. After pointing toward Marshall Field's, they scurried away to the doctor's office.

Dejected, Nancy returned to our lookout spot. "I tried to make small talk and asked where I could find a pharmacy. They really didn't want to talk to me."

We waited there a few more minutes. No one else came

around. A man was sitting in a parked Chevrolet sedan across the street, but he seemed to be intent on his Sunday newspaper. "This is ridiculous. We aren't going to get anywhere like this. I'm going to go into the office and have a look around."

"No, don't go in there, Nancy. I think this is a bad idea. It's not like anyone there is going to admit anything."

"It will take me a few minutes. I'll be back in a flash." She ran toward the office with her camera bag bouncing on her hip.

I was on pins and needles while I waited for Nancy. It was mid-fall and the weather was comfortable, at least. A strong breeze blew down State Street, flapping the American flags that were hung from poles attached to the sides of high-rise buildings.

I was gazing at the skyline when a bevy of police cars and a paddy wagon swept down the street and parked beside the office building where Dr. McGrath was located. Police officers, their belts tight around their jackets, spilled out onto the sidewalk and ran into the building. The man with the newspaper left the sedan and joined another plainclothes man on the street.

No, no, it can't be. I couldn't hide under the balcony, shaking in my shoes. I had to rescue Nancy from this chaos. The first step was the hardest. My stride became more brisk until I was only a few feet away from the door of the doctor's office. A uniformed police officer impeded my advance. "No, miss, you can't go in there."

Other curious pedestrians had crowded around to see what was going on. "Stand back, stand back." The officer held out his arms to signal for us to keep our distance.

A woman wearing a hospital gown and a shower cap appeared on the brick stairway; tears streaked down her face as a police officer led her to a squad car. She was followed by a parade of both men and women in the custody of uniformed officers. Two men in white gowns and caps were placed in separate squad cars, while the rest of the apprehended suspects were led into the paddy wagon. The last person in custody was Nancy.

As the officer on watch had temporarily diverted his attention from the crowd, I broke through the invisible line and ran to the paddy wagon. Already locked up inside, Nancy pressed her face against the wire mesh of the vehicle's window. She wasn't crying but her face was drawn and her eyes were as big as saucers.

This had been my fear all along, but I never could have imagined that Nancy would be in my place.

"I'll get you out!" I called as the police convoy left State Street.

As I rode the train back to Clark and Division, it felt as though my heart would pound out of my dress. I ran to the LaSalle apartments and when I reached the second floor, I began slapping a door with my open palm.

The door opened, revealing Harriet with half of her hair in rollers. "What on earth—"

"I need to talk to Douglas. My friend got arrested investigating the doctor's office where Rose had her abortion."

Harriet admonished me for speaking so loud and ushered me into her apartment.

Without a second thought, I sat on her bed. "It's all my fault." I spilled out what had happened.

"Who is your friend?"

"Nancy Kowalski. We work together at the Newberry."

Harriet had a telephone in her apartment—probably because she needed to make calls related to WRA work. She lifted the black receiver and quickly dialed a number that she obviously knew by heart. She turned her head and spoke in a low voice so I couldn't really hear what she was saying.

When she was finished, she placed the receiver back on its black base.

"What happens now?"

"We wait," she said, and went back to her makeshift vanity to complete rolling up her hair.

Out of respect for her help, I stayed silent, but after a while I couldn't take it anymore. "How can you be so calm? Don't you care?"

Harriet glared back at me. "Don't you know that we are putting out fires every day at the WRA office? Girls having babies out of wedlock; Japanese gambling halls getting raided. If I ran around like a chicken with my head cut off, I wouldn't be able to do my job."

I had no idea that I wasn't the only one dealing with such problems.

"You need to take charge of your life, Aki. Make something out of yourself, for Rose's sake."

Harriet's reprimand burned. Was I, in fact, hurting my sister's legacy by being consumed by it?

A few minutes later, the phone rang, making me jump. Harriet angled her head so she could hear the speaker on the other end of the line. "Yes, yes, okay," she said, and turned to me. "Douglas says that Nancy is at the East Chicago Avenue police station. It's around the corner on Chicago Avenue. Do you need the address?"

"No, I know where it is."

• • •

The police officer with the greasy white hair was manning the front desk again. I braced myself for another unwelcome reception.

"I want to speak to Sergeant Graves," I said to him.

"He's not available today."

He wasn't available? How strange. I knew that it was Sunday but you would think that it would be all hands on deck for this large-scale bust. At any rate, I would have to make my plea to this terrible specimen of a gatekeeper. "You have to release Nancy Kowalski. She had nothing to do with this. It's a big misunderstanding."

The officer checked over some paperwork fastened onto a clipboard. "She's been charged with conspiracy to commit abortion."

"That's ridiculous. She's not even pregnant."

The officer was not in a mood to hear my arguments. "If you want her out, you'll have to pay her bail."

"How much?"

"Two hundred and fifty dollars."

I nearly fell over. That was more than two months' worth of my salary. I had no savings to speak of. There was only one person I knew who might be in a position to help. I ran out of the police station and flagged down a cab. I was determined that Nancy would not spend one night in jail.

Luckily I had written down Roy's address in the notebook that I kept in my purse. In the light of day, his and Ike's apartment was less impressive. I noticed that the paint outside was a bit dingy and the yard in front was unkempt. It took two knocks before Roy opened the door. He must have been taking a nap because his hair was in disarray and he was only wearing a sleeveless T-shirt and Bermuda shorts.

"I'm a bit desperate," I told Roy.

"Come in, come in." Roy rubbed the sleep out of his eyes and invited me in.

I didn't bother to take a seat on his couch and remained standing on the Oriental rug. "I need some money," I blurted out.

"What have you done, Aki?" He sounded more weary than concerned.

"I have a friend, a co-worker. She's in trouble." I gripped the handle of my purse so tightly that blood was rushing down to my knuckles.

"What kind of trouble?"

"I'd rather not say."

"What is it with you and Rose?"

I took a step back, preparing to receive criticism from Roy. "I don't know what you're trying to say."

"Rose asked me for money, too. A few days before she died."

"Why didn't you tell me?" I couldn't believe that he was revealing this so many months after her death.

"To tell you the truth, I didn't remember until now. She came to my place and she stood in my doorway like you just did."

"Did you give her money?"

"I gave her some cash. At least what I had on hand. Maybe twenty dollars."

"Did she say what it was for?"

Roy shook his head. "I hadn't seen her for so long, I was grateful that she came to me." Roy put on a plaid short-sleeved shirt that he had hung over the back of a chair. "I wish

I could help you, Aki," he said as he secured a few buttons. "I've enlisted."

"What?" I sunk down into his couch.

"I've enlisted in the army. I've had to wire all my savings to my sister to help the family relocate out of camp. My father is finally out of Santa Fe."

All the Nisei men around me seemed to be disappearing for the warfront.

"No, I understand." I knew as much as anyone how expensive it was to start over in a brand new place where you had no connections. "But why did you sign up, Roy? You've heard about all the casualties. Especially the Nisei boys."

"I've followed the rules all my life, Aki. You know. I've done everything that my parents have wanted. I can't do that anymore."

I remembered what Ike had said about the Italian girl Roy was dating. Roy didn't mention her, so I didn't dare to bring that up.

I pushed myself up from the couch. "Be sure to tell me when you're leaving. I want to give you a good send-off. And my parents will want to, too."

"I'd appreciate that." He grabbed his wallet from the table, pulled out a twenty-dollar bill and handed it to me.

"No, no. Your family will need that."

"You're family, too," he said. I wouldn't fight him on that point and accepted the money.

We didn't hug. It would be inappropriate to do that, with Roy and me alone in his apartment and him wearing only Bermuda shorts. We did lock eyes and I realized that for all Roy's weaknesses—his temper and how he wore his heart on his sleeve—I did care for him like a brother. My restored affection for Roy, however, didn't solve my problem—how to raise the rest of the bail money to release Nancy from jail.

I supposed that I could sell the gun that was in the locker at the subway station, but it would feel absolutely criminal to walk around Clark Street with a firearm—besides, who knows, I might need it for protection. There was only one other solution—an option that I dreaded.

I went home and went into my second drawer. There in the corner underneath my underwear was the little blue box that Art had given me. It was Aunt Eunice's precious engagement ring from her Japanese husband, the symbol of a love worth risking the loss of American citizenship. But on the other hand, there was Nancy, my friend and co-worker, practically the only person in Chicago who had stood beside me while I tried to uncover the last weeks of my sister's life. I pushed away any thought of Art toiling through military exercises in the heat of Mississippi. I felt awful but what else could I do?

CHAPTER 23

When I returned to the police station, Nancy's whole family had arrived. They peppered me with questions and all I could say was that it was all a misunderstanding. Letting Nancy's older female relatives take a seat on the wooden bench, I stood outside on the steps of the station to wait until the line shortened. The sun was going down and I felt miserable. I had let everyone down: Nancy, one of the few friends I ever had, Art and Aunt Eunice. I was so lost in my thoughts that I didn't recognize the man walking up the stairs toward me.

"Aki." Douglas wore a fedora and held himself straighter than usual.

"What are—"

"I'm going to see what I can do."

I felt a rush of relief. Finally, I had a *hakujin* advocate, a government worker to boot. Surely the police had to listen to Douglas, didn't they?

"Here." I handed him a fat envelope.

"What's this?"

"Bail money."

Douglas hesitated, as if he was going to ask me where I had gotten the cash. He must have thought better of it, because he closed his mouth and nodded before he entered the police station.

I had gone to the first pawnshop that came to my mind—the one next to Aloha. It was strategically located to serve down-on-their-luck gamblers who had used their last nickel but still had a watch around their wrist to exchange for cash. The pawnbroker took out a loupe and examined the diamond in my engagement ring. He quoted a price and I didn't haggle. It was enough for Nancy's bail, and that's all that mattered.

I rubbed the ring finger on my left hand. I'd get the ring back, right?

It seemed like an eternity until Douglas finally reappeared, his hat in his hands. The sky was dark and the streetlights were flickering on at the same time. "The police will be releasing her," he said, putting his fedora back on and readjusting its brim.

"Thank goodness." I exhaled and turned toward the door.

"I wouldn't go in right now."

"Why not?"

"I think her family is pretty upset. They are devout Catholics. Can't understand why you'd put Nancy in that position."

She volunteered, I thought. But yes, I should never have involved her in the first place.

"Let time pass. It will eventually blow over." He turned his face toward the streetlight. His silhouette was strangely comforting to me.

When I finally arrived back at the apartment, I was expecting my parents to be upset that I had been gone so long. Instead, they assumed that I had been having such a good time with my friends that I lost track of time. If they knew the truth,

I would probably be prohibited from leaving the apartment for the rest of our stay in Chicago.

After my parents were asleep, I tried to call Nancy a couple times, but every time I did, the person on the other end hung up on me when I introduced myself. I had become an anathema in the Kowalski household.

The next morning, when I reported for work, our supervisor, Mrs. Cannon, came by the desk. "Miss Kowalski has resigned. We'll be finding her a replacement soon."

Phillis and I exchanged glances.

"What happened yesterday?" hissed Phillis after Mrs. Cannon had left.

I gestured for her to follow me into a back room. "You were right, Phillis. Nancy had no business coming with me to Dr. McGrath's office." As I recounted everything that had happened on Sunday afternoon, Phillis's dark eyes widened and her mouth fell open.

One of the library's pages delivered a stack of newspapers for us to prepare for patron circulation. I immediately noticed the headline on the front page, TWO PHYSICIANS SEIZED IN ABORTION RAID, and began reading the story. Phillis was doing the same with another Chicago newspaper. "This is not good," Phillis said. "This is not good at all."

I was relieved at least that the only suspects mentioned by name were Dr. McGrath and his associate. "Nancy got off on bail. I'm sure that the police will drop all charges against her. She was in the wrong place at the wrong time."

"Sometimes being in the wrong place at the wrong time is the worst thing possible," she said.

As we perused the newspapers, Professor Rip Van Winkle rapped the desk. "Is Miss Kowalski here today?" he asked.

Nancy was his favorite. Professor Rip Van Winkle, whose real name was Alexander Muller, was a retired professor with a grizzly beard long enough to braid. Nancy was the only one among us three to listen to his stories about the Lincoln presidency and North-South divide.

"No, she won't be in today. In fact, she's resigned."

The retired academician staggered back a few steps. "She mentioned nothing to me. What has happened?"

I absorbed his dismay. This wouldn't do at all.

I shrugged and fetched the books that he had requested. By the time I returned to the desk I knew what I had to do.

"Phillis, you have to call her," I insisted. "No one in her house will accept my calls."

"I don't know."

"Please. I know that you don't want to be involved, but this is about Nancy and this job. And you said that we're friends."

Phillis pursed her lips. She was not the type to say anything that wasn't true, and the fact that I was repeating her exact words weighed heavily on her.

"Fine," she said. "During our break."

Phillis went to the rotary phone, which was reserved for calls to academic institutions. I looked in my notebook and recited the Kowalski phone number. Phillis, who had elegant fingers but unusual flat-shaped fingernails, took her time dialing the numbers. I waited patiently as the circular dial turned back in place before the next number in the sequence was selected. When the dialing was completed, I put my ear next to Phillis's by the receiver.

"Hello." Nancy's voice sounded uncharacteristically subdued.

"Nancy, it's Phillis. What happened? Why did you quit?"

"Hold on, okay?" We heard some muffled voices in the

background with Nancy telling someone, "It's Phillis from work." Returning to the phone conversation, she explained, "My parents said that as long as Aki is working at the Newberry, I can't work there anymore."

I was aghast. The good news was that the charges were being dropped against Nancy. The bad news: the police had confiscated her camera.

I grabbed the receiver from Phillis's grip. "Nancy, it's me. Come back to work. They won't have to worry about you being around me."

Nancy didn't reply, but I heard movement and footsteps. Finally, she whispered, "How did you get the money for my bail?"

"Don't worry about that. I was responsible. You were doing me a great favor." I swallowed, fully understanding the ramifications of what I would say next. "I'm going to quit working here, Nancy. You can come back."

Nancy hemmed and hawed, but I insisted. "I'm thinking of going to college, anyway," I said, surprising myself. I had announced to the Nakasone family that I wanted to become a nurse. Maybe this was the time for me to do so.

The head librarian, Mr. Geiger, didn't quite know what to make of my announcement that I was going to resign. He removed his reading glasses, sat back in his chair and studied me from the other side of his expansive desk. "Has something happened in the department?" he asked.

"Nancy Kowalski is coming back; that's all that I can say," I said. "And I will be leaving. I'm hoping to go back to college."

Mr. Geiger pulled at his sideburns. "We'll miss you, Miss Ito," he proclaimed. "You've been an asset to the library."

As I gathered my purse and brown-bag lunch to leave, Phillis watched from a distance behind a stack of monographs, looking almost betrayed. We had become an odd yet complementary threesome over these past five months. Our kinship was hard-earned and I had managed to throw it away on one Sunday afternoon.

I wasn't sure what I would tell my parents. They knew how fond I was of working at the Newberry and they boasted about my job to other Issei they met at the temple or English conversation classes. I was relieved to come home to an empty apartment without any pressure to devise a story. I took a brown-water bath and tried to pretend that I was soaking in tea instead of who-knows-what.

While I was in the bathtub, I heard a rapping on our door but ignored it. I figured if it was important enough, the same person would return. After dressing myself in my striped dress, I went to the door and checked to see if anything had been left for us in the hallway. As it turned out, there was a white envelope placed against the wall.

The envelope was addressed to Mr. and Mrs. Gitaro Ito. The return address was the Chicago Coroner's Office. It had been five months since Rose's death, and I couldn't imagine why they were communicating with us now. Unable to wait for my parents, I opened the envelope—not carefully with a knife as my father would have done, but by ripping it. I pulled out the contents, a two-page pathological report, from the jagged mouth of the envelope.

As in the death certificate, cardiac arrest was listed as the medical cause of death. The force of the subway car had severed the brachial artery in Rose's arm, leading to death in a matter of minutes. I was thankful, at least, that Rose hadn't suffered long. The coroner reiterated that she had committed suicide by intentionally flinging herself into the path of the oncoming subway car. *There was no evidence of the incident being an accident or the result of foul play*, the coroner stated. I let out a breath of contempt. Had the coroner done any kind of investigation to come to that conclusion?

I scanned the second page. There was nothing about Rose's abortion.

I remembered that in my meeting with the coroner, he had insisted that he had to include the procedure in his report. Had he had a change of heart? But why five months later? I checked—the report had been amended with yesterday's date. It didn't make sense.

As I sat at the table, staring at water dripping from our leaky faucet, someone knocked at our door. Perhaps the same person who had left the report? I quickly went to the door and opened it without even asking who was there. It turned out to be a big *hakujin* man in a dark-blue uniform carrying a heavy canvas bag over his shoulder.

"Iceman," he announced. He had a full mustache the color of butterscotch and his chest was wide like an anvil.

"Oh, is that today?" I said stupidly. I was unaware of our household schedule since I usually worked during the day.

"You must be the daughter," the iceman said, walking toward our Coolerator. He removed the leftover ice and put it in our sink before easily lifting the full block from his sack and placing it in the top compartment.

"My parents didn't tell me."

"Monday of every week. Came a little early today, so I'm glad you're here," he said. He had lines on his forehead and on the sides of his cheeks. He might have been a decade younger than my father. "Do you have the coupon?"

"Ah, coupon." I knew that my mother had purchased

some kind of coupon book for the iceman. I looked through our one drawer in the kitchen. There it was, *Booth's Ice*, in red ink. I paged through the book and found tickets in the back, each stating *20 lb.* on the edge.

I carefully tore out one of the tickets and handed it to him. As I did, something on the ticket seemed so familiar. That *20* in red ink—wasn't it the same typeface as was on that piece of paper in Rose's diary?

His work boots scraped our linoleum floor as he made his way to our door. Before he left, I asked him, "By the way, does your company have any Japanese icemen?"

He turned, the lines on his forehead becoming deeper. "No one full-time. But we do have a Japanese boy who helps us from time to time. He has another job, too. He's the desk clerk at the Mark Twain Hotel."

The muscular Nisei with the curly hair—what was his name? Ken, Kenichi, no, Keizo. I was lost in my thoughts and didn't notice at first that the iceman had left. I ran to the bedroom and pulled out the envelope that I had left in my purse. Taking it to the dining-room table, I fished out the ripped stub, the piece of evidence that had been left behind. I compared it to the tickets in the ice company's coupon book. A perfect match. Had Keizo been the one who had taken my sister away from me?

CHAPTER 24

I stood outside the Mark Twain Hotel, glancing at my notebook as if I was waiting for someone on the corner. Instead of Keizo, a middle-aged *hakujin* man with a funny nose that looked smashed in was at the front desk, organizing some papers on the counter. I wasn't sure what I was going to do when I saw Keizo. I wanted to look into his eyes and see what he would do—avert his gaze in shame and guilt, or perhaps stare coldly with no trace of humanity.

"Aki, what are you doing out here?" Peggy had her hands full with a bundle of shampoo smocks and a bag of folded towels.

"Oh, let me help you." I put the notebook in my purse and took the bag from her.

As we walked into the lobby, I searched for Keizo perhaps hiding in the wings. My imagination was getting the best of me.

I waited for Peggy to open the door of her shop. Once we were in, she turned on the lights and dropped the smocks onto an open chair.

"You're a lifesaver," she said, taking the bag from me. "I hope I didn't keep you from something important. Were you meeting someone?"

My heart started racing and I tried to slow down my thoughts. I didn't want to say anything improper in front of this woman whom I had become so fond of. "I was wondering, how well do you know the Nisei boy that works the front desk? Keizo?"

"You're not dating him, are you?" Peggy's usual sunny face took on a grim expression.

"Oh, no."

Peggy looked relieved. "I didn't want to say anything. I think he's a bit troubled. He's scared some of my customers, the young ones. He actually followed one of them to her apartment, can you believe that? I had to have a talk with him a couple of weeks ago, and now he stays away from me." She went to put on her beautician's smock, which was hanging from the wall. "Why are you asking?"

I didn't want to reveal too much, because I was only going by my hunch and had no evidence. "He has some information that I need about iceboxes. Do you know where he lives?"

Peggy shook her head. "I really don't know much about him at all. I don't even know his last name."

I wondered if I should try to speak to his manager or maybe a co-worker. I had to be careful, because I didn't want to tip him off in any way.

"Here, get into a chair. I'd like to trim the sides of your hair. It's getting a bit shaggy. Free of charge."

I tried to politely refuse but Peggy was insistent. She considered it her mission to make sure that my hair was in the best possible shape. A few snips here and there, and my face instantaneously appeared thinner. Peggy was a magician with her hair clippers. Being alone with her in the shop like this made me want to share my secret. "I'm engaged," I blurted out.

"What?" Peggy grabbed my hands to look at my ring finger and I blushed.

"Ah, we're not telling anyone. That's why I'm not wearing the ring," I lied.

"Who is he?"

"His name is Art Nakasone. He's actually from Chicago. He got drafted so he's away at basic training."

"Oh, honey, that must be so hard for you."

So much had happened lately that I hadn't had much time to really miss Art. I began to worry that meant something was wrong with our relationship.

"Is that why you wanted a Lana Turner hairdo the other day?"

I nodded.

"I thought it was for someone special." She dusted the loose hair off my smock before taking it off. "I won't tell a soul. I'm good at keeping secrets."

Peggy had confirmed that Keizo was worth scrutiny, but where could I find him? The Nisei weren't staying put long enough to have telephones, and if they did, they wouldn't be listed in the phone book. I stopped by the front desk after getting cleaned up by Peggy. The snub-nosed worker had big bulging eyes, which made him look like a sick goldfish. When I asked about Keizo, he responded with a blank stare.

"You know, the Japanese fellow. He works here." I tried my best not to sound exasperated.

"Oh, he's off today."

"Do you have a home address for him? Maybe a last name?"

"He keeps to himself," the desk clerk declared and moved on to a guest waiting behind me.

Harriet would have been my next choice in getting information about a Nisei resettler, but after the fiasco surrounding Nancy's arrest, I wasn't sure how open she'd be to my prying. Still, I had to determine if Rose was connected to Keizo, so I trekked to my sister's old apartment. I didn't expect anyone to be home, but I went there anyway, just to check.

After I knocked, Louise swung open the door. She was dolled up in an adorable copper-colored jumpsuit and had a flowered scarf around her head. "Aki! I haven't seen you in ages. I'm off to meet Joey."

"Oh, I wanted to ask you about something."

"I'm walking over to the Olivet." Louise locked the door behind her. "Come with me and we can talk on the way there." Olivet Institute was located about a mile away at 1441 North Cleveland in Old Town, where Joey both worked and lived. The Olivet was a social service agency that had previously worked with Italian immigrant youth before the Nisei arrived en masse. Joey was an early Japanese American hire and now he was reaching out to young Nisei boys.

Louise's stride was long and quick; I was practically running to keep up. "How's Art doing?" she asked.

"I think he's lost some weight." I thought about his last letter: *I'm down ten pounds, darling. I wonder if you'll recognize me.*

"He didn't have much to lose in the first place."

"It's all that running in basic training."

"I bet you miss him like mad."

Again, another reminder that my affection for my fiancé might be lacking.

We stopped at a busy intersection and waited for the light to turn green. Louise readjusted the knot in her scarf that was tied at the nape of her neck. "You wanted to talk to me about something?"

I caught my breath. "What iceman do you use?"

Louise wrinkled her nose at my ridiculously mundane question. "We use Booth's Ice. Why?"

"Do you remember a Nisei boy coming around from the company?"

We started crossing the street.

"A Nisei? No, I've solely dealt with Mr. Booth."

So much for my suspicion.

"Wait a minute, there was a Nisei who would come sometimes. Last year, when Rose, Tomi and I were all living together."

"Was his name Keizo?"

"I don't know. He stopped coming around this winter. I never really talked to him but I handled his deliveries because I was the one most likely to be home in the mornings. We can ask Joey if he knows him. He knows everyone."

By this time, we had arrived at Olivet's gym, one of its main features. Joey was playing basketball with a handful of high-school students, both Italian and Nisei. Somehow all his awkwardness disappeared when he was on the court, catching the basketball and throwing it toward the hoop.

Placing her hands in her jumpsuit's pockets, Louise slouched against the wall and grinned at him. I wouldn't be surprised if they officially announced their engagement soon.

After their game was over and the group dispersed, Joey wiped the sweat dripping down his face with a white towel that had OLIVET stamped on it. "Hi, Aki," he finally acknowledged me.

"You're pretty good."

"Do you know anything about basketball?"

"You're supposed to get the ball into the hoop, I know that much. And you did it a couple of times."

"Aki's not here to cheer you on, Joey," Louise interrupted. "She wanted to ask you about a Nisei iceman."

"An iceman?"

"His name is Keizo. He also works the desk at the Mark Twain Hotel."

Joey shook his head. "Sorry. Should I know him?"

"I wonder if Hammer would know him," I mused out loud. "Or maybe Manju."

When I mentioned Manju's name, Joey and Louise exchanged looks.

"What?" I wanted to know what was going on.

Joey, still hanging on to his towel, put his hand on his hip, while Louise crossed her arms.

These two were in the know, and I was determined to uncover the scuttlebutt. "Tell me. Hammer doesn't want to have anything to do with him."

"That doesn't surprise me," Louise said.

Joey reached for his glasses, which he had placed on a chair, and put them on. "Manju's been on the run from the police."

"For what?"

"They are still looking for the hold-up man in the Near North. Robbed a jewelry store."

"You don't mean . . ."

Roly-poly Manju? He didn't seem like he could hurt a fly. Hammer was the one who seemed to be full of piss and vinegar, at least before he started to sing in the choir.

"He's been hanging out at a Japanese club, Blossom, on the South Side. It has ties to the mob. The whole place was raided and the next day, everyone was back at the club as if nothing happened." According to Joey, the club was located down the street from the Southside Community Hall, the meeting place of the new Buddhist temple.

Even though we were the only ones in the gym, Louise spoke in a low voice that was barely audible. "And Aki, we heard that Manju has been dealing in guns."

"You can't be serious." Upon hearing "guns," I couldn't help but think about the gun in the bento box, Rose's gift to Tomi.

"You better stay away from him," Louise said. It was as if she had read my mind. I said my goodbyes to the couple, the future Mr. and Mrs. Joey Suzuki, and headed to the exact place that I had been warned not to go.

I sensed a difference between Blossom and Aloha. Aloha had a big picture window showcasing its pool table and the bar in the back. Blossom, on the other hand, was completely underground. I had to walk up and down the street a few times before I observed Japanese men going down some stairs from the street into what looked like a basement apartment.

There was no gatekeeper, guard or voluptuous woman waiting behind the heavy metal door when I cracked it open—simply a dingy hallway lit with a bald light bulb hanging from the ceiling. I heard the rumble of mah-jongg tiles and the clicking of poker chips as I made my way into an open room. The gambling den wasn't raucous and the men didn't seem to be as inebriated as the ones in Aloha. Instead, they seemed to nurse their drinks and savor their smokes, keeping their eyes wide open on their cards or mah-jongg tiles. Most of them wore fedoras and they seemed older. They didn't look lecherously at me as I passed by. In fact, they looked right through me as if I were invisible.

I would not dare to address any of them. I definitely got the message that I, as a woman, should not speak. I had to find Manju solely based on my own powers of detection.

As the customers here seemed like high rollers, Manju was probably part of the staff. There were a few croupiers in vests running the roulette wheels and a black cigarette girl who didn't look like the glamorous ones in movies. Instead, she, like me, had what Mom called *daikon ashi*, radish legs that were thick and muscular. She wore a plain denim dress and her hair was styled in two giant braids. Another black woman who looked my mother's age served drinks, expertly balancing them on a round tray. She kept replenishing her tray with visits to a makeshift bar, two card tables stuck in a corner. Pouring those drinks was a heavy man whose shirt tightened around his belly. Manju.

I walked around the perimeter of the tables and stood in front of the rows of distilled spirits. Manju automatically held out a tray of drinks before he recognized me.

The tray almost took a tumble. "What are you doing here?" he said.

"Shouldn't I be asking you the same question? What happened to Clark and Division?"

"I work here now."

"I need to talk to you. About an iceman named Keizo. He also works at the Mark Twain Hotel."

Manju didn't verbally respond, but his nostrils flared as if he knew who I was speaking of. He signaled to a twenty-something black man to take over his spot.

We walked outside of the gambling den into the hallway. "Yeah, I know him," he said, breathing hard. He pulled a cigarette out from behind his ear and lit it with a match. "Why are you asking?"

"What do you know about him?"

Manju gripped his cigarette in a funny way, holding his fingers back as if he was getting ready to claw someone. His fingers were meaty, like overstuffed sausages. He looked like he was sucking on a straw rather than smoking a cigarette. "Not much. Don't be alone with him."

The cigarette smoke, having nowhere to vanish, filled the hallway. My body felt cold and clammy. "What are you saying?"

"A girl at Playtime told me that he broke into her apartment about a year ago. He was there when she came home."

My stomach turned. This information confirmed what Peggy had told me earlier.

"He's a lock picker. You know, housebreaker. He's done some jobs for other people, but I guess he likes to work alone."

"What happened to the girl?"

"You know what happened. Luckily her boyfriend came in, so he didn't get very far. He chased Keizo away and threatened to kill him. He's stayed out of Playtime since then."

I felt the blood pumping through my arms and even my fingertips. My breathing became shallow. "Why didn't she tell anyone?" I said.

"Who's she gonna tell? The cops? She's a prostitute."

"Well, somebody's got to do something. He can't get away with it."

Manju practically rolled his eyes. "Goody Two-shoes. How are you gonna survive here like that? You have to be more like your sister. Though she didn't make it, did she?"

Manju's comment infuriated me. I didn't care that he was almost a foot taller than me and weighed a hundred pounds more. I pushed his chest, which was more solid than it looked.

He smiled, his eyes becoming thin in his full face. "Sorry, sorry. Maybe you got some of your sister in you."

"Are you the one who got Rose the gun?"

Manju was at first stunned, dropping his half-smoked cigarette onto the ground. Then the grin returned to his face. "You found it. I'm glad it was you and not your parents."

"Why did you do that?"

"She asked for it. Paid good money, too. I did her a favor. Wish I could have helped out more. Especially when she came to me for a loan."

I immediately reacted. "What loan?"

"She came to see me in May. I could tell she was desperate."

I was bewildered. Based on Chiyo's memories of the bloody sheets, Rose had had the abortion at the end of April. Why would she need more money in May? "Why do you think that she was desperate?"

"Because she was nice to me." Manju's attempt at humor fell flat. "I had no idea why she needed the money—only that it was important for her to get it."

Had Rose been preparing for our arrival? Was it to secure the apartment? We had wired her some money but perhaps it hadn't been not enough.

"I was low on money, so I couldn't give her anything. I wish I could have."

"You never told Hammer about this?"

"Oh, no. Hammer was so sweet on Rose." Manju sounded like a jilted lover. "If he knew that she had come to me for help, he'd never get over it."

For the life of me, I didn't understand Manju and Hammer's relationship. I was about to directly ask him about it, but stopped myself. I recalled Roy's admonishment: some topics were not my business.

The cacophony of voices echoed from behind the closed door. "I better get back inside," said Manju, leaving me by myself in the dingy hallway.

I couldn't wait to get out of Blossom. The gambling den left a film on my skin, but it wasn't only from the smoke of Manju's cigarettes. There had been a darkness in that room, a lack of humanity. Life had been portioned into two categories: money and more money. If you had none, you didn't exist.

When I got out of the subway car at Clark and Division, I headed toward the row of lockers. How could Keizo have hurt and scared so many girls and women without any fear of getting caught and punished? I felt as though we were like the jackrabbits in the fields of Tropico, leaping and enjoying nibbling on the grass, only to be caught and destroyed. I located my locker and fished for a coin in my purse. I had no idea if the locker had been cleaned out. It had been several weeks, after all. I slid the coin into the slot and opened the door. I could see the outline of the pink *furoshiki*. Standing on my tiptoes, I tugged at the cloth until the parcel slipped into my hands. As I didn't have a bag to put it in, I held it close to my chest, not caring if anyone saw the package or not. Learning about Keizo's abuses had emboldened me. I dared anyone to try to hurt me or any other Nisei women.

CHAPTER 25

Elmer Booth at Booth's Ice was a man of few words. I found his phone number in the resettlement pamphlet that Harriet had given me five months ago. He answered on the second ring.

"Booth's Ice."

"Hello, this is Aki Ito. I live in an apartment on LaSalle and we get ice from you. Well, we had a bit of a mishap and we'll need another block."

"When?"

"Uh, the thing is, I understand that you have a Japanese man. We've decided that we would feel more comfortable with a Japanese man."

"When?"

I gave him a time the next day when both Mom and Pop, who was interviewing for a new job, were out of the apartment. I needed to keep them safe.

The next morning, I dressed as if I were going to work because I hadn't told my parents that I had resigned from the Newberry. I chose one of my old dresses that was frayed at the hem. I had been meaning to get rid of it, anyway. It wouldn't matter if it was ruined or irreparably stained.

"No coffee?" my mother asked, noticing the cup that I usually used was empty.

I shook my head. I wouldn't be able to keep down any food or drink. Pop, meanwhile, was finally attempting to fix our leaky faucet with a wrench that he had brought home from Aloha.

"*Yamenasai.*" Mom told him to stop it. The leak was, in fact, getting worse, with a fine spray spurting out from where the faucet was attached to the basin. My mother was right. Based on Pop's other home-improvement efforts, we might soon be underwater if he continued.

As both of them left the apartment, my mother said, "*Ittekimasu,*" as she always did, a sign that they were on their way out. I replied, "*Itterasshai,*" the Japanese phrase for wishing them well, something that I never said in response. Mom narrowed her eyes, as if she sensed that I might be defying them again.

After they were gone, I went to my dresser and retrieved the bento box from its hiding place in my underwear and dress drawer. I removed the gun from the box. In terms of firearms, I only had experience with Pop's shotgun, but I knew enough not to accidentally aim the barrel toward me. After practicing how to hold it a couple of times with both hands, I checked the cylinder and counted four bullets. I only had four chances to get this done right.

I choreographed the scene before the iceman's arrival. I pictured how he would enter, where I should hide the gun underneath a dish towel on the table and what I would do next. Surprisingly I didn't feel nervous or jittery. I felt calm, almost without feelings, as if my emotions had left my body. I was ready for this. I had been ready from the time I had seen Rose's dead body.

If nothing else, he was punctual. His knock was like a gun going off at a drag race. This was starting.

"Come in," I called, maintaining my position by the dining-room table.

He entered wearing loose brown coveralls, carrying the block of ice in a canvas bag. Even though he was young, he was a little out of breath from carrying the ice up three flights of stairs. Perhaps because of his physical exertion or the turn of my head, he didn't seem to recognize me from the Beauty Box.

He went straight to the Coolerator, put his canvas bag down and opened the ice-block compartment, only to see that our recently delivered ice was still largely intact.

That was when he registered that something was wrong and quickly turned toward me. I was in position and pointing the gun at him.

Keizo didn't say anything. He watched me with his piercing eyes, while the melting ice block remained on the floor, darkening the canvas bag that held it.

"Put your hands up," I told him. He slowly complied. His upper body was strong and wide, like the young sumo wrestlers I had seen competing against each other in Little Tokyo. I knew that if he got close enough, he could easily overpower me.

"You killed my sister, Rose Ito," I said to him.

Finally, an expression came over his face. His eyebrows pinched together into a *V*. "I haven't killed anyone," he said.

"I know all the awful things you did to my sister. And all those other Nisei girls. You've gotten away with it. But not anymore." Now my voice cracked and tears started to rush to my eyes. *Darn it, Aki, stop*, I told myself.

Keizo didn't bother to deny the accusations of rape. He raised his chin in defiance. "Who's going to report me?"

And that was what had protected him all these months.

No one was going to the police. There was too much at stake if we did. As a result, we kept quiet. And Keizo freely went from one apartment to another, taking advantage of our silence.

Could I pull the trigger and kill him? That was the plan. I had been convinced that I could do it, but now my arms were shaking. Keizo smirked as if he knew that I was weakening.

He took a few steps toward me. "Shoot me then."

"I will," I said. And then softer, "I will." More tears dropped down my cheeks, some landing on my lips. I was a coward. I hated myself and hated the situation our family was in.

"What's going on?" A familiar voice roused me. Pop, for some reason, was back in the apartment. I didn't dare look at him because I wanted to keep my eyes focused on Keizo.

"This man forced himself on Rose and made her pregnant. And then killed her."

I feared that Pop would take the gun from my hands, but instead he took the wrench that he had left by the sink. He marched over to Keizo, who still had his hands up in the air, and walloped the side of his neck with the wrench. Keizo collapsed in pain and Pop, like a mad dog, was all over him, furiously pounding him with the wrench. As Keizo raised his arms to absorb the blows, I heard the slapping and tearing of flesh. Keizo thrashed violently like a fish on dry land, seeking an escape from the pummeling, occasionally landing punches on my father's upper body. I felt some sense of vindication to witness Keizo's victimization, but then I realized that Pop had gone too far.

"Stop, you don't want to go to jail for killing him," I called out.

"Gitaro-*san, yamenasai*!" my mother screamed. I had no idea when Mom had entered the apartment.

I aimed the gun at Keizo's head as Pop stumbled away with

his weapon, grimacing as he clutched at his right shoulder with his free left hand.

Keizo's face was swollen, a pulpy mess; he almost didn't look human. His lower arms were battered and torn. "I didn't kill her," he said, blood seeping from his gums and staining his teeth red. "But I saw her in the subway station. I saw who she was with."

"Stop lying!" I shouted, continuing to point the gun at his face.

"It was a cop. It was a cop."

"Nice story." I had regained my confidence. I was ready to shoot him right then and there when I absorbed what he was saying. I took a couple of quick breaths. "Wait. Wait. What did he look like?"

I expected to hear tall, dark and burly.

"He was blond. And average height. Thin."

As soon as he said that, my heart sank. *It could not be.* I lowered the gun for only a moment, but it was time enough for Keizo to break free and make a mad dash for the door. Although his face and arms were mangled, his legs were still strong.

"Stop!" Pop called out from the floor by the hallway where Mom was trying to tend to his injured shoulder. He attempted to get back on his feet but my mother kept him down.

Leaving the gun by the sink, I ran down all three flights of stairs after him, but it was too late. He had escaped, leaving behind a trail of his own blood.

My whole body felt depleted as I trudged back up the steps, smearing the drops of blood with the heels of my shoes. My *boro* dress was wet with perspiration. At the top of the second flight of stairs, Douglas stood.

"What happened?" he asked.

"Nothing," I told him. The WRA was the last agency I wanted to get involved in this.

"Wait," he commanded, and went back into Harriet's apartment.

I was too exhausted to defy him and stood still, feeling a breeze coming through the open front door down below and cooling my body.

He returned with an envelope, which he handed to me.

"What's this?"

"I picked up the bail money for you."

I gratefully accepted it, not having the energy to actually say "thank you."

By the time I returned to the apartment, the water in the tub had been turned on, presumably for Pop's bath, and the bloodstains on the floor had been all mopped away. My mother struggled to push the new ice block into our Coolerator next to the one that was already there. I hurried to help. With much pushing, we were able to complete the task together.

As we stood hip to hip by the sink, washing our hands, my mother asked in Japanese, "That boy killed Rose?"

"I'm not sure," I said truthfully, wiping my hands on a dish towel. "But he did hurt her. And some other girls, too." My hands still damp, I removed the gun from the metal counter and went into the bedroom to put it away in the bento box.

Neither one of us shed a tear. My mother said nothing about the gun. We remained quiet in different rooms, listening to the splashing of water in the bathroom as my father made himself clean.

• • •

I didn't leave the apartment until late afternoon the next day. My parents both had called in sick and stayed in bed, exhausted from the trauma of the day before. My mother had chipped away at our extra block of ice to create a cold compress for Pop's sore shoulder. At around four, I rode on a bus that took me directly to the county morgue, where Pop and I had gone when we first had arrived in Chicago.

It was almost official closing time and most of the clerical workers were preparing to leave for the day.

The coroner was sitting at his desk, the stacks of manila folders standing even higher around him like inebriated sentries. I knocked on the frame of the open doorway. He looked up, his blue eyes still as arresting as I remembered from months ago.

"Oh, Miss Ito." He spoke as if he had been expecting me to appear in his office.

"Did you leave a revised coroner's report at our door this week?" I stood in the middle of the doorway, my hands on my hips.

The coroner readjusted his reading glasses. "I had one of our staff members hand deliver it."

"There's nothing about the abortion in there."

"I didn't think that you wanted it. That's what the police officer told me. He had been hounding me for a while to remove it and finally when he visited me a few days ago, I reconsidered and amended it."

Why would the police be concerned about such a detail?

"What police officer?"

"Sergeant Graves of the East Chicago Avenue precinct. He told me he was making the request on your family's behalf."

It was rush hour when I took the bus from the morgue to Clark and Division. I didn't have a place to sit, and stood elbow to elbow with some secretaries. It had been weeks since I had seen Sergeant Graves with his clean-cut haircut and faint freckles dotting his skin. He had expressed empathy for our plight as Japanese American resettlers. He had stopped Officer Trionfo from verbally attacking me. He always seemed open to listen to my plight. But why was he now interfering and removing all mention of Rose's abortion? Why had he lied to the coroner and said that he was doing it on our behalf? It didn't seem like an accident that this had occurred about the time the abortion clinic was being raided.

My parents were in bed when I arrived home. They must have awakened to eat supper because there was a fresh sandwich left on the table. And a piece of mail addressed to me from Mississippi.

I took the letter, the sandwich and a chair out to the hallway. I liked sitting there the best because I could look out the window and see the skyline. It was already dark, but at least the tops of other apartments were visible, the illuminated windows and silhouettes of moving bodies, providing evidence that life existed outside of our building.

I ate half of the sandwich before putting the plate down on the floor and wiping my fingers clean. I carefully opened the envelope, imagining Art's tongue licking the seal. Art was more expressive in his writing than in person, and I could see why he was training to be a journalist.

Dear Darling,

I haven't heard from you in a few days, so I am dropping you a quick line to see how you are doing.

Mississippi is finally more comfortable. The

temperatures are in the seventies now, so not that different than Chicago.

A new man took the bed next to me. His last name is Funabashi, but he looks as white as he can be. His mother is Irish and I told him about Aunt Eunice. He's from New Jersey. His brother was in the army before the bombing of Pearl Harbor, and the higher-ups didn't know what to do with him until the 100th Battalion formed with the Nisei in Hawaii.

Since we both weren't in camp or from Hawaii, we are both outsiders. Some of the other Nisei don't know quite how to take us, but we like it that way.

On the bed on the other side is a Nisei who spent most of his life in Okinawa. Get this—he was drafted into the Japanese army while he was on a boat back to America. He was drafted by two enemy countries! He doesn't speak English all that well, but we somehow can understand each other. He has a big, blocky body. I'm sure he'll end up holding the Browning. (That's a machine gun.)

It's strange to think that we are all segregated together, as if we shouldn't be with the white men. We are as different from each other as we are the same. Anyway, I shouldn't go too far with this because I don't want to be censored.

Please write when you get a chance. I want to know what you've been up to.

Love you madly.
Yours truly,
Art

I refolded the letter and put it back in its envelope. I was storing each of Art's letters in an old cigar box that Pop had brought home from Aloha. Beside them was the locket holding the sand from our first real date, and the returned bail money. I knew that I had to get my engagement ring back as soon as possible. The pawnshop wouldn't release my ring without my consent, but there wasn't much I really trusted about the businesses in the red-light district of Clark Street.

I walked up Clark Street, this time hoping to run into Georgina and her friends. I wasn't scared of Georgina anymore, especially now that I knew her name.

It was probably too early for the dancers to be out on the street, because all I saw were *hakujin* gamblers scurrying to get a bite to eat before another night of card-playing.

The pawnshop was still open, its show window filled with watches and jewelry displayed on black felt-covered stands. I cringed as I looked for my engagement ring. Thankfully, it wasn't among these baubles for sale. My ring should be safely stored behind the counter.

As I entered the narrow shop, a bell rang from the top of a door. The pawnbroker, chewing on his supper, entered from the back room.

"I want my ring back." I opened up my purse, plucked my claim ticket from an interior pocket, and brought out the envelope full of bail money and Roy's twenty dollars to cover the interest.

The broker looked surprised, as if this didn't happen very often.

After the exchange was made, I strutted home with the ring on my finger, thinking about Art the entire time. I owed him a letter and wondered what I should share with him. Could he accept me for who I really was?

CHAPTER 26

Art must have also written to his family to ask them to check on me, because in a couple of days, I received a phone call from Lois.

"We want to have you over for Sunday supper," she told me. I could hear the twittering of the parakeet in the background. "It's nothing special, only tuna casserole."

Since we didn't have an oven, tuna casserole sounded heavenly.

When I arrived, it was like coming home to my extended family, not because I really knew them—this was only my third time coming to their house, after all—but because they were all happy to see me. I didn't have to prove how pretty or brilliant I was. Aki Ito herself was good enough for them. That's why I debated whether to reveal my recent activities to them. I wanted to remain in their good graces, but their impression of me was based on falsehoods. I was so tired of the fact that much of our existence had been erased. Our house in Tropico. Pop's job. Our daily lives revolving around the produce market and the Japanese community in Southern California. If I was going to continue in this world, I had to hold on to pieces of reality, no matter how disturbing they might be.

I was seated at the head of the table, while Mr. Nakasone sat across from me on the side closer to the kitchen. Mrs. Nakasone, wearing the same flowered apron as before, was on her husband's left while Eunice sat between us. Lois, her long hair styled in two braids, was on my left. We spoke about Art's weight loss and the Nisei he was meeting through basic training. Nothing, however, about when he would be deployed into the combat zone. None of us dared to state it out loud.

"We had some excitement in the neighborhood," Aunt Eunice said, changing the subject. The skin all around her eyes was papery thin, like folded tissue paper. Her hair was a frizzled gray and tied back in a bun. "They arrested the Nisei stick-up man."

I took a quick gulp of water, causing some to drip down the sides of my mouth. I quickly dabbed my face with a napkin.

Mrs. Nakasone shifted in her chair as if she hoped that this turn in the conversation would soon be over.

"He was coming out of a liquor store on South Parkway. I think that the police had been following him. They nabbed him right after he purchased a pack of Camels."

"How would you know, Auntie?" Lois asked.

"I have friends in high places. The criminal's name is Manjiro or something like that."

I felt my throat close and feared that my heart would stop right there at the Nakasones' dinner table. If Manju was indeed arrested for the robbery, wouldn't someone remember that a Nisei woman fitting my description had recently gone into Blossom to talk to him?

"Haven't seen anything in the newspaper," Mr. Nakasone commented in Japanese, casting doubt on Eunice's story.

"Maybe the police have bigger fish to fry." Aunt Eunice had an answer for everything.

News of the arrest made my stomach turn. I tried to continue eating, but all I ended up doing was moving my casserole from one side of the plate to another. I couldn't keep quiet one minute more. "I want you to know that I'm not who you think I am."

The whole Nakasone clan stopped eating and stared at me.

"I'm not a nice girl. And Art doesn't even know."

Aunt Eunice's milky eyes intently followed mine as I spoke.

"I held a gun on a Nisei man. A man I'm pretty sure attacked my sister when she was alive. I think that he might have been the one who hurt Betty, too. I was ready to kill him."

I felt that the air had temporarily left the room.

"But I didn't. I'm ashamed that I didn't. And I'm ashamed that I confronted him like that. I didn't know what else to do. The police weren't going to do a thing."

"What happened to him?" Mrs. Nakasone said.

"He ran off. I checked where he worked, the Mark Twain Hotel and Booth's Ice. He's called in sick."

"Maybe he won't come back," Lois said hopefully. That was wishful thinking. But if he wasn't in Chicago, he was somewhere else, ready to break into some other woman's apartment.

"I hope that he doesn't try to retaliate in some way," Mrs. Nakasone said.

"I don't think he will. My father made sure of that." I didn't get into the gruesome details.

I knew that they were all curious about the gun. I didn't know how to explain it, so I decided to say nothing unless asked.

"I'm glad that our Art is dating a fighter," Mrs. Nakasone declared.

Mr. Nakasone returned to eating and grunted.

We sat in silence eating the last bit of casserole. The noodles stuck in my throat and I could barely swallow. Was this the end of my association with the Nakasone family?

Mrs. Nakasone and Lois started to remove the dirty plates and I got up to join them, but Aunt Eunice held on to my wrist. "You stay," she commanded. Her grip was strong, especially for an older woman, and I dared not disobey. Mr. Nakasone, meanwhile, retreated to his kingdom of Japanese foodstuffs in the other room.

"Art doesn't know any of this?"

I shook my head.

"He has no idea how tormented you are about your sister's death."

I winced. It was almost painful to hear those words spoken out loud, but it was true.

"You know Ren and I had no children, don't you?"

I couldn't respond either way because I had never really thought about it.

"Art and Lois are like my children, too. I know them like the back of my hand." Aunt Eunice's breath smelled fishy from the tuna casserole. "I know something about marriage, too. When you have no children, you get to know your spouse, because there is nobody else. We had a hard time of it. Ren's parents back in Japan didn't approve. My parents didn't approve. So we were on our own. We had to learn to talk to each other. Even though Ren's English was terrible."

I stifled a laugh out of respect of her solemn tone.

"Marriage is very, very difficult, Aki. I don't know how it is for your parents. I don't know what they have taught you."

Mom never said anything to me about those kinds of relationships. I only got the message that divorce was scandalous, based on my mother and her Issei friends' reactions when a Japanese couple's marriage dissolved.

"My mother had an arranged marriage," I explained. "I don't think she really understands how it works in America." From the kitchen sounded the clatter of dishes and cups being washed.

"Well, then, you are going to have to lead the way. If you really love Art—and I'm assuming you do—you have to tell him what is going on in that head of yours."

I looked down at my hands in my lap. I never considered saying how I felt about things. How could I, when I always seemed to be grasping in the darkness to understand where I stood?

"I'll give Art back your ring," I said softly.

Aunt Eunice tightened her grip around my wrist. "This is what I'm talking about. Don't make rash decisions. Open up your heart. Open your mouth. Write him a letter." She then released me and called out to Mrs. Nakasone in the kitchen. "I thought we were having apple crumble for dessert."

We did have the crumble, along with some coffee. After making my confession, I felt much lighter and even held Polly, the white poodle, in my lap while Lois stroked the cat, Crockett. Duke sat right next to me, waiting for a scrap of food to drop onto the ground. Would life someday feel this carefree all the time? It seemed surreal and out of reach, but I was thankful to enter this world from time to time, to remind me of what could be.

The sun had gone down, so it was time for me to leave. As I moved toward the door, the whole family congregated around me to say goodbye.

"*Hai.*" Mr. Nakasone handed me a package of dried squid. "For your fatha."

Mrs. Nakasone gave me a hug. "It'll be all right. You and your family have been through so much. Don't try to solve all your problems on your own. You can talk to us. Really, you can."

Lois walked me out to the screened porch with Duke and Polly following her. Crockett emerged doing figure eights in between Lois's legs.

"Do you really think the same man hurt Betty across the street?"

"I'm not sure," I told her. "He could have."

"They moved to the farm that the candy man opened up."

I remembered that Roy had mentioned that his employer had a potato farm in an area called Marengo near the Wisconsin border. I hoped that Betty would find peace there, but I also knew that you couldn't run from tragedy, no matter how hard you tried.

I walked out of the Nakasone house feeling liberated. I hadn't realized how my secrets related to finding Rose's killer had been weighing me down. Art's family seemed so empathetic, but I didn't know how Art would take it. He probably would feel guilty that he was hundreds of miles away. He wouldn't be able to save the day.

Down the street, the brownstone with the small front yard beckoned me. I walked down to gaze at the yard, which was full of weeds and dandelions. The entryway was neat and swept clean of dirt and leaves. I unlatched the low metal gate and approached the door. I wouldn't have blamed her if she and her family kicked me out.

I pressed the doorbell once; I heard its piercing ring. No one answered immediately and I took that as my sign to leave. As I turned, I heard the door open. "Hello." It was a black woman about my mother's age. She wore oval glasses and had a slight overbite like Phillis had.

"Hello, I'm Aki Ito. I used to work with Phillis at the Newberry."

"Oh, yes, you're the Nisei girl. I'm Phillis's mother."

I was surprised to hear Mrs. Davis use the term *Nisei* instead of *Japanese*.

"Is Phillis here? I was visiting the Nakasones up the street and thought I'd stop by."

"Come in, dear." Mrs. Davis led me into an elegant living room with a thick maroon carpet and ornate furniture that made me think of the Elizabethan times. There was a big cross on the wall, in addition to a portrait of a young black man in uniform, who I assumed was Phillis's brother.

She had me sit on one of the chairs, which made me feel like a queen on her throne, and called Phillis to come to the sitting room.

"Aki." Phillis descended a staircase made of dark wood. As usual, I couldn't tell if she was happy to see me or not.

"Would you girls like something to drink?"

"Oh, no, I'm fine. I had supper at the Nakasone house," I said.

"Well, I'll leave you two alone." Mrs. Davis excused herself and went up the stairs.

Phillis assumed a seat on the couch, which had the same lion's paw feet as the chair. Her hair was back in victory rolls, except now she had many instead of two.

"Hi," I said.

"Hi."

"You're probably surprised that I'm here." The room had a strong perfumy smell that was starting to overwhelm my senses.

"I am." Phillis wasn't the type to wrap anything in shiny paper. It would be best if I was straightforward.

I clutched the wooden armrests. "I miss you and Nancy.

I don't have many friends." I only had one, Hisako, and I wasn't sure where she was.

Sitting erect on the couch, Phillis continued to look at me without much reaction. It was always difficult to determine how she was feeling. "We've missed you, too," she said in a mechanical fashion, as if she were typing the words. "Come back to work. Nancy talks about you all the time. She told her family all about what happened to your sister and, well, everyone understands why you wanted to go see that doctor."

"I'm the type of person who likes to see things through," I said.

"You should call her. Call her tonight, in fact. The Newberry hasn't hired anyone to replace you yet, so maybe you can get your job back."

It was too late for that, at least in my mind. I had moved on, committed to applying to nursing school. But I still wanted both of them as my friends. I glanced at the framed photo of Reggie.

"How is your brother, by the way?" I asked.

Phillis managed a smile. "He's good. He'll be back in Chicago soon. On medical leave."

"I bet that you can't wait to see him."

Phillis nodded. "It will be good for him to be home. For my mother's sake."

Not to mention yours, I thought, but didn't vocalize this opinion. I got to my feet. "I think I'd better go."

Phillis walked me to the door. "Bye, Aki," she said. The light of dusk reflected off of her face and I realized that Phillis, with her dark, observant eyes, was indeed beautiful. Why had it taken me so long to notice?

I left the Davis house, feeling like I had accomplished one piece of Aunt Eunice's advice: I had opened my mouth.

When I got home, my parents were both asleep again.

Pop had quit Aloha and taken a new job as a janitor at the Henrotin Hospital. He started his job at seven, so both he and Mom were now on the same schedule. I was relieved that he wasn't making that trek through the illicit businesses of North Clark five days a week anymore.

It wasn't too late to make a phone call, so I did. This time, Nancy answered instead of a member of her family. "Oh, Aki, it's so good to hear your voice. Phillis told me that you might be calling."

Nancy launched into breathless chatter about everything from her family to Professor Rip Van Winkle.

Like someone finding a break in a double Dutch jump-rope session, I inserted myself into the conversation when Nancy took a pause. "I'm sorry, you know. For getting you involved with the doctor."

Enough time had elapsed that Nancy made light of it. "It was kind of interesting to be a jailbird. I made friends with the other girls in the paddy wagon, especially the doctor's receptionist. Did you know that the police were blackmailing girls who had gotten abortions? Can you even imagine that?"

That revelation seeped into my brain. "Say that again."

"The police would find out who had abortions and go over to the girls' homes to extort money from them. The receptionist told me all about it." Nancy was proud of this new friendship and prattled on about how she had consoled the young woman the whole time they were behind bars.

I couldn't focus on the rest of the phone call. I only thought about the missing piece that Nancy had gifted me: the reason why Rose had been asking for money in May. And also why Sergeant Graves was attempting to sweep away any mention of Rose's abortion.

• • •

First thing next morning, I went straight to Harriet's apartment. I was thankful that Douglas was there when she opened the door. I saw his thin figure seated on her bed. He didn't have his shoes on; somehow seeing his stockinged feet made me feel profoundly self-conscious.

After Harriet invited me in, I told them of Keizo's observation that a policeman had been with Rose at the subway station before she died. I left out the part about the gun because, while I was beginning to be more open with them, I didn't trust them completely. "I was told that the police responded fifteen minutes after the incident happened. If a police officer was already with Rose, why the delay? And why didn't he explain what had happened?"

"It's curious," agreed Douglas. "But it's been more than five months. Will this Keizo talk to the district attorney?"

I shook my head. "That would be impossible. But I have a feeling about who this police officer might be."

Douglas took a deep breath. "You don't have anything solid, Aki. If someone pushed Rose into the path of that subway car, I want them to be prosecuted as much as you do. But without a reputable witness, I don't think you have much."

"What if the officer admits to it?" I asked.

Harriet, who had been puckering her lips in thought, jumped in. "And why in the world would he do that?"

We went back and forth on this. Harriet thought the scheme that Douglas and I had come up with was absurd. Maybe it was. But I had to at least try.

When I returned to the apartment, I was surprised to see my parents were still at home, sitting at the dining-room table. On the surface of the table was our metal tea kettle sitting on a potholder, next to two handleless Japanese cups and a tiny blue box. My ring. I could not take my eyes off of the box.

"You left this on top of the dresser," my mother said in Japanese. My father looked weary. His hair, which hardly had any gray back before the start of the war, was now completely white. The hair on top of his head was thin and I could see his scalp.

"Oh," I said. "It's from Art. We're engaged."

I expected that my mother would shriek in happiness, but she and my father sat like statues in our hard chairs.

"When are you planning to get married?" Mom asked.

"Maybe when he's on his military leave." I had no idea when that would be.

"Are you sure about this?"

I frowned. "I thought that you'd be happy. Especially you, Mom. All you've talked about with me and Rose is getting married."

"I don't want you to rush."

"No runnin' away because of Rose," my father added in English.

"I like Art—we both like him," my mother continued. "But there's been so much change. Too much change. Maybe to add more change is not good right now."

I swiped the box from the table. *What do you know?* I wanted to say to them. *It's not like you two got married for love.* In the back of my mind, I knew that my mother was imparting a bit of truth, but I had no time to reflect on it.

Douglas hired a messenger to deliver an envelope addressed to Sergeant Graves to the police station. I had handwritten the note:

Dear Sergeant Graves:

I need you to come to my apartment at two o'clock today to discuss a most pressing matter involving my sister, Rose. I have evidence that her death was no accident. It was not suicide. Before I take this information to the press, I hope that you will meet me in person to discuss this matter.

Sincerely,
Aki Ito

Sergeant Graves had taken my note seriously; from the window I saw him walk toward our building a few minutes before two. He rapped on our door with authority. After I let him in, he walked past me, went into the hallway and checked the bathroom and bedroom. When he was convinced that we were alone, he took a seat across from me at the dining-room table. "What's this about?" he asked. His face had lost all the warmth and decency that had been on display during our previous meetings.

I brought out Rose's journal. "This is my sister's diary. One that I had made for her in camp. Someone had ripped the back pages from it, so I had no idea what she had written during the last days of her life. Until her old roommate recently mailed them to me." I brought out some bogus pages of the journal, which I had carefully folded to fit a standard-size envelope.

"She wrote down what you did to her. Blackmailed her for getting an abortion. She was asking everyone for money but she couldn't raise enough."

"What do you want?" Graves glowered at me with an intensity that normally would have shaken me. But not today.

"A witness has come forward. He told me that he saw you

with my sister. In the Clark and Division subway station, moments before she was killed."

Graves abruptly got up, pushing the chair back so forcefully that it almost toppled over. "I don't know what you're insinuating."

I knew that I was on thin ice now. I had to be careful and prove that I had enough evidence to be a threat. "I know that you lied to the coroner's office and eliminated my sister's abortion from her forensic records. You didn't want anyone to be looking into her procedure."

"Who is this witness? And the pages of a journal? Anyone can fabricate that."

Graves was obviously not going to admit any of his crimes. I couldn't stand it anymore. "You pushed my sister into that train at Clark and Division," I shouted, loud enough for the neighbors to hear.

Graves shook his head, releasing curse words first softly and then more emphatically, like he was reciting an incantation. "Something's wrong with you people. No one told her to jump in front of that train. I didn't kill her. That was all her doing."

His words rushed out before I could organize and process them in my mind. So wait—Rose had killed herself? Was it because she couldn't come up with the money? Or because she couldn't let Sergeant Graves get away with his blackmail scheme?

I was so stunned for a moment that I didn't anticipate Sergeant Graves's long reach to grab the fake pages of Rose's diary.

He tucked them inside of his police jacket. "No one would believe you, anyway," he said before making his way to the door. "I consider your sister's death a closed case, Miss Ito. Don't bother me anymore."

"You won't get away with this." I wasn't going to back down.

Graves released the doorknob and turned back to me. "I'll tell you what I told your sister. If she got herself arrested, there would be no Chicago for the rest of the family. I could have prevented you all from coming. But I didn't."

Oh, what a humanitarian, I thought bitterly.

"I have the power to make your family's life very difficult here. I'm sure you wouldn't want anything to happen to the rest of your family, especially your father. He has a bit of a drinking and gambling problem."

His words chilled me. The police sergeant had obviously been keeping tabs on us this whole time.

Graves grinned, perhaps in the same way that he had responded to Rose when she hadn't been able to produce the blackmail money. I could see her there on the platform, listening to Graves's threats against our family's future and well-being.

She wasn't going to let him win. She had obliterated his power over her by jumping in front of the train.

He left our apartment, the door closing quietly behind him. Still trembling, I walked to the window. When I saw that he was on the street, I finally opened the closet. Douglas's friend Skip, a reporter with the *Chicago Daily Tribune*, stood crammed against our coats. Unlike Douglas, he was a heavy man with meaty jowls and unkempt clothes. Now that he had some light, he was madly writing in his notebook. I didn't want to interrupt him, so I went downstairs to fetch Douglas from Harriet's apartment.

"He's left the building," Douglas said as he appeared in the hallway. "Did you get it all down? Did the sergeant admit to killing Rose?"

I blinked away tears. "It wasn't what I thought," I murmured, and slowly climbed back up the stairs.

Douglas was right behind me. "What are you saying?"

Oh, Rose, you didn't have to take it on all by yourself. But that's what she had always done, carried our family on her back. There was even a Japanese word for it: *onbu*—short, sweet and powerful. Mom had told me that's what her mother, the grandmother whom I had never known, had done in the rice fields. She put my infant mother inside the back of her kimono and secured her in place with a special long fabric sash. With her baby against her naked back, my grandmother could tell if her daughter was breathing and doing well.

The reporter was leaning back in a chair when we arrived.

"Well?" Douglas said.

The reporter smiled. He had the look of a big dog who had stolen a T-bone steak from his master's dinner table. "He pretty much admitted that he blackmailed Rose Ito. And if these other girls confirm that they had been targeted for blackmail, we'll have a story."

"But killing Rose—" Douglas said.

Skip shook his head. "It wouldn't make any sense, anyway. Why would he try to get rid of a potential source of more money?"

I had to agree, reluctantly. "Yes, I think that she did kill herself." Saying it out loud was painful. "She did it for us."

CHAPTER 27

The reporter worked fast. The story appeared later that week on the front page of the *Chicago Daily Tribune* under Skip Cooper's byline with the headline POLICE BLACK-MAIL SCHEME UNCOVERED. Sergeant Graves was named by three anonymous females and one middle-aged housewife who went on the record. Rose's name was left out of the article since she wasn't alive to be quoted.

I called Skip to express my appreciation.

"Couldn't have written the story without the interview with the receptionist and those other girls," he said. I had Nancy Kowalski to thank for that. Nancy was the one who had convinced the receptionist to talk to Skip. The receptionist, in turn, provided him with sources who had been blackmailed by Graves, who threatened them with jail time for engaging in an illegal procedure.

"The DA is going to charge Graves with bribery," Skip continued. "He's bringing down other officers in the station." It didn't surprise me that Trionfo was one of them.

We said our goodbyes. I didn't want to be late for my morning appointment at the WRA office.

Once I arrived, the same long line snaked out of the office. Even more Japanese Americans were entering Chicago; I had heard that it was in the several thousands. Where would the WRA place all these newcomers? There had been some conflicts between Nisei workers and established unions. Had we come to Chicago to work as low-wage laborers and take away American jobs? The only thing was, most of us were American-born, too.

Instead of waiting in the line, I stuck my head in the doorway and waved at Harriet, who was distributing a list of job openings. She gestured for me to enter and this time, unlike the first time I entered the office, I didn't feel self-conscious. I had an appointment.

Harriet introduced me to a *hakujin* woman about my mother's age. Her plaid suit accentuated the curves of her strong, wide body. Her curly hair was the color of pennies.

"This is Mrs. Sappenfield. She's a representative of the National Japanese American Student Relocation program."

"Well, hello there." Mrs. Sappenfield warmly shook my hand. She wore no lipstick. Her bare face made me feel more at ease. As if she felt that she didn't have to impress me. "You can call me Linda." Of course, I wasn't going to call her by her first name.

She began to open up brochures promoting various nursing programs and I felt my pulse quicken. I learned that quite a few hospitals were accepting Nisei women into their nursing programs and that through the US Cadet Nurse Corps, my tuition might be waived.

Mrs. Sappenfield gave me an application to fill out. "I understand that you were in the Manzanar hospital's nurse's aide training program."

I nodded.

"We've placed a number of you in schools across the nation."

A warmth spread throughout my chest. Was this what hope felt like?

My heart soaring, I promised to return with my completed application. Could this really be my new life? Once I stood on the street, I felt the full force of the autumn wind swirling trash and old leaves from the ground. I thought about my Manzanar friend, Hisako Hamamoto, the first person to tell me that I'd make a good nurse.

"Hisako, it's happening," I murmured, hoping that one day I could tell her face-to-face.

As I walked home, I stopped by the Mark Twain Hotel, my regular routine when I was around Clark and Division. The same snub-nosed *hakujin* clerk was at the desk. Georgina, her hair in curlers, was reading a magazine while sitting in a green armchair in the lounge.

"Oh, sweet Aki, what brings you here?" she said.

"Have you seen Keizo?"

"Who?"

"You know, Keizo. The Nisei man who works the front desk."

Georgina sucked on her bottom lip. "Come to think of it, I haven't seen him for a few weeks."

"He's hurt some girls, women. Including my sister."

Georgina put the magazine on her lap. "We'll keep our eyes peeled. We'll make sure that he doesn't have a place on Clark and Division anymore."

When I arrived back at the apartment, my parents were ready to go send Roy off. I put the brochures away in my drawer and picked up a letter that I had written to Art. I wasn't sure what was going to happen to us, but I had written the whole story about Rose. I even mentioned that his first visit to my apartment had been based on a lie—I hadn't been sick. I had been recovering from the black eye that I had gotten at Aloha. I pictured Art in his mud-soaked khakis reading my multipage letter in Mississippi. Would the real Aki Ito still hold a place in his heart?

"Don't be *guzu-guzu*, Aki," my mother prompted me. "We don't want to miss Roy."

We splurged and took a taxi. Who knew when we would see Roy again? We ran into Union Station, the same place that Roy had met the three of us that miserable day in May. A tight knot of Nisei friends had already gathered to see him off. Ike and Kathryn were now officially a couple, leaving Chiyo out in the cold. When her parents arrived from Heart Mountain, Wyoming, Chiyo moved from the Clark Street apartment and, as she had predicted, was no longer able to attend as many Nisei dances and social events. She had become more involved in the new Buddhist temple a few blocks away, and there was even talk of a Young Buddhist Association chapter being formed there.

"I like how you let your eyebrows grow back," I told her on the platform.

"Really? I think they look ridiculous. My mother said that my plucked eyebrows made me look like a call girl."

Roy's thick locks, on the other hand, were gone as a result of the mandatory military buzz cut. The younger Bello brother at the barbershop had done the deed, and my mother had been the one to sweep up the cut hair and put it in the trash.

"Hope that you're not like Samson and lose all your powers with your hair gone," Ike said.

That comment went over my mother's head and she merely bowed toward Ike, dazzled that he was going to be a doctor.

Roy's hair actually didn't look bad. He had become a

different version of Roy, one who had definitely left his produce market and Manzanar days behind.

"Seems like all we do lately is say goodbye," I said.

"We'll see each other again," Roy said.

"Probably not here, though."

"No, not Chicago. But back in California." As soon as Roy mentioned our home state, a warm feeling spread throughout my stomach. Could we return home someday?

"The winter's coming, Aki." Roy readjusted his grip on the handle of the duffel bag he was carrying. "I doubt that you can survive a Chicago winter."

I thought back to the story of when Roy feared that his toes were frostbitten during that cold snap earlier in the year.

"No, I will," I said. That much I was definitely sure of.

ACKNOWLEDGMENTS

First of all, I am indebted to Erik Matsunaga and Bob Kumaki, who guided me through Chicago's Japanese America, both past and present. Erik, like me, is a social historian with a passion for maps and geography. Look for his work on Chicago on the website Discover Nikkei. Erik also introduced me to Catherine Grandgeorge at the Newberry Library in Chicago; thank you for directing me to documents that described what it was like to work at the library in the 1940s.

Bob and his wife, Mary Collins, kindly hosted me in their home and introduced me to touchstones of Japanese American life in Chicago: the Buddhist Temple of Chicago's chicken teriyaki fundraiser and festival, Montrose Cemetery, and various Chicago neighborhoods, including Uptown, home of the Aragon.

My Soho Crime editor, Juliet Grames, pushed me to make the voice of Aki Ito as real and immediate as possible. Truthfully, it was a process, but I'm so happy to have gone through it to honor the experiences of Japanese Americans who struggled to make a life for themselves after being released from America's wartime detention centers. Thanks to Soho Press publisher Bronwen Hruska, and everyone else under her leadership, including those I've directly interacted with—Amara Hoshijo, Rachel Kowal, and Steven Tran.

Filmmaker Janice D. Tanaka generously shared her research, including photographs and newspaper clippings, with me. These and anecdotal stories helped give life to the characters in *Clark and Division,* who represent real people who have remained hidden after all these years.

Contributing their knowledge and observations to the rewriting process were Janet Savage, Amisa Chiu, Jane Yamashita and Eileen Hiraike. Also providing certain concrete details were Gwenn Jensen; Clement Hanami and Jamie Henricks, both of the Japanese American National Museum; Karen Kanemoto of Chicago's Japanese Mutual Aid Society; Tim Asamen; Michael Masatsugu; Duncan Williams; Yukio Kawaratani; and Lily Havey. What would Japanese American historic scholarship be without Arthur A. Hansen and Brian Niiya? Thanks to both for their careful reading.

The City of Pasadena Individual Arts Grant made it possible for me to develop the beginning of the book, as well as engage in discussions at the Pasadena Central Library and the La Pintoresca Branch Library. My gratitude to librarians Christine Reeder and Melvin Racelis, as well as fellow presenters Sharon Yamato and Lynell George.

The Los Angeles Public Library has remained a vital source of material, even providing archival books from Chicago published in the 1930s and 1940s. The Hill Avenue Writers, namely Kristen Kittscher, Kim Fay and Désirée Zamorano, helped me to produce parts of the first draft by merely sharing their creative presence. Thanks to the Hill Avenue Branch of the Pasadena Public Library for providing a space for our gatherings. Helping during the rewriting process were accountability partners: Sarah Chen, San Gabriel Valley Women Writers and members of the Crime Writers of Color.

As I was very remiss in failing to credit Kathryn Matsumoto in my final Mas Arai novel, *Hiroshima Boy*, I must mention her here. Mea culpa for my earlier omission.

My agent, Susan Cohen, has been a steadfast cheerleader for this project, making me realize that a story like Aki's deserves a place on library bookshelves and in people's personal libraries, digital and physical.

For keeping me sane and balanced, I thank my husband, Wes; my mother, Mayumi; my brother, James, and sister-in-law, Sara; and my best nephew, Rowan. Tulo will always be the best dog companion of the 2020 pandemic.

MORE READING AND RESOURCES

° ° °

For those who want to read nonfiction accounts of this "resettlement" period in Chicago, I first highly recommend the Japanese American National Museum's *REgenerations Oral History Project: Rebuilding Japanese American Families, Communities, and Civil Rights in the Resettlement Era*, helmed by Arthur A. Hansen and Darcie Iki. The Chicago interviews were organized and predominantly conducted by Mary Doi, who did a splendid job. It is all available online via Calisphere.

The extensive papers of Charles Kikuchi include interviews with sixty-four Japanese Americans who had moved to Chicago in the 1940s from World War II detention camps. These papers are part of UCLA's Special Collections and are accessible through the Online Archive of California.

Erik Matsunaga has mapped historic Japanese American communities in Chicago and documented stories of notable individuals through interviews. You can find his maps and stories online at Discover Nikkei and @windycitynikkei on Instagram.

The Japanese American Service Committee in Chicago has the best collection of historic material regarding the resettlement under one roof. Their digital archive provides photographs from the 1940s, capturing the life of young Nisei in the Windy City. Moreover, Ryan Yokota's Nikkei Chicago website is a wonderful repository of "untold stories of Nikkei (Japanese Americans in Chicago)." The Nikkei Chicago article, "The Forgotten Story of Japanese American Zoot Suiters," by Ellen D. Wu is especially illuminating in envisioning a character like Hammer Ishimine. I can also heartily recommend her book, *The Color of Success: Asian Americans and the Origins of the Model Minority*.

Alice Murata's book, *Japanese Americans in Chicago*, published by Arcadia, provides a good photographic overview. She's also written numerous essays on the Nisei experience in Chicago.

The Great Unknown: Japanese American Sketches by Greg Robinson unveils little- known stories, including accounts of those who lived outside of the West Coast and were of mixed race. Also, his groundbreaking *After Camp: Portraits in Midcentury Japanese American Life and Politics* analyzes the experience of Japanese Americans as they left wartime confinement. Furthermore, I can recommend Valerie Matsumoto's *City Girls* for documentation of activities embraced by Nisei women before and during World War II.

Charlotte Brooks has also done extensive research on the topic of Japanese Americans in Chicago. Refer to her article, "In the Twilight Zone between Black and White: Japanese American Resettlement and Community in Chicago, 1942–1945," in the March 2000 *Journal of American History*.

Densho remains the best digital source of Japanese American history in general. Their encyclopedia entries on "Hostels" (Brian Niiya) and "Resettlement in Chicago" (Ellen Wu) contain succinct information on those respective topics.

To get a snapshot of what the prevailing thoughts were of the different communities in Chicago in the postwar era, *Chicago Confidential* (1950) is quite illuminating. Its characterizations can be offensive in several places, but its cynical outsider's point of view provides an unvarnished take on various neighborhoods.

For information about African American soldiers during World War II, I can recommend *The Invisible Soldier: The Experience of the Black Soldier, World War II*, compiled and edited by Mary Penick Motley. *Bridges of Memory: Chicago's First Wave of Black Migration* contains illuminating oral histories about African Americans moving into Chicago.

Regarding the history of abortion in the US, Leslie J. Reagan's *When Abortion Was a Crime: Women, Medicine, and Law in the United States, 1867–1973*, is a must-read. It contains specific arrests in Chicago in the 1940s.

I've been enamored with the region in Los Angeles referred to as Tropico ever since I heard the name spoken by a Nisei interviewee. My good friend, Heather Lindquist, resides in the area and her love for walks around the Los Angeles River, especially during the pandemic, helped me to envision Aki's attraction to the neighborhood as well. Our friendship was forged through exhibition work at the Manzanar National Historic Site and co-writing the book *Life after Manzanar*, which includes some material on Chicago. Another friend,

Donna Graves, has written about the early Japanese immigrant presence in Tropico. Other sources of information include Laura R. Barradough's *Making the San Fernando Valley: Rural Landscapes, Urban Development, and White Privilege*; Kevin Roderick's *The San Fernando Valley: America's Suburb, Los Angeles*; and two books published by Arcadia, *Early Glendale* and *Atwater Village.*

Another Arcadia book, *Chicago's Polish Downtown*, written by Victoria Granacki in association with the Polish Museum of America, provides an overview of this ethnic community, while *Polish-American Politics in Chicago* by Edward R. Kantowicz features more analysis.

For those seeking to dive into the archives about law enforcement in Chicago, I can direct you to *The Police and Minority Groups* issued by the Chicago Police Department in 1946; *Chicago Police Problems*, issued by the Citizens' Police Committee of Chicago, published by the University of Chicago Press in 1931; and *Criminal Justice in America/ The Kohn Report: Crime and Politics in Chicago*, edited by Aaron Kohn.

And last of all, periodicals from the 1940s, not only mainstream newspapers, can provide interesting details. All ten Japanese American camp newspapers are available via the Densho website and certain libraries. The archive for past issues of the *Pacific Citizen* can also be found on its website.

BEHIND THE BOOK

∘ ∘ ∘

GETTING TO KNOW NAOMI HIRAHARA

∘ ∘ ∘

The author, on a visit to Hiroshima at the age of three.

Naomi Hirahara was born in Pasadena, California. Her father, Isamu (known as "Sam"), was also born in California, but was taken to Hiroshima, Japan, as an infant. He was only miles away from the epicenter of the atomic bombing in 1945, yet survived. Naomi's mother, Mayumi, or "May," was born in Hiroshima and lost her father in the blast. Shortly after the end of World War II, Sam returned to California and eventually established himself as an independent gardener in the Los Angeles area. After Sam married May in Hiroshima in 1960, the couple made their new home in Altadena and then South Pasadena, where Naomi and her younger brother, Jimmy, grew up and attended secondary school.

Naomi received her bachelor's degree in international relations from Stanford University and studied at the Inter-University Center for Advanced Japanese Language Studies in Tokyo. She also spent three months doing volunteer work in Ghana, West Africa.

She was a reporter and editor of *The Rafu Shimpo* during the culmination of the redress and reparations movement for Japanese Americans who were forcibly removed from their homes during World War II. During her tenure as editor, the newspaper published a highly acclaimed inter-ethnic relations series after the LA riots.

Naomi left the newspaper in 1996 to serve as a Milton Center Fellow in creative writing at Newman University in Wichita, Kansas.

After returning to Southern California in 1997, she began to edit, publish, and write books. She edited *Green Makers: Japanese American Gardeners in Southern California* (2000), published by the Southern California Gardeners' Federation. She then authored two biographies for the Japanese American National Museum, *An American Son: The Story of George Aratani, Founder of Mikasa and Kenwood* (2000) and *A Taste for Strawberries: The Independent Journey of Nisei Farmer Manabi Hirasaki* (2003). She also compiled a reference book, *Distinguished Asian American Business Leaders* (2003), for Greenwood Press and with Dr. Gwenn M. Jensen co-authored the book *Silent Scars of Healing Hands: Oral Histories of Japanese American Doctors in World War II Detention Camps* (2004) for the Japanese American Medical Association. Under her own small press, Midori Books, she has created a book for the Southern California Flower Growers, Inc., *A Scent of Flowers: The History of the Southern California Flower Market* (2004). Other Midori Books projects include *Fighting Spirit: Judo in Southern California, 1930-1941* (co-authored by Ansho Mas Uchima and Larry Akira Kobayashi, 2006).

Summer of the Big Bachi (Bantam/Delta, 2004) is Naomi's first mystery. The book, a finalist for Barbara Kingsolver's Bellwether Prize, was also nominated for a Macavity Award.

Receiving a starred review from *Publishers Weekly*, *Summer of the Big Bachi* has been included in the trade magazine's list of best books of 2004, as well as the best mystery list of the *Chicago Tribune*. *Gasa-Gasa Girl*, the second Mas Arai mystery, received a starred review from *Booklist* and was on the Southern California Booksellers Association bestseller list for two weeks in 2005. *Snakeskin Shamisen*, the third in the series, won an Edgar Award in the category of Best Paperback Original. The third Mas Arai book was followed by *Blood Hina, Strawberry Yellow, Sayonara Slam and Hiroshima Boy*, all currently published by Prospect Park Books. The seventh and final Mas Arai mystery, *Hiroshima Boy*, was nominated for an Edgar Award in the category of Best Paperback Original, an Anthony and a Macavity.

Naomi also has two books in her Officer Ellie Rush bicycle cop series, *Murder on Bamboo Lane*, winner of the T. Jefferson Parker Mystery Award, and *Grave on Grand Avenue*, both published by Penguin Random House. Her new series set in Hawai'i featuring Leilani Santiago is connected to the world of Ellie Rush. The series begins with *Iced in Paradise*, released by Prospect Park Books. Her only book for younger readers, *1001 Cranes* (Delacorte), received an honorable mention in Youth Literature from the Asian/Pacific American Librarians Association.

Her nonfiction books include the multiple award-winning *Terminal Island: Lost Communities of Los Angeles Harbor* (Angel City Press), co-written by Geraldine Knatz, and *Life after Manzanar* (Heyday), co-written by Heather C. Lindquist. Naomi has also curated exhibitions at Descanso Gardens and the Los Angeles Maritime Museum.

Naomi and her husband, Wes, make their home in Southern California. Naomi served as chapter president of the Southern California chapter of the Mystery Writers of America in 2010.

THE INCARCERATION OF JAPANESE AMERICANS DURING WWII

∘ ∘ ∘

"Barracks at Manzanar concentration camp, California, c. 1942.," *Densho Encyclopedia* https://encyclopedia.densho.org/sources/en-denshopd-i34-00170-1/ (accessed Feb 9, 2021).

The incarceration of Japanese Americans during WWII remains one of the most traumatic events in US history. Altogether about 120,000 Japanese Americans were forcibly removed from their homes and relocated to concentration camps, many losing everything in the process—land and homes they owned, businesses, possessions. It was a mass violation of human rights the United States is still coming to terms with.

Japanese American history begins much earlier, in the 1880s, when the United States and Hawai'i started seeing an influx of migration from Japanese laborers in search of the American Dream: farmers, fishermen, mill workers, and railroad workers. Their path to the American Dream, however, was not an easy one. Not long after their arrival, anti-Japanese movements blossomed in many Western states. Japanese laborers were regularly subject to workplace harassment, and formal laws were passed to block Japanese immigrants from various aspects of American life. In 1913, states began enacting legislation that prevented people of Japanese descent from owning land, beginning with the California Alien Land Law. In 1922, the federal government ruled that people of Japanese descent could not become naturalized citizens. Two years later, Congress passed the Immigration Act of 1924, which halted all Japanese immigration to the United States.

Despite the discrimination they faced in both government policy and their personal lives, Japanese immigrants and their American-born children settled and built communities and institutions, often centering around "Little Tokyos" consisting of churches, newspapers, youth organizations, and other cultural and social organizations.

In the early 1940s, as the threat of a possible war with Japan was growing, several US federal agencies began surveillance on Japanese American communities, putting together a custodial detention list of "enemy aliens" to be arrested if war were to come, on the grounds that any Japanese or Japanese American persons living in the United States might be saboteurs or embedded agents for Japan. On December 7, 1941, when Japan attacked the US military base in Pearl Harbor, the ramifications in the Japanese American community were swift and devastating. First, community leaders—heads of Japanese Association branches or priests of Buddhist temples—were apprehended and imprisoned. But West Cost political leaders were calling for stronger measures to be taken.

On February 19, 1942, President Roosevelt signed Executive Order 9066, which established new "military zones" across the West Coast—Alaska, Washington, Oregon, California, and Arizona—from which the military could exclude anyone. This paved the way for "voluntary evacuations"—that is, the forced removal of Japanese Americans from their homes and into concentration camps called "War Relocation Centers." The first such camp was Manzanar, in Southern California, and another nine followed. The government downplayed the prison-like conditions of these facilities. These centers were surrounded by barbed wire fences and guarded by soldiers. "Inmates" lived in blocks of barracks, sharing communal bathrooms that were sometimes no more than rows of toilets without any walls for privacy.

Although most Japanese Americans cooperated with the incarceration, a few did openly defy them. Gordon Hirabayashi decided that it was his responsibility as a citizen to defend the constitutional rights of Japanese Americans and turned himself over to the FBI in principled resistance to "internment." He took his case all the way to the Supreme Court.

In 1943 and 1944, with the encouragement of the War Relocation Authority, many young Japanese Americans left the concentration camps and headed east to cities like Chicago, Denver, and New York. Home was no longer the West Coast, as they were prohibited to return—they wouldn't be allowed back into the exclusion zones they had been forced from until 1945. With no other option but to start over, Japanese Americans slowly worked to rebuild their communities in new places.

In the 1970s, long after the war was over, Congress finally created a commission to examine the causes of the WWII incarceration. The commission found that there had been no military necessity, that the real reasons behind the removal of Japanese Americans from their homes were race prejudice, war hysteria, and a failure of political leadership. This eventually led to the Civil Liberties Act of 1988, which consisted of a presidential apology and a $20,000 payment to 82,000 surviving former detainees.

Today, this story has never been more relevant as America grapples with the controversies of immigration, terrorism, the infringement of civil liberties, and the ongoing institutionalized racism toward people of color.

When a system of selective service registration was introduced in camps, some men protested the military draft because of the unconstitutionality of mass incarceration. Nonetheless the segregated 442nd Regimental Combat Team was established in March 1943. Japanese Americans came out of confinement to serve on the frontlines of Europe and as military translators in the Pacific. Together with the 100th Battalion, which originated in Hawaii, the 442nd suffered serious casualties with 800 killed or missing in action and became the most decorated unit in US military history for its size and length of service.

DISCUSSION QUESTIONS

◦ ◦ ◦

1. How do the opportunities and choices available to the Ito family—in terms of home, employment, education, and community—change after the bombing of Pearl Harbor? How do euphemisms such as "internment" and "relocation" diminish the harsh reality of incarceration?
2. Besides Aki, which character do you relate to most? In what ways do you think their decisions and actions during this tumultuous time resonate with your own approach and experiences?
3. Aki almost blacks out on the train ride to Chicago. What do you make of her sickness? Were you fearful when Aki heard Rose's voice? How does forced displacement and relocation affect the body, memory, and identity?
4. In chapter 9, Aki translates *kurou* as "a guttural moaning, a piercing pain throughout your bones." How does Aki cope with the grief of her sister's death? How do her parents internalize their pain? How do the physical items Rose left behind take on a new life?
5. Aki seems driven to protect her sister's legacy. Why do you think she takes the investigation of Rose's death into her own hands?
6. How is Aki watched and evaluated differently—at the police station, outside the chocolate factory, inside Art's truck—by *nisei* and *hakujin*?

7. Aki often describes herself as a lesser version of Rose. How does Aki's definition of herself in relation to her sister change over the course of the novel?
8. What do you make of the library scene when the professor belittles Phillis? What type of connection is the author making between the discrimination against Black and Japanese American citizens?
9. Why does Aki initially feel guilty about her relationship with Art? Were you surprised that she did not tell him about her efforts to find out what happened to her sister?
10. How is police sergeant Graves responsible for Rose's death and continued abuse against women? What is the relationship between the Chicago Japanese American community and local law enforcement? Do you think trust can exist between the police and an ethnic, racial, or religious minority community?
11. In chapter six, Aki's mother tells her to, "Never shame us. All we have is our reputations." How does Keizo take advantage of the silence and sacrifices demanded of Japanese American women and girls?
12. Why do you think the author chose *Clark and Division* as the novel's title?

RECIPES

YURI'S SPAM FRIED RICE

Serves 2-3 people

Ingredients:

- 2 cups of white rice (short grain preferred)
- Half a can of Spam (I prefer Lite), cubed into ½" squares
- ½ cup frozen peas
- 5 stalks green onion, diced
- Ground black pepper
- Splash of soy sauce

Instructions:

Prepare white rice as instructed on the package. In a greased large pan or wok, cook cubes of Spam until the edges are browned. Add steamed rice and heat over a medium flame, stirring constantly. Carefully add frozen peas and heat through. At the end, mix in green onions and add a splash of soy sauce and ground black pepper to taste. Serve immediately.

CHICKEN STOCK MISO SOUP

Serves 2 people

Ingredients:

- 3 cups chicken stock
- ⅓ tofu square (firm or extra firm), cut into ¾" squares
- 1 ½ tablespoon miso paste (red or white – I prefer organic low sodium white)
- 2 stalks green onion, diced

Instructions:

Heat chicken stock in a medium-sized sauce pot. Before stock boils, add tofu squares. When some of the squares start to float to the top, add the miso paste and stir until completely dissolved. Serve in bowls and top with green onion. Eat immediately.

BEVERAGE PAIRINGS FOR YOUR BOOK CLUB: SAKE

During the pre-World War II era and even throughout the 1950s, sake was mostly consumed by Japanese who lived in the archipelago and abroad. As the West began their love affair with sushi, sake also began to gain a foothold in the US and Europe.

Today, you don't even have to worry about serving sake warm. To appeal to the American market, Japanese sake distilleries have started producing sake to drink cold or room temperature in wine glasses.

Here are a few recommendations:

HAKUTSURU SAYURI JUNMAI NIGORI

Nigori is the type of unfiltered sake which has a milky or cloudy color. The bits of unfermented rice that sit in the bottom of the bottle add to the richness of the taste.

Hakutsuru Sayuri Junmai Nigori is packaged in a pretty pink bottle reflecting its "sayuri" brand, which means little lily. Remember to refrigerate and shake before serving. 12.5% alcohol content.

SHIRAYUKI EDO GENROKU JUNMAI

For a special occasion, you might consider Shirayuki Edo Genroku Era Junmai, if you can find it at a specialty liquor store or high-end sushi bar. Less water is used to create this ancient sake, giving it an amber color. Taste is close to scotch whisky. 17.5% alcohol content.

Other Titles in the Soho Crime Series

STEPHANIE BARRON
(Jane Austen's England)
Jane and the Twelve Days of Christmas
Jane and the Waterloo Map

F.H. BATACAN
(Philippines)
Smaller and Smaller Circles

JAMES R. BENN
(World War II Europe)
Billy Boyle
The First Wave
Blood Alone
Evil for Evil
Rag & Bone
A Mortal Terror
Death's Door
A Blind Goddess
The Rest Is Silence
The White Ghost
Blue Madonna
The Devouring
Solemn Graves
When Hell Struck Twelve
The Red Horse
Road of Bones

CARA BLACK
(Paris, France)
Murder in the Marais
Murder in Belleville
Murder in the Sentier
Murder in the Bastille
Murder in Clichy
Murder in Montmartre
Murder on the Ile Saint-Louis
Murder in the Rue de Paradis
Murder in the Latin Quarter
Murder in the Palais Royal
Murder in Passy
Murder at the Lanterne Rouge
Murder Below Montparnasse
Murder in Pigalle
Murder on the Champ de Mars
Murder on the Quai
Murder in Saint-Germain

CARA BLACK CONT.
Murder on the Left Bank
Murder in Bel-Air

Three Hours in Paris

HENRY CHANG
(Chinatown)
Chinatown Beat
Year of the Dog
Red Jade
Death Money
Lucky

BARBARA CLEVERLY
(England)
The Last Kashmiri Rose
Strange Images of Death
The Blood Royal
Not My Blood
A Spider in the Cup
Enter Pale Death
Diana's Altar

Fall of Angels
Invitation to Die

COLIN COTTERILL
(Laos)
The Coroner's Lunch
Thirty-Three Teeth
Disco for the Departed
Anarchy and Old Dogs
Curse of the Pogo Stick
The Merry Misogynist
Love Songs from a Shallow Grave
Slash and Burn
The Woman Who Wouldn't Die
Six and a Half Deadly Sins
I Shot the Buddha
The Rat Catchers' Olympics
Don't Eat Me
The Second Biggest Nothing
The Delightful Life of a Suicide Pilot

GARRY DISHER
(Australia)
The Dragon Man
Kittyhawk Down

GARRY DISHER CONT.
Snapshot
Chain of Evidence
Blood Moon
Whispering Death
Signal Loss

Wyatt
Port Vila Blues
Fallout

Under the Cold Bright Lights

TERESA DOVALPAGE
(Cuba)
Death Comes in through the Kitchen
Queen of Bones
Death under the Perseids

Death of a Telenovela Star (A Novella)

DAVID DOWNING
(World War II Germany)
Zoo Station
Silesian Station
Stettin Station
Potsdam Station
Lehrter Station
Masaryk Station
Wedding Station

(World War I)
Jack of Spies
One Man's Flag
Lenin's Roller Coaster
The Dark Clouds Shining

Diary of a Dead Man on Leave

AGNETE FRIIS
(Denmark)
What My Body Remembers
The Summer of Ellen

TIMOTHY HALLINAN
(Thailand)
The Fear Artist
For the Dead
The Hot Countries

TIMOTHY HALLINAN CONT.
Fools' River
Street Music

(Los Angeles)
Crashed
Little Elvises
The Fame Thief
Herbie's Game
King Maybe
Fields Where They Lay
Nighttown

METTE IVIE HARRISON
(Mormon Utah)
The Bishop's Wife
His Right Hand
For Time and All Eternities
Not of This Fold
The Prodigal Daughter

MICK HERRON
(England)
Slow Horses
Dead Lions
The List (A Novella)
Real Tigers
Spook Street
London Rules
The Marylebone Drop (A Novella)
Joe Country
The Catch (A Novella)
Slough House

Down Cemetery Road
The Last Voice You Hear
Why We Die
Smoke and Whispers

Reconstruction
Nobody Walks
This Is What Happened
Dolphin Junction: Stories

STAN JONES
(Alaska)
White Sky, Black Ice
Shaman Pass
Frozen Sun
Village of the Ghost Bears
Tundra Kill
The Big Empty

STEVEN MACK JONES
(Detroit)
August Snow
Lives Laid Away
Dead of Winter

LENE KAABERBØL & AGNETE FRIIS
(Denmark)
The Boy in the Suitcase
Invisible Murder
Death of a Nightingale
The Considerate Killer

MARTIN LIMÓN
(South Korea)
Jade Lady Burning
Slicky Boys
Buddha's Money
The Door to Bitterness
The Wandering Ghost
G.I. Bones
Mr. Kill
The Joy Brigade
Nightmare Range
The Iron Sickle
The Ville Rat
Ping-Pong Heart
The Nine-Tailed Fox
The Line
GI Confidential
War Women

ED LIN
(Taiwan)
Ghost Month
Incensed
99 Ways to Die

PETER LOVESEY
(England)
The Circle
The Headhunters
False Inspector Dew
Rough Cider
On the Edge
The Reaper

(Bath, England)
The Last Detective
Diamond Solitaire
The Summons
Bloodhounds

PETER LOVESEY CONT.
Upon a Dark Night
The Vault
Diamond Dust
The House Sitter
The Secret Hangman
Skeleton Hill
Stagestruck
Cop to Corpse
The Tooth Tattoo
The Stone Wife
Down Among the Dead Men
Another One Goes Tonight
Beau Death
Killing with Confetti
The Finisher
Diamond and the Eye

(London, England)
Wobble to Death
The Detective Wore Silk Drawers
Abracadaver
Mad Hatter's Holiday
The Tick of Death
A Case of Spirits
Swing, Swing Together
Waxwork

Bertie and the Tinman
Bertie and the Seven Bodies
Bertie and the Crime of Passion

SUJATA MASSEY
(1920s Bombay)
The Widows of Malabar Hill
The Satapur Moonstone
The Bombay Prince

FRANCINE MATHEWS
(Nantucket)
Death in the Off-Season
Death in Rough Water
Death in a Mood Indigo
Death in a Cold Hard Light
Death on Nantucket
Death on Tuckernuck

SEICHŌ MATSUMOTO
(Japan)
Inspector Imanishi Investigates

MAGDALEN NABB
(Italy)
Death of an Englishman
Death of a Dutchman
Death in Springtime
Death in Autumn
The Marshal and the Murderer
The Marshal and the Madwoman
The Marshal's Own Case
The Marshal Makes His Report
The Marshal at the Villa Torrini
Property of Blood
Some Bitter Taste
The Innocent
Vita Nuova
The Monster of Florence

FUMINORI NAKAMURA
(Japan)
The Thief
Evil and the Mask
Last Winter, We Parted
The Kingdom
The Boy in the Earth
Cult X
My Annihilation

STUART NEVILLE
(Northern Ireland)
The Ghosts of Belfast
Collusion
Stolen Souls
The Final Silence
Those We Left Behind
So Say the Fallen
The Traveller & Other Stories
House of Ashes

(Dublin)
Ratlines

KWEI QUARTEY
(Ghana)
Murder at Cape Three Points
Gold of Our Fathers
Death by His Grace
The Missing American
Sleep Well, My Lady

QIU XIAOLONG
(China)
Death of a Red Heroine
A Loyal Character Dancer
When Red Is Black

JAMES SALLIS
(New Orleans)
The Long-Legged Fly
Moth
Black Hornet
Eye of the Cricket
Bluebottle
Ghost of a Flea

Sarah Jane

JOHN STRALEY
(Sitka, Alaska)
The Woman Who Married a Bear
The Curious Eat Themselves
The Music of What Happens
Death and the Language of Happiness
The Angels Will Not Care
Cold Water Burning
Baby's First Felony
So Far and Good

(Cold Storage, Alaska)
The Big Both Ways
Cold Storage, Alaska
What Is Time to a Pig?

AKIMITSU TAKAGI
(Japan)
The Tattoo Murder Case
Honeymoon to Nowhere
The Informer

CAMILLA TRINCHIERI
(Tuscany)
Murder in Chianti
The Bitter Taste of Murder

HELENE TURSTEN
(Sweden)
Detective Inspector Huss
The Torso
The Glass Devil

HELENE TURSTEN CONT.
Night Rounds
The Golden Calf
The Fire Dance
The Beige Man
The Treacherous Net
Who Watcheth
Protected by the Shadows

Hunting Game
Winter Grave
Snowdrift

An Elderly Lady Is Up to No Good
An Elderly Lady Must Not Be Crossed

ILARIA TUTI
(Italy)
Flowers over the Inferno
The Sleeping Nymph

JANWILLEM VAN DE WETERING
(Holland)
Outsider in Amsterdam
Tumbleweed
The Corpse on the Dike
Death of a Hawker
The Japanese Corpse
The Blond Baboon
The Maine Massacre
The Mind-Murders
The Streetbird
The Rattle-Rat
Hard Rain
Just a Corpse at Twilight
Hollow-Eyed Angel
The Perfidious Parrot
The Sergeant's Cat: Collected Stories

JACQUELINE WINSPEAR
(1920s England)
Maisie Dobbs
Birds of a Feather